THE ADVERSARY CHRONICLES

Rebellion
in the
Stones of Fire

RANDY C. DOCKENS

Carpenter's Son Publishing

Rebellion in the Stones of Fire

©2022 by Randy C. Dockens

Published by Carpenter's Son Publishing, Franklin, Tennessee

Published in association with Larry Carpenter of Christian Book Services, LLC
www.christianbookservices.com

Edited by Robert Irvin

Cover and Interior Layout Design by Suzanne Lawing

Printed in the United States of America

9781952025662

This book, with permission, utilizes the Sefarad font in several places. Sefarad is a Latin font that simulates Hebrew. Sefarad was developed by Juan Jose Marcos, professor of classical languages, Plasencia, Spain. You can read more here:
http://guindo.pntic.mec.es/jmag0042/hebrew.html

Contents

FOREWORD

In this book I have used the transliterated names of biblical characters. You can tell which these are in the pronunciation guide; there, they will show their Hebrew spelling as well. This is done for two reasons. First, I think it adds some authenticity to the story, and second, I think it adds some originality. I hope you enjoy this aspect of my latest novel.

You will also notice that many of the names are somewhat familiar to how we say them in English, except for one: Eve. The Hebrew name transliterated is *Chavvah*. Doesn't sound much like Eve, does it? Why is this? Well, for whatever reason, Eve comes from the Greek translation of Chavvah in Hebrew to Eva in Greek.

You will also find some ideas are not mainstream thoughts about Adam and Eve and about the worldwide flood. I think this helps to make a well-known story not so well known, adds some originality, and will hopefully make the reader think about the story more closely.

Here are some of the changes from the often-told story about Adam and Eve and the flood.

First, I have the garden not on Earth, but in another dimension. Why? Well, there is a curious verse (Genesis 2:5) which seems to indicate that the earth did not spring into full growth in a matter of seconds. Then, in a later verse, a garden is mentioned. So either the vegetation of this garden grew faster than that of the rest of Earth—which is definitely possible since God can do anything—or this garden was separate from what he was presently creating. Does such an idea pique your interest? I am hoping so. Read on.

Second, I have Satan not possessing the serpent but manipulating the creature to do his bidding, much like he does to people today. Why? Satan is not referred to until verse fifteen of chapter three. While not specifically mentioned, the implication is clearly there. God's curse moved from the physical form of the serpent to the intent of the serpent. Satan is definitely the one who changed the serpent's original intent. Is this how it really happened? No one can say for sure. Yet it does fit with Satan's nature. Either way is definitely possible.

Very importantly, I believe the flood was not God's vengeance on mankind but a result of his love for mankind. I know this is not the usual view, but if we better understand what was really going on in this part of history, perhaps we can see a side we haven't noticed before. Some extra-biblical literature, like the Book of Jasher and the Book of Enoch, give some unique perspectives during this early time of history and enhance some of the ominous biblical references in the early chapters of Genesis.

Finally, let me say this. All of my books have some sort of Jewish point of view as it relates from Scripture. The history of God's people, prophets, psalmists, and Messiah is a Jewish one! But this book is possibly closer to the Jewish viewpoint than any other I have written because it comes from the biblical stories themselves. My books are meant to look at these stories, and God himself, from a different perspective. Thus, I landed on the viewpoint of Mikael (the archangel Michael) for an inside—and yet not human—perspective on these historical events.

May this story provide you hours of entertainment while at the same time make you think a little differently about an all too familiar story.

Hopefully you will discover more to these biblical accounts than you ever realized.

Pronunciation Guide

Av/Aba: אַבָּא/אָב (äv/ä' bä): Father/Dad

Adam: אָדָם (ä däm'): Adam

Akrab (ăk' răb): constellation Scorpio

Arakiba (ä răk' ə bä)

Archangel (ärk' ān gəl)

Ari (är ē): constellation Leo

Artel (är' təl)

Ar'yel (är' ē əl)

Azel (ä zěl')

Bakba (băk' bä)

Betulah (bə tū' lä): constellation Virgo

Caylar (kā' lär)

Cham: חָם (käm): Ham

Chanok: חֲנוֹךְ (kăn' ōk): Enoch

Chavvah: חַוָּה (kăv vä'): Eve

Dagim (dā gěm'): constellation Pisces

D'li (dě lē'): constellation Aquarius

Edna (ěd' nä)

Eldad (ěl' dăd)

Elohim: אֱלֹהִים (ěl' ō hēm)

Gabriel: גַּבְרִיאֵל (gä' brə yāl)

Gedi (gě' dī): constellation Capricorn

HaKodesh (hä' kō děsh)

Halayim (hä lā' ěm)

Hebel: הֶבֶל (hä' běl): Abel

Ima/Em: אֵם/אִמָּא (ī' mä/ām): Mom/Mother

Isha: אִשָּׁה (ĭsh' shä): wife/woman

Jahvan (yä' văn)

Jepheth: יֶפֶת (yě' fěth): Japheth

Kajin: קַיִן (kä' yĭn): Cain

Kasshat (kăs' shăt): constellation Sagittarius

Kesil (kěs ĭl'): constellation decan Orion

Kezia (kěz' ē ä)

Lemek: לָמֶךְ (lä měk'): Lamech

Lucifer (lü' cə fər)

Mezarim (mě' zär ēm): constellations of Ursa Major and Ursa Minor

Mazzaroth (măz' ză rŏth): Constellations

Methushelach: מְתוּשֶׁלַח (mě thü' shě lăk): Methuselah

Mikael: מִיכָאֵל (mē' kä āl): Michael

Moznayim (mŏz nā' yĭm): constellation Libra

Naamah (nā' ə mä)

Nacash (nā' kăsh): constellation decan Draco

Nephel (něf ěl')

Nephilim: נְפִילִים (nəf' ē lēm)

Noach: נֹחַ (nō' äk): Noah

Quentillious (küĭn tĭl' lē ŭs)

Raphael (rä' fā ěl)

11

Rayneh (rā′ nĕ)

Rebkah (rĕb′ kä)

Ruach: רוּחַ (rü′ äk)

Saba: סָבָא (sä′ bä): Grandpa, or
Grandfather

Samyaza (sä mī′ ä zä)

Sarton (sär′ tŏn): constellation Cancer

Savta: סַבְתָּא (săv′ tä): Grandma, or
Grandmother

Shem: שֵׁם (shām)

Sheol: שְׁאוֹל (shə ōl′)

Shor (shōr): constellation Taurus

Tartarus (tär′ tä rŭs)

T'leh (tĕ lā′): constellation Aries

Teomim (tā′ ō mĭm): Constellation Gemini

Tima (tē′ mä)

Uriel (yür′ ē əl)

Yahweh (yä′ wä)

Zander (zăn′ dər)

CHAPTER 1

Disturbance in the Force

Mikael approached two of his fellow warriors who were engaged in animated conversation. His left hand rested on the bejeweled hilt of his sword to keep the weapon from impeding his quick gait. He nodded to both as he came to an abrupt halt. Both stopped their conversation in mid-sentence and looked at Mikael expectantly.

"Raphael, have you or Uriel seen Ruach today?"

Raphael gave a wry smile as he brushed his golden-colored hair over his shoulder. His blue eyes twinkled with amusement. "Seen? Is that a trick question?"

Uriel chuckled but then stopped when he saw Mikael's extremely serious expression. Mikael didn't crack a smile.

"Mikael," Raphael said. "What's wrong?"

Mikael shook his head slightly. "I'm not sure." He too brushed his long blond hair, which was somewhat darker than Raphael's, over his shoulder. "Last time I saw him, he looked . . . different."

Raphael and Uriel looked at each other. Both gave a slight shrug.

Raphael turned back to Mikael. "I'm not trying to be anything but serious. But how can you say he looks different? We can barely see him as it is. He's *Ruach HaKodesh*, Elohim's Spirit. He has a form, but he is transparent for the most part."

Mikael sighed. They were taking him too literally. "Yes, Raphael. But he produces a feeling, a presence, an aura . . . that is powerful yet calming."

Raphael nodded. "Yes, that's true."

"His aura, as we sometimes say, felt different . . . troubled. Unlike any time before."

"Well," Uriel said, "he does have a great deal of stress to unite both the love and justice of our Creator so they can both exist within him." He shook his head. "Such stress likely takes its toll on him now and again. That's a lot of tension to keep harmonious."

Mikael rubbed his chin. "Maybe. This . . . this felt different, though."

Uriel shrugged and patted Mikael on his shoulder. "We'll keep our eyes out for him and let you know if we find out anything or hear anything."

Mikael nodded to his friends. "Thanks. I'll let you know what I find as well."

Mikael walked on, wondering where to look, when he suddenly got the idea to head to the throne room. *Ruach*.

Ruach HaKodesh often sent telepathic messages to these warriors to let them know the will of their Creator. Going to the throne room sounded serious—definitely not a place to approach lightly. There were only a few select cherubim and seraphim, special angels, who had access to the Creator in his throne room. Mikael wondered: *Why does Ruach want me there?*

The throne room was not hard to miss. Since the place contained the Shekinah glory of the Creator, his brilliance was so bright the light would penetrate any crevice existing in a structure. In addition, with the throne room composed of various types of colored crystals, the place gave off a magnificent glow that could be seen from extremely far away. Not only was the throne room colorful, the area also sat on the highest place in the middle of the kingdom, a dimension in and unto itself. Mikael looked up and followed the path upward toward the glow—a glow he had always considered comforting knowing his Creator's presence was always with him. Now he would enter his Creator's dimension. That, he thought, was not as comforting.

As Mikael neared the throne room, he paused. *Am I supposed to enter?* There would be grave consequences if he entered uninvited. He looked around. His eyes caught a slight blur of something against the glow of the throne room. He approached.

"Ruach. I received your message. What is wrong?"

Only a vague outline of a Person could be observed. Although transparent, he appeared like heat waves between an observer and an object. "Thank you for coming. I didn't want to alarm the others. You're the archangel, the leader of our Creator's heavenly host."

Mikael often wondered why he was the leader of an army. *Shouldn't an army have an enemy?* They certainly trained as if there was one. But everything here was so perfect. What was the need for such a force? Unless . . . Ruach was about to now tell him.

Mikael took a step closer to Ruach. He lowered his voice. He was unsure why he did, but doing so seemed the appropriate thing to do. "Ruach, tell me what's going on."

Ruach shook his head. "Mikael, I can't yet reveal what is going on. All I can say is, I have felt a change, and it's not a good change. There is a disturbance brewing. I can't tell you what it is or who it is, but . . . " His voice trailed off.

Mikael cocked his head. "But what? You can at least tell me where this disturbance is originating from, can you not?"

Ruach nodded.

"Okay. So, where?"

"That's why I called you here." Ruach's form turned toward the throne room.

Mikael looked from Ruach to the throne room and back, realization slowly dawning. In almost a whisper he said, "What? *Here?* But . . . why? *How?*"

Ruach turned back to Mikael. "That is why I need your help."

Mikael put his hand to his chest. "*My* help? But you're the one who can sense all. What do you need with my help?"

Ruach put his hand on Mikael's shoulder. Mikael could not see his hand, but he could feel it, as well as the warmth now radiating from his shoulder down through his very being. "That's the point, Mikael. The time of choices is approaching. I need you to question the cherubim to see what they know. If a rebellion is brewing, I don't want them to think I know."

Mikael's eyes widened. "*Rebellion?* Here? How—" He paused, his mind trying to catch up to such a thought. "How is such a thing even possible?"

Ruach shook his head. "It is a mystery. But a mystery you need to get to the bottom of."

Mikael nodded slowly, then stopped. His heart sank. "Wait. You said 'them.' Why did you make this plural?"

Ruach seemed to look down and then back to Mikael. "It *is* plural, I'm afraid. The feeling I've received has gotten stronger over the last several days."

Mikael took a step back in shock. "I can't comprehend even one of us rebelling, much less several. Are you sure?"

Ruach slowly nodded. "Yes. I am certain."

Mikael glanced back at the throne room. "And you think the rebellion is from one of the cherubim?" He shook his head. "They are the closest to our Creator. They reflect his glory back to him. How could rebellion be in one of them?"

"It is either one of them, or one of them knows something. You must find out what they know."

"But how do I do that? They are in the throne room almost constantly. They come out only rarely, and for short periods of time."

Ruach nodded. "Yes, that is true. And that is why you have my permission."

Mikael cocked his head slightly. "Permission? For what?"

"To enter."

Mikael's mouth fell open. "The throne room!?" His voice was one of disbelief. "But won't they know something is amiss if they see me in the throne room? Only the cherubim and seraphim are allowed."

"Others are allowed with permission."

Mikael swallowed hard. As far as he knew, no one—at least as yet—had ever entered the throne room except for select cherubim and seraphim.

"The glow of one has faded," Ruach said. "Likely almost imperceptible, but perhaps you can notice so you will know where to direct your questioning. Don't approach directly.

Not yet at least. Let's talk after your visit. Don't engage. Just observe."

Ruach stretched out his transparent arm and directed Mikael's attention toward the entrance of the throne room.

Mikael's eyebrows raised. "You mean, *now*?"

"Is there any better time?"

Mikael knew the answer was no, but he wasn't sure he was ready for this step without further preparation. He started to ask if the Creator was expecting him but caught himself as he realized Ruach HaKodesh was one component of the Creator-Trinity. Ruach giving permission was the same as the Creator giving permission.

Mikael slowly walked toward the entrance of the throne room. Two large angels with broad shoulders and a muscular build stood next to the doorway. Each had blondish-colored hair and blue eyes that highlighted their tanned appearance. Both wore a sky-blue robe that contrasted with the golden sash around their waist and the other across their chest that was in place to hold a large, sheathed sword along their back.

"Hello, Azel," Mikael said.

Azel nodded. "Ruach has already informed me to allow your entrance."

Mikael nodded. "Thank you." He paused briefly at the entrance. Would the portal to this dimension open?

He briefly glanced at Azel, who merely smiled.

The entrance seemed to simply fade, revealing a myriad of colors within. Mikael swallowed hard and stepped through the opening and into a dimension few—if any—had ever been invited into.

CHAPTER 2

The Throne Room

Mikael was not prepared for the sensory overload that hit him as he stepped into his Creator's throne room. The color and sound were overwhelming. Mesmerizing.

The first things to capture his attention were the four special cherubim, who moved like lightning under the clear expanse upon which the Creator's throne sat. Each cherubim had four distinct faces. Mikael had heard these represented characteristics of his Creator, and these cherubim reflected these reminders to their Lord. He knew this was a different dimension from the one outside, and so he could not fully comprehend the features of these specially created beings. These cherubim came together, wings touching, and then moved apart in all four directions. Yet their movement was so quick they were almost a blur, somehow forming the shape of a cube. Their movement created air friction and static electricity that produced brilliant lightning and air currents that kept the clear expanse above them aloft and the throne elevated.

Next to these winged cherubim were spectacular compound wheels composed of some type of brilliant material—there were spots of color along each rim of the wheel structure—with each rim perpendicular to the other, and all of this forming a spectacular blur of color due to the speed of the movement. The entire structure moved in a circular path—able to turn in any direction without having to physically turn, somewhat like a marble rolling on a floor. These structures also moved as quickly as the cherubim, and their blur appeared to form the shape of a sphere.

Mikael thought about these two shapes produced by the cherubim and these wheel structures: cube and sphere. He knew the cube represented perfection. The sphere was a close second. A cube, he knew, was a zonohedron: every face with point symmetry. And if the lines are turned into arcs, a sphere is formed. Mikael smiled. It made sense his Creator would have such perfection in his throne room.

It wasn't only the shapes that were meaningful. The colors—reds, golds, blues, cyans, and greens—shown brilliantly as the white lightning passed through nine large crystals standing in the middle of where these creatures traveled, arranged in rows of three, again forming a cube, and producing what looked like flames of fire. Two of these nine were also colorless crystals refracting all the varied colors of the others. These acted as prisms creating a kaleidoscope of color that emanated from the midst of the cherubim, who seemed to be ablaze with the color. As Mikael looked upward to where his Creator sat on a bluish-colored throne above the clear expanse, he noticed these same colors were emanating from the being of the Creator as well. The whole throne room was alive with fire and color under the throne, and these same colors swirled around the throne itself. He knew the very particles of creation were surrounding him—the very essence the Creator used to display his creativity.

As Mikael's eyes tried to adjust to all this brilliance, he noticed someone moving through these colorful crystal stones who seemed to be ablaze. *Lucifer.* He seemed to glow from the fire and the colors. Mikael couldn't get over the beauty of this one who, technically, was a cherub, but who also had many traits of a seraph as well. At that moment, Mikael realized he was aware of the melodic songs of the seraphim who hovered around the Creator's throne. They too appeared to be ablaze as their wings allowed them to hover in a serpentine pattern, each producing beautiful melodic song. Their melody seemed to be alive and penetrate Mikael's very being, all of this making him want to join them in songs of praise to his Creator. All these sensory impressions also left Mikael wanting to simply remain in this place and revel in the beauty of both sights and sounds.

Mikael watched as Lucifer donned a type of vest that had stones mounted to the front. The colors of these stones were identical to those of the large crystals among which he was walking. Now, in all his brilliance, he rose and hovered between the throne of the Creator and the fiery stones beneath him. Mikael realized Lucifer's name now had even more significance: *light-bearer.* Lucifer was reflecting the brilliance and color emanating from the Creator's throne back to him. It was no wonder the other angels regarded him as special. No one else had this position. No one else was able to stand before the Creator, see Trinity as a single being, and reflect the Creator's glory back to him and his throne. *What an honor,* Mikael thought.

Mikael then remembered his mission. He observed the cherubim, seraphim, and Lucifer himself. All were so brilliant, so special, so beautiful. Ruach had stated something was wrong. But as Mikael stood and watched, he could only see beauty in motion. His eyes moistened as he watched. He became overwhelmed with the privilege of being in his Creator's presence. Those here had the special honor of being with his Creator continuously. He shook his head. Any other angel would give anything to be in these positions. Surely, those here felt this privilege. *Didn't they?*

Unsure how long he remained in his reverie, Mikael came back to himself and headed back to exit the throne room. As he began to leave, he looked back again before the entrance closed. Now on the outside, he felt regret having to leave such an experience.

"Hello, Mikael. I didn't realize you were in the throne room."

Mikael looked at the angel who spoke to him, his voice familiar. "Uriel?" He looked around. "Where's Azel? Don't tell me you have taken over his post already."

Uriel laughed. "Yes. Quite some time ago. I've always heard time stands still in our Creator's presence. I guess the rumors are true."

Mikael gave a sheepish smile and nodded. "I guess so. I feel like I was there for only a short time, and still I didn't want to leave."

Uriel leaned in. "So what did you find out?"

Mikael shook his head. "Nothing."

Uriel stood in an even more erect position. "You didn't notice anything out of the ordinary?"

Mikael chuckled lightly. "Ordinary? Believe me, Uriel. There is nothing ordinary in our Creator's throne room."

Uriel playfully pushed Mikael on his shoulder. "You know what I mean."

Mikael nodded. "Yes, I know. But, still, everything seemed so wonderful, so special. I can't imagine the throne room being more awesome. Even though something is now, apparently, amiss."

Uriel gave a slight shrug. "So what now?"

Mikael put his hand to his chin. "I'm not sure." After a few seconds of silence, he looked at both angel guards standing there. "You two see the cherubim and seraphim enter and leave more than anyone. Have you noticed anything?"

Uriel looked at his partner. "Jahvan, your expression seems to indicate you've noticed something."

"Well . . . " Jahvan looked as though he had been caught doing something he shouldn't have. "It's probably nothing, so don't take this too seriously." He glanced between Mikael and Uriel. "Please!"

Mikael patted him on his shoulder. "It's okay, Jahvan. Ruach wants me to investigate, not interrogate. Anything you have is worth noting and checking up on."

Jahvan gave a large sigh. Uriel gave him an encouraging nod.

"Okay," Jahvan said. "It's Lucifer."

Mikael thought that very odd. What he had observed in the throne room—what Lucifer had done—was so amazing and beautiful. What could possibly be wrong?

"What about him?" Mikael asked.

"Like I said, the change is subtle," Jahvan softly answered.

"That's okay, Jahvan. Just tell me. At this point, anything is worth at least checking. Our Creator expects perfection, so if you notice something about Lucifer not living up to that standard, telling me is for the good of him as well. You'd actually be doing him a favor."

Jahvan gave a slight nod. Mikael could tell he was still nervous about attempting to articulate what was on his mind.

"All the cherubim and seraphim appear extremely humble when they enter and appear very rejuvenated when they exit. It's Lucifer, I'm afraid. He just appears less humble than the others. He used to appear just as humble and rejuvenated as the others. As I say, the change is subtle—barely even noticeable. I just get the impression he is becoming conceited." Jahvan held up his hands in the form of a slight shrug. "Don't get me wrong. I'm not saying that for sure." He paused. "It's just an impression."

Mikael looked at Uriel. "What about you, Uriel? Notice anything?"

Uriel shook his head. "No. Sorry." He glanced at Jahvan. "But Jahvan is at this post at the entrance to the throne room probably more than any of us. So I'd take his impression seriously."

Mikael noticed Jahvan had stiffened when Uriel first spoke, but then relaxed a bit when Uriel seemed to back his perception.

"Thanks, Jahvan." Mikael glanced between Uriel and Jahvan. "Let's keep this among us for now. Okay?"

Both nodded.

Mikael left his two friends at their post and walked alone. He wondered if he should find Ruach.

What would I tell him?

CHAPTER 3

Choir Practice Revelation

Mikael decided to wait a bit before he talked with Ruach. He wanted to get a feeling from others, to take the pulse among the angel community, so to speak, before he made an accusation he might later regret.

For the moment, everything seemed normal. As was customary, Mikael went to listen to choir practice. Often he joined in, but this time Mikael mainly wanted to listen. Closing his eyes allowed him to revel in both the melodic voices of the other angels and their words of praise. He always left uplifted after taking in this scene.

Mikael sat ready to listen. There seemed to be an audition happening up front. Several angels were vying for a solo role. Mikael closed his eyes and listened to several of the angels sing the same tune and same words. He smiled. He was glad he wasn't the one who would have to decide. Each one sounded as beautiful as the next. It did seem to Mikael, though, that the last one who sang had a slightly better baritone nuance to his tonal quality. Mikael greatly enjoyed this performance.

Feeling someone sit next to him, Mikael opened his eyes. "Halayim!" He sat up straighter. "I thought you were judging the singing."

Halayim sat back, slouching. "I am."

Mikael grinned. "And?"

Halayim now sat up straighter and turned to face Mikael. "I need your help."

Mikael held up his hands. "Don't get me involved in this. I just came to listen. The last time I stated my opinion, I felt ostracized by too many."

Halayim laughed. "That was because you didn't choose Lucifer."

Mikael squinted. "He wasn't even in the running!"

Halayim grinned. There was clearly something he wasn't saying.

Mikael's eyes widened. "You set me up!"

Halayim patted Mikael's shoulder. "Sorry about that. I needed someone other than the obvious choice. We can't choose him for everything."

Mikael sat back and crossed his arms. "Thanks a lot, buddy. Way to use a friendship."

Halayim laughed and leaned back again. "I do need your help, though, in this selection."

Mikael's eyes widened. He smiled. "You expect me to participate after what you just told me?"

Halayim jabbed at Mikael's shoulder. "Come on. That's water under the bridge. Besides, I have my mind made up— sort of. I just want your confirmation."

Mikael gave him a stern look. "Lucifer is not in the running?"

Halayim laughed and shook his head. "No, not this time."

"Well, I really liked the baritone undertones of the last singer."

"Zander?"

Mikael nodded. "Why? Who did you choose?"

Halayim laughed. "The same." He gave a wry smile. "Now I can tell everyone he was your choice."

Mikael shot to an upright position. "You wouldn't."

Halayim patted the air. "Don't worry. I'm kidding. Just kidding."

Mikael gave a stare Halayim's way. "You'd better be. Being shunned is not a good feeling." He paused. "Not now, anyway."

Halayim had stood, but now he leaned on the seat in front of them. "Want to explain that? Something wrong?"

Mikael patted the seat next to him. Eyebrows raised, Halayim took a seat again.

"I can't really tell you anything, but I need to ask how the rehearsal went," Mikael said. "Did you hear anything out of the ordinary?"

Halayim shook his head slowly. "No, just Caylar wanting to sing everything in B-flat."

Mikael laughed. "How devastating."

With a small smile, Halayim replied, "That's as devious as things got." He cocked his head. "What's troubling you, Mikael?"

Mikael waved his hand. "Nothing." He paused. "Well, I'll explain everything later."

Halayim rose. "If you say so." He took a few steps, then turned and pointed toward Mikael. "I expect an explanation later." He walked toward the front, clapping his hands.

"Okay, everyone," Halayim called to the group. "Places! Zander, take the score from the top. Caylar, you sing backup."

He pointed Caylar's way. "And no, you can't sing your part in B-flat."

Mikael smiled, sat back, and closed his eyes. Zander's tone was lovely. He soon heard others finding a seat behind him, but he simply concentrated on the music—until he heard some of the others begin to speak. He kept his eyes closed as if not listening—but tried to pay attention to what everyone was saying at the same time.

"Of course Zander got the part."

"Well, he does sound excellent," another said.

"I wonder what Lucifer will think?"

"What? Why would he care?"

"The song is about *him*, about the fiery stones in the Creator's throne room."

Mikael heard the other shift in his seat. "You think the part should be given to him?"

"He did write the words, after all."

"But I saw Halayim go over the piece this morning. I thought he wrote the song."

The other gave a huff. "Edited it, you mean."

"Well, I think Zander sounds wonderful."

"Of course he does. But listen to the words."

"I am," the other responded. "They sound correct." He paused. "Listen."

Then came the beautiful words, in melody.

He walks among the fiery stones
Absorbing the glow of the crystal cones
He dons his vest full of colorful tones
Reflecting back the glory from the Creator's throne.

"Yes," the other said. "But the words were supposed to read: *He walks unique among the fiery stones / absorbing the glow of the crystal cones / he dons his vest full of colorful tones / reflecting back <u>his</u> glory to the Creator's throne.*"

Mikael's eyes shot open. Blasphemy! Why hadn't that been obvious to him when he was in his Creator's throne room observing Lucifer? Was Lucifer that good at hiding his true feelings? The words were subtle, but their meaning totally opposite from what Zander had just sung!

Mikael wanted to jump up right then and find Ruach, but he knew he had to wait. Otherwise, the two behind him would know they'd been overheard. He wanted to know who they were, but he couldn't place their voices. He reclosed his eyes, trying not to move, yet mentally willing these two to leave as soon as possible.

It was several more minutes before he heard the two behind him stand and leave. Thankfully, they walked toward the front and then left the large room. He was unsure of their names but remembered these were two who had shunned him previously. They were obviously deeply connected with Lucifer.

Are they part of what Ruach is sensing?

Once he knew the two had left and were not returning, Mikael slowly rose and left the room. He caught Halayim's eye and gave him a thumbs-up to let him know the song Zander and Caylar had sung was spectacular. Halayim grinned, nodded, and turned back to his students.

As he stepped from the room, Mikael's smile faded. He had to find Ruach and see what his next steps should be.

CHAPTER 4

Another Will Emerges

Ruach paced. At least, that's what his movements made it appear he was doing. After a couple of minutes, Mikael put his hand on Ruach's shoulder, but his hand simply went through Ruach's image. Ruach stopped and turned his way.

"Ruach, surely you have a plan," Mikael said.

"It's a bigger problem than first realized," Ruach said. "I can feel the discontent growing even now."

Mikael's eyes widened. "Then we need to put a stop to this discontent growing further. Surely that's possible."

Ruach nodded. "Possible, but not necessarily the wisest course of action."

Mikael cocked his head. "Would you mind explaining that?"

"I'm afraid what you have been training for will now come to pass," Ruach said simply, straightforwardly.

Mikael gave Ruach a blank stare. He barely whispered the word: "War?"

Ruach nodded. "I'm afraid conflict will be inevitable."

Mikael felt numb. He shook his head. Suddenly, an idea dawned. "Ruach, if everyone could see what I saw in the throne room, its awesomeness would surely change their mind. The place is so beautiful, so mesmerizing, they would certainly have a change of heart."

Ruach put his hand on Mikael's shoulder. *Why did his touch always have such a calming effect?*

"The throne room is not a place for public display," Ruach said. "Plus, it is exactly there where this rebellion has started."

Now Mikael found himself pacing. He suddenly stopped and turned Ruach's way. "So, how many are we talking about? Surely only a handful, right?"

Ruach shook his head. "Thousands."

Mikael took a step back and nearly fell, his legs weak. "What? How could such discontent and division possibly be in so many?"

"Unfortunately, Lucifer is influential. He was created that way but has now turned his Elohim-given trait toward his own gain."

Mikael put his hands to his temples; he was just trying to comprehend the words. He didn't want to be disrespectful, but he had to express that he couldn't understand why this was happening.

"You and the Creator are going to let this happen?"

"*Let?* No. Prevent? No."

"But . . . why?"

"You, and all the angels, are our messengers. You don't know all that is planned. Angels were made to be either for or against. There is no gray. The choice has been given, but the consequences are irrevocable. It has been deemed so. If a war is fought, the event will seal you on one side or the other forever."

31

Mikael found himself shaking—literally. This was serious, very serious. He looked back at Ruach. "Can you prevent the war?"

"Yahweh himself will be speaking to everyone today. We do not give up the hope. Neither do we back down from the decision. Every angel has to decide."

Mikael bolstered his resolve, reminding himself he was an archangel, a leader of Elohim's heavenly host. He would do whatever was asked of him.

"What do you wish me to do?" he asked Ruach as calmly as he could.

"Come back to the throne room. I think all will become clear. As the leader of the Almighty's host, you should understand the terms and the reason for them."

Mikael followed Ruach back toward the Creator's throne room. Nothing more was said between them. While he wanted to ask many more questions, Mikael knew Ruach would state that all would be revealed in its time.

When Mikael arrived at the throne room, Azel and Uriel were guarding the entrance to this holy place. Both smiled. Mikael smiled back, but he felt his greeting was somewhat forced. He didn't feel like smiling. He was afraid of what was going to happen once he entered the room.

The portal dissipated and he stepped through into the swirl of mesmerizing color.

The four special cherubim with four faces were performing as before, moving with blurring speed which produced lightning and set the colorful crystals ablaze. Lucifer was again in his position of reflecting back the glory and color of the Creator's throne. This time, though, the Creator and Lucifer were conversing. This had not happened last time. Mikael was unsure if this occurred often. If they were in each other's presence frequently, though, doing so made sense.

"Lucifer, I have decided to create again."

"Very good, my Lord. I know that is a passion of yours."

Mikael noticed Lucifer trying to shine brighter. Yet Mikael couldn't tell if this was his way of showing approval of what the Creator said, or a way for him to hide his disapproval.

"I will create in the image of the four cherubim who represent Yahweh," the Creator said.

Mikael noticed the four cherubim increase their speed, producing more lightning, and, in turn, more color from the crystals. This created for Lucifer the challenge of matching their intensity in color for him to radiate. He glanced back at them, seemingly annoyed, but his demeanor returned to one of contentment when he faced the Creator.

"Why so, my Lord? Are they not subservient?"

"Subservient? They are special, just as the seraphim are special."

"But not unique."

"Unique? Uniqueness cannot create uniqueness. My new creatures will be mortal, but with a potential of eternality, and have a spirit of their own, but with an inner desire of a connection with Ruach. They will desire and need friendship and intimacy, but with an inner desire of an eternal connection. They may not know this, but Yahweh and Ruach will guide them."

"But what is their purpose, my Lord?" Lucifer pressed on. "They sound inferior."

"Through weakness comes strength. Through belief comes eternality. They will be lower than my angels during their life, but greater when glorified."

"Why do you need more, my Lord? Am I not sufficient?"

"Lucifer, you are my light-bearer, the brilliant one, the one who walks among the stones of fire. I have made you for this purpose, but not for an end-all purpose."

Mikael then saw what he had dreaded the thought of. Lucifer's glow faded—a visible fade.

"Lucifer?" the Creator questioned.

"You cannot replace me. I am unique," Lucifer said. "You cannot replace me with someone inferior."

"You are not being *replaced*," the Creator responded with complete calmness. "This is part of a larger plan."

"But I *am* unique. What plan can be greater?"

"Lucifer, I have explained. Uniqueness cannot create uniqueness. Therefore, you are not unique. Yes, there is no one created to do what you can do. You are the most perfectly formed creature I created, the first I created so you can fulfill a special purpose. Your special design contains the characteristics of both cherubim and seraphim. But you are created. That means you are not unique. Special—most definitely special—but not unique."

In the words which came next, Mikael heard great empathy in the Creator's voice. "Lucifer, you are more special to me than you can ever realize."

Lucifer either did not hear or did not take the Creator's words to heart. *How could he not feel such love and caring from his Creator?* Mikael thought.

"I will not be part of this plan?" Lucifer questioned. "I do not see myself in this plan. I must be part of this plan."

"Lucifer, do not forget your place. Your place has not changed. My plan for you has not changed. All plans do not include everyone already created."

"That is unacceptable."

The words stunned Mikael even as he heard them come from the light-bearer.

"Lucifer, be careful of your words," the Creator said.

"Is that a threat?"

"It is a warning, Lucifer. My love for you has not changed, but there are consequences to actions. I am unique. I cannot change. You of all my creations should know this."

Lucifer shook his head. "I *can* be unique. I *am* unique. My will shall thrive. I can, and will, become greater."

"I think not." The Creator's tone in making this short statement was nearly one of regret—but at the same time spoken with force.

With that statement, Lucifer's vest fell from his torso. He no longer reflected the colors from the Creator's throne. Lucifer's arm went to his eyes to protect them from the blinding color now facing him. He yelled in pain and fell through the expanse to the chamber below where the cherubim still moved in their constant blurred action. The lightning now seemed to hurt him. He yelped in pain and ran from the throne room.

Mikael noticed the Creator's gaze turn his way. His eyes widened, and he immediately genuflected.

"Arise, Mikael, my archangel, head of my heavenly host."

Mikael did so, but he also kept his head bowed in deference. The Creator had never spoken to him directly in such a form.

"Look at me, Mikael."

Mikael did so. The brightness was nearly overwhelming. He wasn't sure why he did not need to shield his eyes. Apparently, the light shining through the expanse above him muted its intensity. Still, the brightness was nearly too much to take in.

"My Lord. What are your wishes?" Mikael asked.

"Are you, unlike Lucifer, my greatest creation, on my side?"

"Absolutely, my Lord. I wish to be on no other."

"Gather all the angels. Yahweh will talk to them today." He paused. "Prepare yourself and your closest subordinates for war. A war greater than you can imagine."

Mikael genuflected once more and then bowed. "Yes, my Lord."

"Mikael." Although spoken in a commanding tone, the Creator's voice was, at the same time, filled with kindness.

Mikael looked up at this One he knew he would do anything for.

"Rest assured," the Creator said. "What is coming will be a great battle with many losses. But one in which you *will* be victorious. Great things are in store for the victors."

Mikael bowed again. "Yes, my Lord."

Mikael bowed a final time and left the throne room.

CHAPTER 5

Warning from Yahweh

Both Azel and Uriel flinched as Mikael practically fled from the throne room.

"Mikael!" Azel exclaimed. "What's wrong? You look almost fearful."

"A war is coming, Azel."

"What?" Azel's eyes widened. "A *what*?"

"Please command all the angels to gather. Yahweh is speaking." Mikael looked directly into Azel's eyes. "Tell them all. Gather! Gather now!"

Mikael left without another word. He gave a quick glance back as he hurried to relay the message to others. It was then he noticed that Azel and Uriel were quickly moving toward him. He stopped and turned to meet them.

Uriel spoke first. "Ruach asked us to follow you to have everyone assemble. Jahvan will guard the entrance to the throne room."

Mikael knew having one guard was unusual, but Jahvan was one of the most formidable angels he knew. Mikael nodded and continued to walk to the Sacred Altar of Stones. Mikael never thought about why they had been given this name, but this was the meeting place when many angels gathered.

All three stood next to the stones with their backs forming a small triangle. Each held their swords with both hands and held them in front of them with arms raised. The swords began to resonate with each other, and the blades of the swords emanated brilliant shades of color from hilt to tip. At first the colors transitioned slowly but then began to increase in speed and intensity. After a short while the colors moved upward, far above their swords, turning into a beacon for all angels to see—a symbol for all to gather.

The angels began to appear. Slowly at first, but more and more in quick succession. Some flew in using their giant wings to arrive softly. Some, without wings, teleported in to arrive, while others, likely close when they saw the beacon, walked up. In only a matter of minutes, tens of thousands of angels surrounded Mikael, Uriel, and Azel.

The light of the beacon began to shorten in length. As all looked up, they saw Yahweh descending. All genuflected.

"Arise, my angels," Yahweh said.

All stood. Yahweh stood on top of the altar of stones with a clear smile. A genuine smile that was almost mesmerizing. *He always makes everyone feel at home and special when in his presence,* Mikael thought. His clothing was pure white yet trimmed in scarlet and azure blue. His kittel had deep splits on the sides to allow free range of motion for the white trousers underneath. He wore a sash of deep purple trimmed in gold around his waist.

Yahweh held his arms open in a welcoming gesture. "My sons. I have much news to tell you. Much of what I can say is good and wonderful." His smile suddenly vanished. "But some is not—and very concerning."

His smile brightened once more. "First, the good news. Trinity has decided to create again."

There was much commotion throughout the angel throng. Mikael looked around to see if most were happy to hear this news—or somehow concerned. As he looked at the faces he could see, most seemed mainly curious.

"We will call these new creations *humans*."

"My Lord," one of the angels said. "What will be their purpose?"

Another spoke up. "Are we not enough for our beloved Creator?"

Yahweh smiled. "My dear sons. We do not create because you are not enough. We create for you as well as for us." His smiled broadened. "We cannot change. Being creative and diverse in our creations is one of our traits."

"What have you envisioned, my Lord?" another angel asked.

"I am in the process of creating another dimension in which these humans can live. This dimension will be a place of diversity and beauty. A place where they can procreate, give glory back to their Creator, and also be a place in which you can help us minister to them."

"Procreate?" one of the angels asked.

Yahweh smiled. "Yes, they will be of two genders, where Trinity will allow small humans to grow inside the female, thus giving birth to another human. This born human will be small, almost helpless, and grow into an adult human."

"They will be weak, then, my Lord?" still another angel asked.

Yahweh laughed lightly. "They will be weak, but wonderful. For a time they will be indecisive and need help choosing and understanding their Creator. Yet being parents to their young will help the humans understand love, and, thereby, their Creator. At the end of time, they will become glorious and more than you can imagine."

"End of time?" one of the angels asked. He had a confused expression and looked at those standing near him. "I don't understand that term."

"That's because such a word hasn't been created yet," Yahweh said as he chuckled lightly. "You experience the passage of events, which many of you refer to as 'time,' but you are eternal beings living in an eternal dimension. Yet 'time' for humans will be a demarcation of events based upon their dimension and the world on which they will live. Their dimension, their world, will not be eternal. Their world will have an end."

The angel's eyes widened, and Yahweh gave a broad smile. "There is much wonderment to come." Yahweh's expression quickly changed to one of sadness. "But your question, Quentillious, is one which will change everything." His gaze swept over the angel crowd. "For everyone."

Murmuring went through the crowd again for a few moments. All eyes soon turned back to the Master.

"The creation of a dimension of time will be the initiation of our new creation and will be the determination of each angel's fate."

The angels looked at each other, eyes wide, and turned back to Yahweh.

"What do you mean, Master?" Quentillious asked.

"Whose will do you serve?"

Quentillious's stature stiffened as if the statement shocked him. "Yours, of course, my Lord." He glanced at the other angels and then back to Yahweh. "There can be no other."

"Unfortunately," Yahweh said, "another will has already been initiated."

Mikael heard gasps through the angel crowd. This was such a foreign concept to almost everyone here. *That's a good thing,* Mikael thought. Surely their lack of understanding meant rebellion was not yet too widespread. Yet Ruach's words came back to him. Mikael shook his head lightly. How could such a thing happen here within the Creator's presence? Although he was pleased to hear that such a concept seemed preposterous to Quentillious, he hoped the same was true for most.

"Once humans are created and have been trained to establish a kingdom in their dimension under my rule, all angels will have a choice to make," Yahweh said.

Every angel looked confused. Many shook their heads, not understanding.

Yahweh went on to explain.

"You were created to be my messengers. All your duties have not yet been assigned to you. I know you are happy with me." He smiled as he continued. "And I am more than happy with you." Yahweh stood straighter as if delivering a very important message. "Yet humans will need guidance and teaching. You all will help in this regard. You will be more than merely ones who return glory to me, you will be my instruments in helping humans understand my glory and love for them. As stated, they will be a different creation: one who starts out weak and lowly, but one who ends in strength and victory."

His gazed panned the angel throng once more. "You, my friends, my children, will be a big part in this."

"We are excited to serve you in this way, Master," Quentillious said.

Mikael laughed to himself. It seemed Quentillious couldn't contain his excitement without expressing it. Mikael could see excitement on most faces as well.

Yahweh gave a brief laugh. "Thank you, Quentillious. I'll be sure and make the first mission yours."

Quentillious stood straighter and gave a broad smile.

Yahweh turned serious in tone. "You all were created differently, however. You do not procreate and have been created to be loyal. That requires your will be sealed with mine. I need messengers upon whom I can depend explicitly."

"You have it!" one of the angels shouted.

Yahweh gave a quick smile and turned somber again. "Each of you will be asked to make a decision very soon. You will be for me or against me. A war is coming. Whose side you choose is a decision that will be irrevocable."

Again there were murmurings in the crowd, but this time the reactions of the angels were much louder and more animated than before.

"My Lord," Quentillious said. "Such a thing is unthinkable."

Yahweh nodded. "Indeed, Quentillious. It is. Yet, have I ever lied?"

Quentillious shook his head. "No, my Lord. Never. Impossible."

"So be on alert, Quentillious." He scanned the entire crowd, deliberately. "All of you. Be alert. You will be asked to choose. I hope you choose wisely."

Yahweh disappeared from their presence; it was almost as though he turned into a beam of bright light and shot upward out of sight. All the angels stood motionless for several seconds as if dumbfounded with the news they had just heard.

The angels then slowly began to head off in groups of twos, threes, and fours, likely discussing what they just heard.

A realization then dawned on Mikael, and it hit him as directly as a beam of light piercing between his eyes.

Lucifer had not been present.

CHAPTER 6

The Creative Dimension

ikael sat on a rock, leaning back while using his hands to brace himself. He was glad the Creator had allowed his angels to come to this dimension. This was where the Creator had used his imagination and diversity to create a world beyond comprehension and beauty. The colors of this world were spectacular. Sitting on the rock he could hear a brook bubbling nearby, see colorful shrubbery everywhere, and spy multicolored creatures peeking out from the grasses in the near distance. Occasionally he would see a colorful creature fly by, land, and give a beautiful song. Each variety seemed to have a different type of trill with each being almost as relaxing as a touch of the Master himself. He wondered, several times, why none of the creatures or foliage had been given names. He was sure, though, that Yahweh had a plan for that.

He looked up and saw Azel approaching and then take a seat next to him. "This place is so peaceful," the large guardian angel said.

Mikael nodded.

"What did the Creator name this place?" Azel asked.

"Eden," Mikael answered. "A place of paradise. Our dimension is wonderful, but this one . . . well, this dimension just has an indescribable beauty."

Azel nodded and then grinned.

Mikael gave him a quizzical look. "What?" He sat up. "You know something."

Azel laughed and nodded again. "I heard that some of this beauty will become part of our Creator's new world that he is creating for his humans."

Mikael's eyes widened. "Really?" He looked around again. "If it's half as beautiful as this, his new world will be wonderful." He looked back at Azel. "What do you know?"

"Not much. Just that he will start very soon. His new dimension will not just be a world, but a universe—a place to give humans a reason to praise their Creator and give them many things to investigate and figure out. Apparently he plans to make them a very curious creation." Azel smiled. "It seems he will give them a great deal to ponder."

Mikael stood and smiled. "This is all so exciting. I can't wait to see what he does."

Azel nodded. "Heading back?"

Mikael shook his head. "I was going to walk around. Care to join me?"

Azel stood. "Certainly. I love looking around in this dimension. Every time I get a chance to visit here, something new is almost always present to enjoy."

Mikael laughed. "Yes, it seems our Creator just can't help himself. Creation seems to exude from him."

Azel nodded. "That seems true." He stopped and looked at a plant displaying a colorful top with fuchsia petals and cobalt-blue, delicate-looking stamens with bright silver spots in periodic places. As the gentle breeze blew, the stamens seemed to twinkle. "See, I don't think this was here before."

"It's magnificent," Mikael said.

Azel nodded. "Everything here is."

As they walked they admired the totality of the beauty around them. Azel suddenly put his arm in front of Mikael.

Mikael gave Azel a curious look. "What's wrong?"

Azel nodded his head to his left. "Look."

Mikael looked in that direction. Lucifer was talking to a creature—a beautiful but unusual creature. The creature had arms but didn't seem to have any feet and moved in a serpentine manner while using an extremely muscular type of tail. The two seemed to be in conversation.

"I don't recall seeing this creature before," Azel said. Then, in nearly a voice of awe, he added, "But it is magnificent—almost as if it has scales. They glisten in the sunlight and throw off various hues."

Mikael nodded. "I've never seen a creature here that speaks. Maybe we can talk to it after Lucifer leaves."

Azel shot Mikael a quick glance. "Why do you think Lucifer is talking to it? You don't think this creature is part of Lucifer's rebellion, do you?"

Mikael shrugged. "I don't know. But if this creature is new, how could it?"

"So you're not concerned?"

"Oh, I didn't say that," Mikael said, eyes wide. "I just don't want to immediately arrive at a conclusion. After all, if we discovered a new creature here able to speak, we'd be talking with it as well, wouldn't we?"

Azel squinted. "So, why are we being secretive and not just walking up and introducing ourselves to a new creature in the Master's creative dimension?"

Mikael gave Azel a blank stare. "You know, you're right. Let's go introduce ourselves."

As they approached, Lucifer stopped his conversation when he saw the creature turn its gaze toward them. The creature elicited a smile and gave a slight wave. "More new creations. Hello."

Azel waved. "Hello. We thought we'd come over and introduce ourselves."

The scaled creature smiled. "It's always great to meet someone new who can talk. I haven't found anyone else here who can do so except you three."

Mikael nodded to Lucifer. "Can you introduce us to your friend?"

Lucifer gave a smile, but his expression looked forced. "This is Serpent. I call him that because of his serpentine gait."

Serpent laughed. "I haven't been given a name yet. Thank you, Lucifer, for giving me one. Names help so greatly in having conversations."

Serpent turned Mikael's way. "And you are?"

Mikael smiled. "Oh, forgive me. I'm Mikael. And this is Azel."

Serpent nodded. "Very pleased to meet you. Lucifer was telling me about your dimension. Although different from mine, his description sounded wonderful." Serpent looked at Lucifer and then back to Mikael. "At least you can travel between yours and mine. I cannot do the same."

Mikael smiled. "Oh, we come here because of the Creator's beauty and the wonder he has created. This dimension is always spectacular to visit. You should feel blessed to be here."

"Oh, this place is wonderful." Serpent turned up what appeared to be his brow. "Hard to talk to the other creatures, though." Whispering and putting his hand to the side of his mouth, he added, "They're a little dense, I'm afraid."

Mikael and Azel laughed.

"Beautiful, though," Azel said.

"And you whispered that . . . because?" Mikael asked.

Serpent chucked. "Just in case some of them can understand. Don't want to start out on the wrong foot, you know."

"So you are new?" Azel inquired.

"I think so. I don't recall anything before yesterday."

Lucifer forced himself in the conversation in a not-so-subtle fashion.

"I'll talk with you later, Serpent," Lucifer said. "I need to get back to my duties."

Serpent nodded. "Please come back soon. I enjoyed our conversation."

Lucifer disappeared. Mikael knew the Master had not yet taken any action against Lucifer with the exception of not allowing him back into the Trinity's dimension. So what duties did Lucifer have if he wasn't allowed back inside the throne room?

Serpent gave a slight gasp. "Where did he go?"

"Oh," Mikael said. "He just went back to our dimension. He teleported: disappearing from here and reappearing there."

Serpent's eyes grew wide. "Oh, you angels are quite lucky to be able to teleport like that. Doing so must be pretty awesome."

Mikael never thought about this ability before. Teleporting was something he could always do. He never thought about another creature desiring to do so. Actually, he realized he had never met anyone like Serpent: intelligent yet limited. He wondered if this was a prelude to the Creator's human creation. Maybe Serpent was a creature who could keep the new beings from becoming lonely.

"So, Serpent," Azel said. "What do you think of our Creator's new dimension that he has created?"

"Oh, it's quite wonderful—and beautiful. I feel fortunate. He did tell me there would soon be other creatures I would be able to converse with. When I met Lucifer, I thought perhaps he was that one. Yet, I guess not." Serpent sounded a little disappointed. "Lucifer is a great conversationalist, though." After a slight pause, and almost as an afterthought, Serpent added, "With very creative ideas."

"Oh?" Mikael asked. "Like what?"

Serpent gave a smile, but one which seemed more wry than a genuine smile. "Oh, just in general. He seems to know a lot about almost everything. I'm very new here, so learning is something I treasure."

"I'm sure the Creator will give you plenty of instruction and a life mission," Azel said.

Serpent nodded. "I'm sure he will. I look forward to what he will tell me."

Mikael could hear the Serpent's stomach growl. "Oh, excuse me," Serpent said. "Sorry about that. I think it's time for me to eat." He laughed. "I enjoyed our conversation so much, I forgot about the need to eat."

Mikael had never thought about eating or someone needing to do so. "Oh, please, go right ahead," Mikael said. "We should probably be on our way, anyway. We too have things we need to do."

Serpent smiled. "My Creator gave me many choices of things to eat. He mentioned something he called a fig. I thought I'd try that today. His description made the fruit sound delicious."

"Oh, I'm sure it is. Our Creator makes nothing but the absolute best."

Serpent gave a slight nod. "I'm sure. Maybe next time we meet I can tell you how delicious figs are."

Mikael nodded and gave Serpent a smile as the creature headed farther into the foliage. Serpent remained upright but traveled in a serpentine manner as he propelled himself forward. Both angels watched until the creature was out of sight.

"Well, Serpent seems pleasant enough," Azel said.

Mikael nodded, putting his hand to his chin. "Yes, true. But . . ."

Azel cocked his head. "Something's bothering you. What is it?"

Mikael shook his head. "It could be nothing. It's just the smile Serpent gave. The expression looked . . . deceptive." He shrugged. "Maybe I'm just making something out of nothing."

Azel got a concerned look on his face.

Mikael gave a slight smile. "Sorry. I didn't mean to worry you."

Azel shook his head. "No, I've found your instincts are usually quite good. It's likely worth keeping an eye on both Lucifer and Serpent."

Mikael's eyebrows raised.

"You did say Lucifer was looking for recruits," Azel said.

"Angel recruits."

"Maybe Lucifer is thinking outside the expected."

Mikael gave a blank stare at Azel and then placed his hand on the large guardian's shoulder. "Azel, sometimes you're brighter than you look."

Azel smiled. "I'm always bright. Maybe things look brighter to those who are dull."

Mikael jabbed at one of Azel's stump-thick arms. "Come on. Let's get back and see how to stop a rebellion."

CHAPTER 7

Dimension of Time

Mikael headed down the walkway parallel to the path leading to the Creator's throne room. He noticed Lucifer talking to four other angels. Mikael slowed his pace to see if he could determine anything from their interactions, though he could not hear what they were saying.

He was startled by Azel suddenly grabbing his arm. "Mikael, you have to come and see."

Mikael nearly lifted from the ground in his surprise. "Azel! Give an angel notice, will you?"

Azel laughed. "It's starting, Mikael! It's starting!"

Mikael grabbed Azel's shoulders. "Calm down, Azel. Tell me what you are talking about. *What's* starting?"

"The humans—well, *eventually* the humans. Our Creator is starting to build his dimension of time which will contain the humans."

Mikael glanced back at Lucifer and the other angels. Could this be what they were talking about? They looked just as solemn as Azel did excited.

Azel pulled on his arm. "You have to come see. We're allowed to see what he does."

Mikael's eyes widened. "You mean we're permitted in the time dimension as it's being created?"

Azel nodded enthusiastically. "He's asked Halayim to have a choir and soloists sing as he does his work." Azel pulled on his arm again. "Come! It's going to be glorious!"

Mikael wanted to know what Lucifer was up to, but he definitely didn't want to miss this. Such a creation would be a once-in-an-eternity production.

Almost all the angels had gathered to see the event. Everyone kept asking another how their Creator was going to do such a thing. No one had seen him create before. Often, when they went to his creative dimension, they were astounded by something he had created, but they were never present when the new creature, animal, or plant was formed. His creation was always a joy of discovery. This was taking that wonderment to a new level. They would get to see a side of their Creator never before witnessed.

A beam of light suddenly emanated from the top of the Creator's throne room.

"Where is he going?" many of the angels could be heard asking. One suggested going to the creation dimension to see what might be occurring.

Mikael was glad for the power of teleportation. He as well as many of the angels teleported to this dimension to see what their Creator would do. Amazed, Mikael stood watching an expanse form, and it appeared to get larger and larger.

It seemed many of the animals could somehow tell something was happening as they scurried deeper into the dimension and away from its center. As Mikael stood with Azel in amazement as the dark expanse got ever larger, Serpent approached them.

"What's going on? Why is everyone so excited?" Serpent asked.

Azel looked at the creature in amazement. "The Creator is creating the time dimension. You don't find that exciting?"

"Oh, it's happening now? Of course I'm excited. When did he start creating?"

Azel stood with mouth slightly open. "When did he start? He's creating right now!" He pointed. "Don't you see the expanse growing?"

Serpent looked in the direction Azel pointed. The creature furrowed its brow and shook its head. "Everything looks the same." Serpent looked dejected. "I wish I could see it. You angels have all the fun."

Azel's countenance changed; he realized that because of their higher dimension they could see things Serpent likely could not. "Oh, I'm sorry, Serpent." He glanced back at the forming expanse and then over to Serpent. "It is spectacular, though."

"Well, please tell me about your experience when it's over. That way I'll know when I'll have someone I can talk with," Serpent said.

Serpent glided off, leaving Azel and Mikael looking at each other with a sorrowful expression. "Poor creature," Azel said.

Mikael nodded. Yet he quickly forgot about Serpent as they continued to watch in amazement as the expanse formed. As the newly created area grew larger, many of the angels began teleporting into it. Halayim's choir began singing, and this made the whole event even more glorious.

Mikael watched as what seemed to be dense and black grew larger and larger. He now noticed it filling with water.

"What is the Creator doing?" Azel asked.

Mikael shook his head. "I'm not sure." Looking around, he saw Gabriel and waved him over.

"Gabriel, Yahweh spends a lot of time with you," Mikael said. "Do you know what's happening?"

Gabriel smiled. "A little, but not everything. Currently, he is taking water from his creative dimension and filling this darkness with it."

"It's getting so massive," Azel said. "Will this new dimension contain water-based creatures?"

Mikael shook his head while thinking of the special cherubim in the throne room who were supposedly a reflection of Elohim. "I don't think so. Yahweh said these new humans would be in his likeness. This must be a prelude to something."

Raphael was next to come their way. "Isn't this exciting?"

Mikael nodded. "But what is the Creator doing?"

"I'm not sure," Raphael said as he pointed. "But look. Ruach is making sure the water is retained as a sphere."

"A gigantic sphere," Gabriel said. "It's so large this sphere could be considered a dimension of itself."

Azel nodded as he stared in awe. "I can't even see the opposite side of the sphere anymore. It's almost as if this whole dimension is water in a dark expanse."

"Look!" Raphael exclaimed, pointing. "How does water produce that?!"

All shook their heads in wonderment and turned to Gabriel. He laughed. "I don't know the answer to everything."

"Well, speculate," Mikael said.

"It would seem the water sphere has become so large the density at its center is producing pressure so high the atoms of the water are being compressed together, likely creating other elements the Creator will somehow use. As photons are the stabilizing force of electrons within an atom, photons are released during this process—which we see as light."

"I don't understand," Raphael said.

Gabriel chuckled. "I'm not sure I do either. After all, this is our Creator, and that is definitely what he is doing: creating."

"Look at Ruach," Azel said. "He's drawing the photons, or light, or whatever you want to call it, to the surface of this darkness. He is dividing the light from the darkness."

As millions of photons came to the edge of the dark expanse, they sparkled in an amazing array of light, each particle seeming to twinkle to the very music sung by the angels.

"They're beautiful. Just astounding," Mikael exclaimed. "And so many."

"With so many photons being generated, it likely means the Creator has created many new elements from the water density and pressure," Gabriel replied. "He'll likely use these photon particles to help stabilize whatever he decides to create within this dimension." He smiled, but in a pleasing, stunned way. "It is so like our Creator to put things in their proper order."

All the photons seemed to congregate along one area in which Ruach traveled, thus creating bright and dark sides to the expanse.

Next they heard the voice of their Creator.

"Evening and morning have been achieved. Day One is finished. All is good."

"What does that mean?" Azel asked.

Mikael shrugged. *Day* was a term he had never heard before. He looked at Gabriel, whose countenance seemed to show an understanding. Mikael raised his eyebrows. "What do you know, Gabriel?"

"Well, I don't. Not really. Yet the term 'day' is likely a division of time our Creator has established."

"Day," Azel said. "A unit of time." He paused in thought. "Yahweh did talk about such a concept." He shook his head. "I still don't think I understand the meaning, though."

Mikael heard the choir stop singing and then saw Halayim and the rest of his group teleport. He, Azel, Raphael, and Gabriel also teleported back to the creation realm.

Mikael waved his arm. "Halayim! Halayim!"

Halayim finished a conversation with one of the choir members and walked over.

"Wasn't that magnificent?" he asked the four of them.

Each nodded.

"But is that all there is?" Azel asked.

"Oh, no," Halayim said. "The Creator has asked us to come back each day. There will be at least six days for which we are to sing as our Creator does his work."

Mikael squinted. "How do you know when to teleport back into the time dimension?"

"It won't be long now. Since we're outside his time dimension, it won't seem as long for us."

Still another light beam seemed to leap from the Creator's throne room.

"Look!" Halayim exclaimed. "It's starting." As he ran toward his choir members, they each quickly teleported back to the time dimension.

Mikael and his friends didn't have to say a word. They did the same.

Ruach was now circling within the large watery expanse, carving out a smaller sphere from the center of the enormous one.

As Ruach was doing this, Yahweh gave a command for the expanse to stretch in all directions. As it did so, the remainder of the water began to thin out as the expanse stretched.

Mikael was so engrossed in this aspect that it took some time for Azel's pounding on his arm to register. He finally looked at Azel, who was pointing at something entering the dimension—evidently from the Creator's throne room.

All sorts of particles flooded the expanse; they combined with each other as well as with the photons which had entered earlier. These particles combined in various ways, producing numerous displays as Ruach continued forming the sphere which he kept separate from the expanse being stretched deeper and deeper.

The Creator was expanding the dimension.

Mikael looked at Gabriel, eyes wide. "Do you know any details of what we're experiencing?"

Gabriel gave a slight shrug. "A little. I don't know all the names, but I know the gluons stabilize the nucleus of each atom he forms, and the photons stabilize the electrons. I could get more technical, but . . . "

"Please don't," Raphael interjected. "You've already gone too far for me. All I know is, our Creator really knows how to create."

All laughed and nodded.

It was almost as if Halayim's choir knew exactly when to crescendo and when to sing softly. Their songs seemed to punctuate each galaxy formed as the expanse stretched farther and farther as the universe formed. At the same time, however, each galaxy appeared dissimilar from the next: some were circular, some more round, others flatter. Then, in various places, nebulae formed, looking somewhat hazy, but all

displaying glorious colors combined to produce beautiful for-
mations and shapes.

Almost in a whisper, Azel exclaimed, "Wow, our Creator
really knows how to use photons."

All laughed, but they also looked at each other in amazement. Azel glanced at Mikael. "This has to be even more glorious than the creative dimension we always visit. The Creator
is really in his most intense creative zone now."

Raphael nodded. "I agree. Look!"

The expanse kept growing as more and more galaxies
formed, many with planets and stars giving light to each
region as they traveled deeper into the universe. Some stars
were so bright they looked as though they would burst from
their intensity. Some exhibited reddish hues while others had
a more blue tint.

Azel pointed. "Look at that one!"

The star pulsed as it spun.

Halayim's choir suddenly stopped singing, but then an
amazing thing became obvious: Mikael could still hear music.
He looked at the other two. "Can you hear it?" he nearly whispered. "Our Creator's expanse is singing its own song."

Azel and Raphael stopped and listened. A smile slowly
crept across their faces as they nodded.

Halayim's choir began to mimic the staccato beat and hum
of the various creations. Soon everything was in harmony.
Quite breathtaking, Mikael thought.

Even as the expanse continued to grow, Yahweh came back
to the sphere Ruach was forming. He created another small
gap between the large ball of water and used some of the water
to make a vapor surrounding the sphere. Some of the vapor
aggregated, forming something wispy and white that constantly seemed to change in shape.

Yahweh then stood upon the sphere of water, lifted his hands, and spoke: "Sky. Day Two is now complete."

Mikael looked at Gabriel, who seemed to be waiting for something.

"What is it, Gabriel?"

Gabriel looked at Mikael with a curious look. "He didn't repeat what he said yesterday."

Mikael shook his head slightly. "Excuse me?"

"It is good."

Mikael gave him a blank look. "Is that important?"

Gabriel nodded slowly. "Yes. The omission must have been intentional."

"So why didn't he say the words?"

Gabriel gave a small shrug. "The only thing I can think is that the work of his command isn't complete. The sky is still expanding. Yahweh's work is complete on the ball Ruach has formed, but not complete throughout the expanse."

Mikael gave a slight smile. "So, more to come?"

Gabriel nodded and laughed lightly. "Oh, absolutely."

CHAPTER 8

Creation Continues

The cycle continued. The angels would teleport back to the creation dimension and return when the Creator started his amazing formation process once more.

"Where is everything previously created?" Azel asked. "It still looks dark around the sphere." He then pointed to the sphere of water which remained from the huge sphere the Creator had made in the beginning. "Is he going to leave that sphere as it is?"

Raphael shook his head. "I don't think so. Look what Ruach is now doing."

Gabriel responded. "I think Ruach is moving in and above the water of the sphere and causing the other elements to coalesce. See, something is rising out of the water."

A large mass of land rose from somewhere within the sphere of water pushing the water away. As the land rose, some of the water became trapped in pools—some large, some small—within the structure of land which formed. In some areas the water seemed to be siphoned up through holes in the land mass and then cascade down and over the rocks and crevasses formed, arriving back at the large area of water.

Mikael could hardly believe his eyes. "The appearance of land is so wonderful."

"And clever," Azel said.

Mikael nodded. "He definitely has something special planned for this part of the expanse he has created."

They each saw areas of green appearing over much of the land mass: trees, shrubs, flowers.

"Impressive," Raphael said in what was nearly a whisper.

"It isn't as lush as his creative dimension," Azel said. "I wonder why."

"Oh, I'm sure he's just getting started," Mikael said with a grin.

Yahweh again stood on the sphere. "Earth is created. All is good. Day Three is now complete."

Azel looked at Raphael and Mikael. "What do you think tomorrow will bring?"

Mikael smiled. "Let's find out."

They teleported, returning with their Creator.

The Creator caused more elements to come together, forming a sphere, and this emitted photons on a massive scale. This sphere appeared similar to some of the stars the Creator had already created, but this one was extremely yellow in color. Mikael noticed the Creator placed this new yellow star near Earth.

"Oh, I get it," Raphael said. "This is to provide light and heat for the plants to grow."

"Look!" Now Azel pointed. "He's making another sphere."

This time, however, the sphere was much smaller in size than Earth and looked more like a large, spherical rock.

Earth then began a very slow circling motion around the star.

The rock began a slow circle around Earth.

Yahweh did the same several times making some of the spheres rocky, some gaseous while displaying various colors, and then set them in motion around the star he just created.

"Oh, how ingenious," Mikael gasped. "From Earth these will look like stars."

"That's only the half of it," Raphael said with a grin.

"Speaking of stars," Azel said. "Why can't we see them from Earth? We're now standing on the dark side of Earth."

All looked up and only saw darkness.

"Curious," Mikael said.

Gabriel pointed upward. Their gaze followed his.

Mikael looked at the black sky and then back to Gabriel. "I don't see anything."

Gabriel looked at Mikael and smiled. "Just look. And wait."

Mikael shrugged and returned his gaze to the darkness. The light of the other stars and galaxies reached Earth simultaneously.

"Whoa!" Azel said as he ducked in shock. Everyone did the same. "That was awesome!"

"Indeed," Raphael said.

Gabriel chuckled. "These will now always be visible from Earth when the sun is not in view."

They continued to stand on the dark side of this planet, Earth, and look into the sky. "Oh, the night sky is glorious," Azel said. "The smaller sphere is reflecting the light of the huge star, and the lights of the other stars are now visible." He nodded. "Our Creator is making something very wonderful for . . . someone."

Mikael could only nod in agreement.

They then heard their Creator speak. "It is good. Day Four is complete."

Mikael looked at the other two. "Let's not head back this time. Let's stay and see how long a day really is in this dimension."

Both Raphael and Azel nodded. "Great idea." All sat in a lush bed of . . . something green that had numerous tiny slivers of plant material sticking upward that felt almost smooth when one brushed their hand across it—someone nearby had called it "grass"—and watched the night sky for several hours.

Azel sat upright. "While we're here, we may as well view everything, right?"

Mikael's eyebrows raised. "What do you mean?"

Azel displayed a wry smile. "Follow me."

They teleported to various nebulae, pulsars, galaxies, and even viewed the sun of Earth up close. Its outer edge seemed to be in constant motion. Occasionally, giant plumes of what appeared to be fire billowed into space and then fell back again in gigantic arcs. The view was simply wonderful to behold.

Before they knew it, they heard their Creator speak again.

"Let the waters teem with creatures of all kinds, and let the Earth flourish with various flying creatures."

The three of them looked at each other with eyes wide. "Let's go see," Mikael said.

The others nodded and followed him back to Earth.

"Wow," Azel said. "This is starting to look more like his creative dimension."

They watched as Ruach flew over the water with new water creatures forming in his wake. Some were small and colorful, others large and quite massive. Many jumped out of the water, into the air, and fell back into the water creating great waves from their splashes, as if these creatures were . . . well, *enjoying themselves. Who can blame them?* Mikael thought.

At the same time Yahweh himself walked over the Earth, his hands waving here and there as flying creatures appeared. These were quite different from the water creatures. Some were quite colorful, whether they had splashes of various hues across their feathers, beaks, or plumes. Others, apparently nocturnal, were darker in color. The four of them laughed and pointed whenever a new variety emerged.

They heard their Creator again.

"It is good. Multiply and fill the earth with your offspring. Evening and morning are complete. All is good. Day Five has ended."

"Let's go back this time," Mikael said. He wanted to see what the other angels were saying. Also, it had been a while since he had checked in on Lucifer to see what he was up to.

On top of that, he felt bad he had not talked to Serpent since the Creator had begun his work in this new time dimension. Serpent had looked so sad knowing he could not see what Mikael and the other angels could see.

Both Raphael and Azel agreed. They teleported back to the dimension of the angels.

CHAPTER 9

Humans

To Mikael's surprise, there was a buzz happening among the angels. He saw Uriel in the distance and walked over.

"Uriel, what's going on?"

"Mikael, unity is breaking down fast."

Mikael cocked his head. "What's the issue?"

"Some are not . . . very happy with the Creator's creation of another dimension."

Mikael was taken back. "But that's why he's the Creator. *Creating* is what he does. No one has ever had issues with him creating anything before. Everyone has loved his creativity."

"I think the problem is Lucifer. Surprisingly, he's very manipulative—and charismatic."

Mikael sighed. "Ever since he was banned from the Creator's throne room, he's become a problem."

Uriel's eyes widened. "I thought you knew."

"Knew? Knew what?"

"He was only banned from the Creator's throne. He still has access to the throne room. He just has to stay below the expanse where the Cherubim reside."

Mikael cocked his head. "But what does he do if he can't fulfill the very duties he was made for?"

"Apparently—now this is just hearsay, I'm afraid—he still talks to the Creator."

"About what?"

Uriel patted Mikael on his shoulder. "That, my friend, is a question for Ruach."

Mikael stood in thought as Uriel walked on. Maybe Uriel was right. He had to find Ruach. But would he be available with all the creation taking place? He headed toward the throne room, then paused and sighed. No, he really had to know. He picked up his pace trying to make himself feel confident as he approached.

Jahvan was standing at the entrance. "Hello, Mikael. I'm sorry, but I haven't received word from Ruach to allow you entrance."

Mikael exhibited a small smile. "Yes, I know. I'm actually looking for Ruach. Have you seen him?"

Jahvan shook his head. "No, not recently, I—"

Mikael raised his eyebrows. "Something wrong?"

A smile quickly spread across Jahvan's face. "Ruach has just now asked you to enter."

"What?" Mikael shook his head. "No, I just wanted to talk to him."

The portal opened and the kaleidoscope of color became visible. Mikael looked at Jahvan with a puzzled look.

Jahvan laughed. "I just do as Ruach tells me."

"Well, I wish he would have done the same for me," Mikael said.

Ruach appeared at the door. "Well, Mikael, I'm telling you now. Enter." If he could see Ruach smile, the great Spirit would most likely be wearing one.

"Ruach, why do you want me to enter?"

"There is a conversation I think you need to hear."

Mikael gave a slight shrug. "Okay. You're the boss."

Ruach laughed. "That's why you need to hear this conversation."

Mikael squinted, but followed Ruach inside without further questions. This time, Ruach evidently made Mikael invisible. No one, not even Lucifer, seemed to notice him.

Lucifer paced through the stones of fire. The fiery crystals were part of the reason for the kaleidoscope of color beneath the expanse. Yet Lucifer was no longer donning the vest of stones, and he was beneath the expanse.

The Creator spoke. "Lucifer, your position is gone, not because I no longer love you, but because you have rebelled."

All Mikael could hear from Lucifer was a "hmmph."

The Creator's tone became softer. "Lucifer, your rebellion was in your heart long before it became visible, causing your light to fade."

Lucifer said nothing.

"And your rebellion, your separate will from mine, is still there. Lucifer, you can't hide this from me. Don't let your pride shortchange your possibilities."

"Oh, I know my possibilities," Lucifer said. "Actually, you're making my plan *for* me."

Mikael looked at Ruach, wondering what that statement was supposed to mean.

Ruach sighed. "Come, Mikael. Let's go."

Mikael felt confused. What did Lucifer mean by his statement?

Once they had left the throne room, Mikael turned to Ruach. "Would you be able to explain what just happened?"

"I'll let the events unfold," Ruach said. "They will become clear. What I can say is this: get your army prepared. The next day of creation will create something marvelous—and lead to something sorrowful."

Mikael pondered what those words meant and why Ruach spoke them as a riddle. He wanted more information, but when he turned to ask Ruach, he was gone.

At that moment Azel and Raphael walked up. "It's time, Mikael. The Creator is starting again."

All three teleported to the time dimension. They saw Halayim's choir gathered around Earth, so they teleported to the Earth's surface as they noticed Yahweh there.

As Yahweh walked along the land, he spoke, and various kinds of land animals appeared, two of each, at his command. The spectacle was awesome to watch as all the necessary components of the earth came together in the twinkle of an eye to create each kind of animal. Yahweh's creativity was simply overwhelming, the variety of animals mind-bending.

Mikael knew he would never be able to think of such things. *Did Lucifer think he could?* Like him, every angel looked in awe at their Creator. Even though they had all seen the wonders in Eden, as it had come to be known, this dimension the Creator had already made, this new wave of creativity did not diminish the awe in their eyes.

Then something unusual happened: the Trinity stood together. "It is time for us to create the human."

All the angels stood for what would surely be a momentous event. Great anticipation was on each angel's face. Even the choir stopped singing to wait for this miracle.

It was amazingly touching to see the Trinity together. Most angels could not see their Creator as one entity. That could only be done above the expanse in the throne room, being a dimension unto itself. They saw three beings, all dressed in bright Shekinah glory, standing together.

Yahweh did not simply speak to cause the human to form. This was far more intimate. Each part of the Trinity passed his hand—or what appeared to be a hand—over the ground between them. No one had a completely unobstructed view, but from where Mikael was looking, he could see the human slowly being formed from the ground. All the elements needed to create the body of what was now being referred to as a . . . *human* . . . were somehow coming together through the divine touch of the Trinity.

As this occurred, Halayim's choir began to sing once more. Their crescendo slowly rose as more and more of the human body formed, almost looking as if the body was slowly rising from the ground. This creative endeavor was a tedious process, but before long the complete body of the human became visible.

Yahweh slowly and lovingly lifted the body. The Trinity then disappeared! This caught everyone off guard. Everyone teleported back to the creation dimension, assuming that was where Yahweh had taken the human form.

Ruach met them there and directed them to a garden he said had just been created. For some reason, Ruach allowed only Mikael to enter the garden and witness what Yahweh was doing with the human.

The first thing Mikael noticed was that the colors in this garden, though lush, were more muted than what he was accustomed to seeing in his master's creative dimension. The plants and animals were reminiscent of what he had observed the Creator making on Earth. Evidently, this was a place for the human. Mikael just wasn't sure why.

The important thing now was to see what Yahweh would do next. Yahweh gently laid the human on soft grass. The man looked muscular and well proportioned, but this was to be expected: Mikael could never think of the Creator making anything inferior.

Yahweh then bent over the human and gently opened his mouth. Yahweh put his mouth over the human and breathed into him. Mikael saw the man's chest . . . gloriously begin to expand! At the same time, the man's body glowed with a tinge of Yahweh's Shekinah glory, almost like an afterglow, and the glow seemed to hide the details of the human's body, but it did not interfere with seeing who he was at the same time. As Mikael looked more closely, the chest of the human began to rise and fall slowly. Certain places on the human's body looked to pulsate as if something was flowing though those areas. The human suddenly sat up and looked around—he appeared alert, intelligent, and somehow knowing his Creator.

Yahweh lovingly put his hand on the human's shoulder and smiled. "Hello, Adam."

Adam smiled back. "Hello, Yahweh, Creator."

Yahweh nodded. "I have so much to tell you." Yahweh stood and held out his hand. Adam grabbed his Creator's forearm and stood. As Adam looked around, he seemed to look right through Mikael—as if he wasn't there at all. Apparently, Ruach had made him invisible in this garden. Yet Ruach allowed him to follow Yahweh and Adam as they began to walk.

Ruach looked at Mikael. "You need to understand what is at stake."

Mikael had questions but knew this was not the time to ask them.

Yahweh put his arm around Adam's shoulders. "I have so much to show you and tell you."

Adam was wide-eyed at every turn. "Everything is so beautiful. Who is all this for?"

Yahweh smiled. "It is all for you, Adam."

"Me?" Adam sounded surprised.

"Or," Yahweh said, "it will be. I want to teach you how to take care of a garden like this. Where you are now is how your home, called Earth, will look once you know how to take care of the land and its plants. I created this replica so you will know you are doing things correctly. Your world is growing even as we speak. Once you know how to take care of everything here, I'll take you there. Then you can make Earth as lush as this garden I have created within my creative dimension, called Eden."

Adam smiled. "I can't wait to learn—and see everything."

"The other thing I have done is put a replica of most of the animals and plants that will be on Earth, where your kingdom will be, here."

"Kingdom?"

Yahweh smiled. "Yes, Adam. Kingdom. Earth will become your kingdom under my rule. How does that sound to you?"

"Very impressive, my Lord. I'm very honored."

Yahweh turned solemn. "Adam, I know you have just arrived here. I have a lot to teach you, and you have a lot to learn. Yet the biggest thing to learn is obedience."

Adam nodded as if he agreed.

"No challenge to that statement?" Yahweh asked the question suddenly, surprisingly—at least it struck Mikael that way.

In a surprised tone, Adam answered, "Oh, no. Of course not. You are my Creator. I can do no greater honor than to serve and obey."

Yahweh smiled broadly. "I am very glad to hear you say that." He paused, looked intently at Adam, then said, "Now come with me. Your greatest lesson begins."

Adam followed Yahweh to the middle of the garden. Mikael noticed the brilliance of the colors of the creation dimension shining brightly.

The brilliance of color was most stunning from two trees. Yahweh pointed to the most beautiful one first.

"Adam, this is the Tree of Life."

Adam gasped. "My Creator, this place is the most beautiful of all the garden." He looked anxiously at Yahweh. "Will this be part of my kingdom?"

Yahweh gave a half smile. "Perhaps. But that decision is yours."

Adam looked contemplative but didn't ask anything further.

Even Mikael marveled at the tree. This was the first time he had seen this creation as well. There was a river flowing through the middle of this garden, and the tree had roots growing on either side of the river, with the most beautiful fruit growing on its branches.

"Adam, this tree will sustain you, growing forever, never fading. This special tree will produce fruit that will periodically change so you will never grow tired of the taste of each kind. This is my gift to you."

Adam smiled. "It truly is a most marvelous tree and different from any other in the garden I have yet seen. This is a most wonderful gift."

Yahweh laughed. "Oh, trust me. There is no tree like this one, and no other tree will ever be like it. There are many other types of trees, each with a different type of fruit. All are for your enjoyment. Yet you must periodically eat from this tree for the continual sustainment of your present state. Do you understand?"

Adam nodded and then motioned to the other brilliant tree. "This other tree also looks beautiful and special."

Yahweh smiled. "Yes, Adam. This tree is also extremely special." His smile faded. He turned to Adam and looked directly in his eyes. "This is the only thing I have chosen to withhold from you." He pointed to the tree. "Eating from this tree is forbidden."

"Forbidden?" Adam cocked his head. "Why is this so?"

"Remember what I told you, Adam. To be here, to earn your kingdom, you must learn obedience."

Adam's brow furrowed at first, but then a smile slowly spread across his face. "I see. Obedience comes with a choice, or it is not obedience."

Yahweh smiled and patted Adam's shoulder. "You learn very quickly, my son. This tree is called the Tree of Knowledge of Good and Evil." He again looked deeply into Adam's eyes. "Remember this. Don't get distracted and make the error of eating from this tree."

Adam shook his head. "No, my Creator." He looked contemplative once more. "I know you have made me understand things, but this tree is a puzzle to me. I do not understand its name." He looked around. "Yet you have supplied so much to take in and learn. This should not be hard to remember."

Yahweh smiled. "Obedience does not require understanding, only trust that I want the best for you."

Adam nodded.

"I have given you some heavy thoughts to remember, and these must sink in. Yet such a beautiful garden can't be for just serious talk now, can it?"

Adam cocked his head, seemingly unsure of how to respond.

"How about some fun for a change?" Yahweh asked. "Ready?"

Adam grinned broadly. "Very."

"Okay. You sit on this rock. I'll have the animals that will be in your kingdom pass by. I want you to name them however you wish."

"Really? I can name them . . . *anything*?"

Yahweh laughed. "Absolutely. After all, they will be part of your kingdom. So you have the right to name them."

Over the next several hours, creature after creature passed by, and Adam provided a name for each kind. Adam found he couldn't just sit and look. He would run his hand over each pair of creatures as they passed to feel the differences in the textures of their skin. Some were large. Some were small. Some felt rough, others smooth and soft. He giggled as he caressed some of the smaller ones. These creatures seemed to greatly enjoy the human interaction.

Once they had all passed, Adam looked at Yahweh. "That was fun."

Yahweh smiled. "I'm glad. Being a ruler has a lot of responsibilities." He leaned in close to Adam and whispered, "But also a lot of fun."

Adam nodded, displaying a broad grin. He then turned solemn. "Yahweh, I have a question."

"Yes?"

"Well, I noticed every creature which came by was male or female, two forms of each type of creature."

Yahweh nodded. "Yes, that is right. They are of two genders so they can reproduce and create more of their kind."

Adam nodded. "Yes, that makes sense." He looked at Yahweh. "Perfect sense. But what about me?"

"What about you, Adam?"

"Well, you've created mates for each kind of animal which I have named. Yet I don't see a mate for me. Do I have one?"

"Do you want a mate, Adam? Am I not sufficient?"

"Well, I certainly enjoy being with you and talking with you. But if I am to be head of a kingdom, I will need more of my kind as well, won't I?"

Yahweh nodded. "Yes, you will." Yahweh smiled. "I wanted you to come to this realization on your own. You are not like these other creatures. I made you special, and you are able to make choices the other creations cannot make. I am incredibly pleased you have come to this conclusion on your own. This, again, is another responsibility of one who rules. Do you understand this, Adam?"

The man nodded. "Yes, I believe I do. I am to teach others of my kind what you will be teaching me. I need to do for them what you have done and are doing for me."

Yahweh smiled. "Yes, Adam. That is it exactly. I will make a mate for you."

Adam yawned. "I feel like I can't keep my eyes open. Is something wrong with me?"

Yahweh put his hand on Adam's shoulder. "Just lie here and sleep, Adam. As you sleep, I will create for you a mate, a *wife*, a special companion. I will make her be a part of you so you two will be connected to each other and helpers to each other."

Adam nodded and yawned again. He slowly knelt and then lay on the ground. In a matter of minutes, he was sleeping soundly.

To Mikael's sheer amazement, Yahweh worked quickly. He sliced open Adam's side, took one of his ribs, and sealed up Adam's side. There was not even a hint of a scar left.

As Adam slept, Yahweh teleported back to Earth and created another human from the ground and Adam's rib in much the same way he had for Adam. Although this human looked remarkably similar to Adam, there were obvious differences. She had softer features to her frame and look than Adam did.

Again, Yahweh carried her to where Adam slept. As he had done to Adam, he also breathed into her, and she also took on a glowing appearance . . .

She awoke, sat up, and smiled. Yahweh helped her to her feet.

As she looked at Adam asleep on the ground, she looked back at Yahweh. "Who is this?"

"Isha, this is Adam. He will be your partner, your *husband.*"

At that moment Adam woke slowly. He sat up, yawned, stretched, and suddenly stopped when he saw the woman. He turned to face Yahweh.

"This is my mate, my wife?"

Yahweh smiled and nodded. "Yes, Adam. Isha is created for you as your wife, and you as her husband."

CHAPTER 10

Serpent

As Mikael walked from the garden into the main part of the creative dimension, he noticed Serpent approaching from the opposite direction. Mikael at first hesitated, then decided to follow him. He didn't realize Serpent would be one of the creations that would become part of Adam's kingdom on Earth. So far, all the animals he had observed in the garden were duplicates of those which also resided on Earth. He had to find out the discrepancy.

Adam and Isha had sat down on a grassy knoll, eating some fruit from one of the nearby trees. Mikael watched as Serpent approached them.

"Are those figs?"

Both quickly turned to see who had spoken. Adam stood and helped the woman to her feet. He spoke first. "They are. How do you know about figs? And . . . where did you come from?"

With his strong muscular tail, Serpent approached the two while donning a smile. "I am Serpent. I ate some figs not long ago. They're wonderful, aren't they?"

Both nodded. Isha replied and nodded toward her mate. "Adam has been showing me all the things the Creator made for us, but we've never encountered anyone like you."

Serpent smiled broadly and gave a slight bow. "Well, thank you. That's a nice compliment. I wouldn't want to be like anyone else, would you?"

Adam appeared hesitant to return the pleasantries. "My Creator did not have you and your mate walk before me as creatures he created for my kingdom. Yet here you stand in the garden with a name. How is that?"

Serpent's eyes widened slightly. "Oh, Lucifer, one of the Creator's high-ranking angels, named me. Maybe that's why the Creator didn't have me with the other animals. I already have a name. Plus . . . " Serpent lowered his head and whispered. "You probably noticed some of them are not too bright, if you know what I mean." He smiled. "But they are all so cute, aren't they? Some, I admit, are intelligent—to a degree."

Serpent looked at Adam while holding up his hands. "But if you, leader of the time kingdom, want to rename me, that is your right." He gave a slight bow. "And I will comply."

Isha put her hand on Adam's arm before he could reply. "Oh, it's a great name. Don't you think, Adam? His name matches the serpentine pattern of his movements. Lucifer must be quite clever."

"Oh, indeed he is," Serpent said. "Maybe I can introduce you to him sometime."

"That would be nice," Isha replied. "Having others to talk with would be wonderful." She paused but then said excitedly, "What about your mate? May we meet her?"

Serpent shook his head. "Unfortunately, she has not yet been allowed to enter your garden."

"Why?" Isha asked, tilting her head as if the reply struck her as strange.

Serpent shrugged. "Somehow Lucifer was able to get me in. He hasn't been able to do that for my mate as yet."

Isha nodded but still looked confused by Serpent's reply.

"So if you had to request to be let in, you will not be part of my kingdom?" Adam asked.

"Maybe the Creator is just testing to see how compatible we will be together." Serpent gave a slight smile and looked at Isha. "Maybe if you told Lucifer you wanted to talk with my mate, he could be more persuasive with the Creator."

Adam shook his head. "The Creator has not allowed us to see or talk with angels."

Serpent gave a forced smile. "Oh, that's right. Excuse me for not remembering that."

"What do you mean?" Isha asked, intrigued.

"Well," Serpent replied, putting forward a sympathetic tone, "I was created outside the garden in the Creator's creative dimension, and so I'm allowed to see angels." Serpent looked around in a cautious manner as if searching to see if anyone was looking.

"Are you all right?" Isha asked, a bit concerned by Serpent's mannerisms.

Serpent gave another forced smile. "Yes, I'm fine." He refocused on the two of them. "Anyway, there is a ranking system here. The higher you go, the more you can see." He shrugged. "That's all."

Mikael knew Serpent was likely wondering if he was limited in who he could see within the garden. Perhaps Serpent couldn't see him here and he would not have to be cautious. Yet Mikael didn't move from where he had concealed himself—just in case.

"That's an interesting thought." Isha pointed to the small pile of figs they had picked. "Would you care to join us for some figs and talk further?"

Serpent's eyes widened. "Oh, that would be lovely. Thank you."

Both Adam and Isha sat down once more. Serpent had his lower extremities coil around themselves so he would be lower and more at eye level with the humans.

After a couple of bites, Adam asked, "Why are you the only other creature who can talk?" He quickly held up his hand. "I'm not complaining, mind you. You're just . . . different."

Isha nodded. "I met a few birds who can mimic what I say, but they can't carry on a conversation like you." She smiled warmly. "What purpose did the Creator assign to you?"

"Purpose?"

Isha nodded. "Yes." She pointed to Adam. "Our Creator is preparing Adam and me to lead a kingdom on Earth. We have talks with him almost every afternoon as he teaches us things we need to know about ruling and taking care of all the plants and animals. If we follow his guidance, one day Earth will look like this garden."

"The Creator did tell me my mate and I are to be the voice for all the animals," Serpent said. He shook his head. "But that doesn't sound very important."

Isha's eyes widened. "Oh, your purpose sounds greatly important. We could work together and make Earth absolutely wonderful." She looked at Adam. "Let's ask Yahweh about this also."

Adam nodded but looked cautious.

Serpent appeared to mull over her statement, seemingly not liking it. It was the first time he seemed less than amiable to the man and woman. "You think I would be under you

in your kingdom? I think I am able to speak, even to angels
. . . "—Serpent apparently added this last statement to empha-
size his perceived ranking order—". . . because I was made
unique." He gave a quick glance to the two of them and then
shrugged. "At least, that's what Lucifer tells me." He took
another bite of fig. "I really like him. He's unique as well."

Adam squinted. "Unique? Both of you are unique?"

Serpent nodded.

"But can two be unique?" Adam asked. "Doesn't unique
imply oneness, one being like no other?"

Serpent replied, "Well, I am the only animal here who can
speak, and he is the only angel who can be directly in the
Creator's presence." Serpent smiled weakly and shrugged.
"That sounds unique to me."

"Oh, different, for sure," Adam said. "I'm not so sure about
unique, though." He turned to Isha. "Let's talk to Yahweh
about this term when he visits this afternoon."

She nodded. "Yes, he is definitely wise and will know the
answer." Isha turned to Serpent. "If you visit tomorrow, we'll
let you know his answer." She gave a genuine smile. "He will
make everything clear."

"Oh, I'm sure he can. After all, he is the Creator, right?"
Serpent said with what seemed the slightest of condescending
tones.

"Why do you say it that way?" Adam asked. "Are you saying
he can't give the correct answer?"

Serpent held up his hands. "Oh, no. My goodness, no." He
chuckled. "He definitely knows the answer."

Isha now looked confused. "He knows the answer but may
not tell us?"

Serpent shook his head lightly. "I'm sorry. I've probably
said too much." He gave a small smile. "I just get so excited

being able to talk with someone. It's just something Lucifer told me, so I probably shouldn't be telling you."

Adam leaned in. "What did he tell you?"

Serpent waved his hand. "Oh, nothing, really."

Adam continued to stare at Serpent, expecting a reply.

Serpent looked from Adam to Isha and back. "All right. I don't know this for a fact, mind you. But it may be that the Creator is not . . . being totally honest with you."

Both jerked their heads back. "That's impossible!" Adam said in astonishment. "He's the Creator."

Serpent held up his hands as if patting the air to calm them down. "I know. I know. I'm not saying he doesn't know, it's just . . ."

Adam raised his eyebrows, waiting.

"He just may not tell you everything."

"Like what?" Adam sounded doubtful.

"Well, you can't see angels, right?"

Both nodded.

"You can't leave the garden, right?"

Both nodded again.

"But he *is* preparing me to lead my kingdom," Adam said. "And preparing both of us for how to tend the earth to make our kingdom as lush as this garden."

Serpent nodded. "Yes, yes, of course he is. But who is in *control* of your kingdom?"

"Well, he is, of course," Adam said. "He's the Creator. I wouldn't have anything without him."

Serpent suddenly sat up slightly higher on his coils. "You know? You're right." He paused, then waved a hand in a dismissive gesture. "Yes, surely you're right." He shrugged. "I mean, what possible reason could he have for keeping you in the dark about anything?" He nodded. "You are most certainly correct."

Adam and Isha looked at each other and then back at the Serpent. They didn't seem to know what to say.

Serpent moved upright, now as fully erect as he could, unwinding the coils of his lower extremity. "Well, I must be off," he said. "I have a meeting with one of the angels. I hope to see you again tomorrow."

Adam and Isha stood.

"I enjoyed talking with you," Isha said.

Adam gave a slight nod with a thin smile.

Serpent headed in the direction close to where Mikael stood. Mikael froze, but Serpent didn't seem to notice him. Evidently, the Creator had made angels invisible within the garden. Despite the innuendos from Serpent, Mikael knew the Creator had a purpose for all he did or did not do. And what the Creator did was always for the benefit of everyone. Who was feeding these half-truths to Serpent?

Mikael could think of only one angel who would do such a thing and do it on purpose.

Mikael debated whether to follow Serpent or wait and see the reaction of the humans from their conversation with Serpent. He decided to stay—at least a little while.

Both humans sat down again. Adam spoke first. "Well, he is certainly an odd creature."

Isha's eyebrows shot up. "Oh, I thought he was nice. Don't get me wrong. Having you and Yahweh to talk with is wonderful. But getting other thoughts and opinions is nice as well. As far as I know, he is the only other creature with whom we can carry on a conversation."

A small, furry creature scurried into Isha's lap. She laughed. "Hey there!" She held the animal and buried her face in its fur. "Aren't you cute?"

Isha looked at Adam. "What do you call these creatures again?"

Adam chuckled. "This little furball is call a squirrel."

Isha smiled and rubbed her hand over its soft fur. "Aren't you a cute little squirrel?"

The creature seemed excited to be in her lap. Isha laughed again as she continuously stroked the squirrel's fur. "Yes, you are."

The squirrel jumped out of her hands and scurried off with another squirrel that came by with a nut in its hands.

Adam laughed. "Well, I think *he* communicated quite well. We rank second to mates and food."

Isha laughed with him. "Yes, that's true." She turned serious again. "But you get my meaning, right? Yes, all these creatures are wonderful, and they give serenity and more meaning to our lives. But conversation is also so important. I enjoyed talking with Serpent."

Adam nodded. "I get what you're saying. Yet . . . "

Isha put her hand on Adam's arm. "What is it?"

Adam shook his head. "I can't really say." He paused. "But he seems to speak in riddles. He says one thing, but his tone seems to imply something different." He shrugged. "Maybe Yahweh can help clear up some of the things he said."

"Adam?"

Adam and Isha looked at each other with great excitement. "He's here!" Isha exclaimed.

Adam nodded and helped Isha to her feet. "We're over here, Creator!"

Yahweh gave each of them a hug. Mikael could see a visible relaxation in their muscles as they hugged. He smiled. Yahweh had an intimate connection with these humans. Mikael had no doubt his Creator loved him as well. Yet theirs was a different kind of connection than this. He had an intimate connection with his Creator—but not like *this* kind of intimacy.

Mikael thought about his relationship with Yahweh. His connection with the Creator was more of a respect with intimacy combined. After all, he was the commander of Yahweh's angels. Their connection was not meant to be like this. Mikael asked himself if he was jealous. He had to admit he admired the special attention the Creator gave these two humans.

Still, no, he was not jealous. He was simply happy for them. And he was happy with his place in his Creator's kingdom. He just didn't yet know what his role was going to be in this new time kingdom Adam would rule.

But he knew Yahweh had a plan.

He wanted to be ready for whatever his Creator had in store for him.

CHAPTER 11

Doubt

As Mikael left the garden, he saw Ruach in conversation with Serpent. He planned to walk by, not wishing to disturb their conversation.

"Mikael!" Ruach called. "Please come over and talk with us."

Mikael did so but noticed Serpent didn't look happy with him encroaching on their conversation. Yet Serpent appeared to try being as pleasant as possible.

"Hello, Serpent," Mikael said. "It's good to see you again. I'll have to tell you about the Creator's new time dimension as I promised." He smiled. "It was quite special."

"I am sure there is no doubt," Serpent said. "Yet Raphael and Azel have filled me in for the most part. I just came from talking to the humans."

Mikael acted as if he didn't know. "Oh, that must have been nice."

"Yes, it was." He glanced at Ruach and then back to Mikael. "Lucifer was able to allow me entrance into the garden."

Mikael raised his eyebrows. "Lucifer *allowed*?"

Serpent waved his hand. "Oh, you know what I mean."

Mikael scrunched his brow. No, he didn't know what this meant, so he turned to Ruach.

"Lucifer asked for Serpent to be able to meet the humans," Ruach answered. "We agreed."

Mikael nodded but still wasn't sure he understood.

Ruach turned to Serpent. "You do know why we allowed this?"

Serpent nodded, seemingly reluctant to admit what he knew. "You said I had decisions to make, and meeting the humans would help me do that."

Mikael looked from Serpent to Ruach, still confused. "Decisions?"

"Go on, Serpent. Explain the meaning to Mikael."

Serpent looked at Ruach, sighed slightly, and turned to Mikael. "The Creator told me obedience demands a choice, and he wanted to provide me with choice."

Ruach added, "Choice is a gift, Serpent. Don't take such a gift lightly. You are the liaison between what is created here in Eden and the Creator."

"As if you don't already know what's going on in the creation dimension," Serpent said with what Mikael noticed was just a hint of sarcasm.

Ruach put his hand on Serpent's shoulder. "Well, of course that is true. But you can influence all these creatures and make this a happy environment for them. They need interaction, touch, and affection. Your mate seems content in this role."

"I noticed," Serpent said. "Too happy, if you ask me."

Ruach chuckled. "She does seem content. Yet you by her side could make her more content."

Mikael noticed the expression on Serpent's face, and this indicated he had not totally bought into this role which had been assigned him.

"You prefer to be in the human domain so you can have more verbal communication?" Ruach asked Serpent.

Serpent looked at Mikael, then glanced at Ruach. Mikael got the feeling he didn't want to answer the question. "Let's just say there are pros and cons to each," Serpent said.

Mikael raised his eyebrows. That wasn't the answer he had expected. He looked at Ruach, who seemed to understand perfectly. "I encourage you to think long-term, Serpent. Short-term goals are not necessarily what is best."

Serpent nodded and then left the two of them behind. Mikael heard Serpent speak under his breath in a whisper: "Riddles. Why always riddles?"

Mikael chuckled. "What's with him?"

Ruach patted Mikael on his upper arm. "Go back to the garden and listen some more. I want you to get a full picture. What you will have to do may prove difficult, and I want you to have enough information to make your choice as well."

Mikael squinted and wanted to ask more questions, but Ruach disappeared. Mikael chuckled to himself. *That's one way to end a conversation.*

Mikael didn't know what to do but comply. He headed back to the garden. Hearing laughter and talking, he headed in that direction.

"That's the way, Isha," Adam was saying, encouraging her. "Separate these flowers so they are not so crowded, then plant them over in the sparse area. They will then grow there allowing more nutrients and light to help all of them grow."

As Isha did so, Adam turned to Yahweh. "That makes so much sense. I mean, I wouldn't have thought to separate them like you said, but your explanation makes the purpose of the action very clear. So if we do this on Earth, we can help the plants spread, grow, and prosper?"

Yahweh nodded. "Sometimes the simple things make the most impact."

Adam laughed. "Even your simple words of wisdom are profound."

After Isha replanted the flowers, she rinsed her hands in a nearby stream. She turned. "So what's next?"

Yahweh smiled. "Walk with me. That's enough gardening lessons for today."

After a couple moments of silence, Adam said, "We met a remarkably interesting creature today. He could talk."

Yahweh nodded. "And what did you think of this creature?"

"Oh, I liked Serpent—a lot," Isha said.

Adam was quiet.

Yahweh stopped and turned to Adam. "And you, Adam? What were your thoughts about Serpent?"

Adam looked down and then back to Yahweh. "Serpent seemed a little condescending."

"Very clever, though," Isha interjected.

Adam nodded. "I'm not denying that. Not at all. Serpent's tone, though, just had a sense of superiority."

Yahweh nodded. "I see. And how did that make you feel?"

"Like I wasn't important—or not as important as this creature thought it was."

Yahweh nodded again. "And what did you want to do about that?"

Adam paused, and then with a slight smile, replied, "Kick Serpent out of the garden."

"Adam!" Isha replied.

Yahweh laughed. "I take it you didn't do that?"

Adam shook his head. "No. We actually invited Serpent back again."

Yahweh laughed even harder. He then turned serious. "As ruler of a kingdom, you may come across many people with a similar attitude as Serpent. You will certainly have the power to banish, but doing so may not always be the best choice."

Adam nodded. "Yes, Creator. I realize that is true."

"Sometimes kindness can actually be a deterrent, as such a response can change one's attitude. Sometimes, though, harsh consequences are needed and appropriate to elicit the desired response."

Adam cocked his head. "How am I supposed to know which to do?"

Yahweh took his index finger and tapped Adam's chest. "You have to love them. Even in spite of themselves, and even if the love is not reciprocated. If you love them enough, you will know the right consequence to give."

Adam nodded. "You are wise, Creator. I just hope I can live up to that."

Yahweh smiled. "It is all a choice, Adam. Obedience does not require a reason, but it does require trust. If they trust you enough, their obedience will follow."

Yahweh gave them each a hug. "That's enough teaching for today. Until tomorrow."

"Aw," Isha said. "Is it really time for you to leave already?"

Yahweh smiled and kissed her cheek. "You make leaving difficult, but I do have to go."

Both waved as Yahweh walked away and then disappeared.

Mikael wondered if this was what he was supposed to have witnessed. It seemed like a great lesson. Was Adam's lesson for him as well? He turned to go, but then heard Adam speak.

"I love our talks with the Creator, but . . . "

Mikael turned. *But?*

Isha took Adam's arm. "But what, Adam?"

"Did he really answer my question?"

"He gave advice—great advice. Incredibly wise advice. What do you mean?"

Adam shrugged. "He never answered my question about Serpent. Why is he the way he is? Was the Creator holding back information?"

Isha tugged Adam's hand in a playful manner. "Now you're just being silly. Your question was about Serpent's attitude. The Creator definitely answered that." She leaned into him. "He's giving you wisdom for when there are more humans than just us to take care of. You and I can make decisions together. But if there were five or six of us, reaching a decision would likely not be so easy."

Adam smiled and placed his arm around Isha's shoulders. "You're right, Isha. Those were great words of advice."

Mikael debated whether to leave or follow Adam and Isha as they began walking deeper into the garden. He saw Adam stroking his chin, so Mikael decided to follow a little longer. After a couple of minutes, Adam spoke quietly, almost as if to himself.

"I wonder what it would be like to have a kingdom of my own."

Isha giggled. "You will, silly. As soon as our training is over."

Adam gave her a strange look, then smiled and gave her a side hug.

Mikael gasped. *Doubt.* A seed of doubt had been planted. Lucifer's pride had now spread to the garden, one of the most protected and praised parts of the Creator's kingdom.

Mikael had heard enough for now. He had to go talk with Ruach. Doubt could lead to disobedience and then to rebellion.

Mikael shuddered. *How does rebellion spread so quickly and so easily?*

At any rate, Ruach should know what he just heard.

CHAPTER 12

Battle Practice

Mikael walked with determination, but he really didn't know where to look for Ruach. He could be anywhere. Seeing movement in his periphery, he turned and saw Azel and Uriel approaching.

Azel spoke first. "Mikael, what's going on? I'm hearing rumors of certain angels pledging their allegiance to Lucifer."

Uriel nodded. "I've heard the same thing. Granted, no one is actually claiming it's them, but the rumors are becoming hard to ignore."

Mikael sighed and shook his head. He couldn't believe all this was happening. "Okay. The two of you round up all the angels for battle practice."

Their eyes widened. "*All?*" Azel asked.

Mikael nodded. "Yes, all. We don't know who will be on our side or not, but we can't let that stop our preparation."

"So, it's true then?" Uriel asked. "War?"

Mikael gave a slight shrug. "I definitely hope not, but . . . " He shrugged again. "We prepare as if conflict will happen, and we pray it does not."

Both nodded. "We'll meet you at the practice field," Uriel said.

As they turned to leave, Mikael asked, "Have either of you seen Ruach?"

Uriel nodded. "I saw him headed to where Halayim conducts choir practice."

"Thank you." Mikael headed in that direction as the other two went to the task of gathering the angels. Mikael couldn't think of why Ruach would be talking to Halayim. It wasn't as though him doing so would be odd, necessarily, but the timing seemed strange.

Just as Mikael reached the building, Ruach was heading out. Mikael breathed a sigh of relief and gave a slight wave.

"Ruach, may I talk with you?"

Ruach turned and smiled, or that's what Mikael thought he was doing. "It's okay, Mikael. And yes, battle practice is a good idea."

Mikael was unsure why Ruach's knowledge of things before he even told Ruach amazed him—but it did so every single time. "I just feel everything is unraveling," Mikael said.

Mikael felt a warmth flow through him as Ruach put his hand on Mikael's shoulder. His touch was extremely calming. *Why did others not want this?*

"Ruach, why is all this happening?" Mikael asked.

"Choice is a tricky thing. It leads to such wonderful things. Or to things only thought possible in nightmares."

Mikael's eyes grew big and he spoke in barely a whisper. "Are we headed into the nightmare?"

"All of creation is coming to a crossroad. Trinity has given choice to its creation. The angels are even now making a choice, as is Serpent, and even Adam. While Trinity is tied to each and every dimension created, choice is still something given freely."

"But what if everyone makes the same wrong decision?"

Mikael felt a pat on his shoulder from Ruach. "Mikael, while choice is freely given, we will not be taken by surprise. We have a solution for every contingency."

Mikael nodded. This didn't really give comfort. While he was glad to know ultimate control was still in the hands of his Creator, that knowledge didn't take away the sinking feeling he had as to what was coming in the near term.

"Now go. Be the leader of the Almighty's host you were created to be," Ruach encouraged him. "We'll talk again soon."

Ruach took a few steps and then disappeared. Mikael stood in place for several seconds. Watching the creation of the time dimension had been so glorious. Would the wonderment really be so short-lived?

*****

When Mikael reached the practice field, almost every angel had arrived. He unfolded his large, majestic wings from his back and rose above the others.

"Angels," he said in a commanding voice, "divide in rank."

The angels did so and waited for further instruction.

"Pair off in groups of seven."

Again, the angels did so.

"We need to ramp up our skills. Count off among your groups. Angels one, two, and three will fight against angels four, five, six, and seven."

The angels drew their swords and took stances. From Mikael's viewpoint, seeing all the angels make these movements essentially in one large synchronous movement was a majestic sight to behold.

"Begin!" Mikael shouted.

Mikael flew above them all, closely watching technique. For those who seemed to be struggling, Mikael would land and give individual instruction as the others continued to fight.

After he felt everyone was performing to their peak ability, he shouted: "Now in the air!"

All the angels took flight and continued their fighting practice. From a distance, the angels' performance looked chaotic, but Mikael could see order in the chaos. He watched how each angel flew as he fought. He knew skill was needed, not only in wielding one's sword, but in the position one needed in flight. Each angel needed to be on the offensive and defensive in any position. Swords glistened and sparks flew as they made contact. Each angel had to fight against the opposite inertia generated by swords making contact.

Mikael saw many going from an offensive to a defensive stance in a split-second, using their wings to counteract the generated inertia of each sword strike, and doing this whether they were upright, upside down, or sideways. Mikael knew these moves, while looking graceful and elegant when executed well, were exceedingly difficult, took great skill, and could only be achieved through a great deal of practice. He again gave instructions to various angels when he saw they were not up to their peak level of execution in various fighting strategies.

Finally, Mikael shouted, "Cease!"

All angels immediately stopped wherever they were and looked at Mikael. "Let's give our praise to our Creator," Mikael said.

All the angels landed, gathered in groups of seven with their backs to each other, and held their swords straight up. The swords resonated with each other producing colorful displays radiating from hilt to the tip of each sword. Then, in unison, all angels shouted, "Praise be to our Creator whom we serve!"

Mikael rose again in the air. His majestic wings moved rhythmically, producing a slight *swoosh* sound in perfect rhythm.

"Very good today," he told his fellow angels. "I am proud of all of you. Some have wondered why we need to practice such maneuvers when we live in such a blessed place." Mikael turned so he could look at all of them.

"You have either heard rumors—or are part of those rumors—that certain angels are against our Creator."

There was a rumbling throughout.

"It is, unfortunately, true. As angels, we are the messengers of our Creator. We don't know all he has in store for us, but we can rest assured of his love for us and that what he does is best for all."

Mikael saw many heads nodding as he spoke—but not all.

"As his messengers, and as his army, he is giving us one moment of choice—a choice that will be irrevocable once made. You will either choose to be on the side of our wonderful Creator or you will choose to forever be against him. I beg of you to choose wisely." Mikael remembered the words of Ruach and repeated them. "Do not just consider what you feel is important in the short term. We are eternal beings. Think long term. Think wisely."

Mikael paused and again circled above them while looking over the vast host. The thought of some of these angels soon becoming his enemy broke his heart and was almost unbearable.

"Again, I ask of you that when you choose, you choose wisely. That is all."

Mikael descended, and his large, majestic wings folded neatly onto his back, looking almost as if he had no wings at all.

Raphael approached. "I think something is already afoot."

Mikael squinted.

"Just follow me," Raphael said.

Raphael had them both teleport back into the creative dimension. Only a short distance away, Serpent was talking with Lucifer.

Mikael looked at Lucifer as he spoke to Raphael. "They seem to talk a lot."

Raphael nodded. "I normally wouldn't think too much about them having conversations with each other, but after what you've told us, their frequent conversations make me uneasy."

"Any idea what they talk about?"

Raphael curled up the corner of his mouth. "Sort of. I've talked to Serpent as well, trying to pry out of him what he discusses with Lucifer without actually being direct."

"He's pretty smart and crafty, though," Mikael said. "I'm sure he knew what you were doing."

Raphael nodded. "Likely. He was pretty vague, but he did say he felt he and Lucifer had much in common."

Mikael raised his eyebrows. "Like what?"

"He kept talking about how Lucifer was created for a unique purpose, and that he had a unique purpose."

Mikael's eyes widened. "They both think they're unique?"

"It would seem so."

"Yes, they were created for specific purposes, but to say they are unique, like no other, is absurd. It's almost . . . "

Raphael looked Mikael in the eye. "Rebellion?"

Mikael nodded.

CHAPTER 13

Disobedience

Mikael paced while trying to decide what to do. He felt like everything was about to whirl out of control. Although he tried to rationalize this in his mind, he couldn't. After all, they all served the same wonderful Creator, so why were some angels against him? He found it befuddling to attempt to understand how Lucifer, also a created being, could think he could provide anything their Creator couldn't. Granted, Lucifer was the Creator's first, and had the most intimate connection of them all with the Creator. Everyone else would love to be able to be as close to their Creator as Lucifer. Mikael just couldn't understand how Lucifer could turn like this and be so persuasive in his anti-Creator ideas. Also, he was having a hard time understanding why the Creator was allowing this.

Choice. Yes, that was what Ruach said, and yes, it did make logical sense. Yet, right now, no choice seemed a better idea. Ruach's other words came back to him: *think of the long term and not the short term.* Mikael nodded. Yes, choice was definitely needed for long-term success. But why didn't everyone make this wise choice?

As Mikael turned in his pacing, Ruach was suddenly in front of him. Mikael pulled to a dead stop and put his hand to his chest.

"Ruach!" He took a couple of short breaths. "You startled me."

Ruach chuckled. "Apologies, Mikael. I appeared just as you turned. I didn't have time to call to you."

"I take it you want me to do something?"

"I need you to go back into the garden. Things will come to a culmination soon."

Mikael was unsure what that meant, but he knew it wasn't good. He nodded. "Okay. I'll head there now."

Ruach put his hand on Mikael's shoulder, gave a light pat, and disappeared.

Mikael sighed, turned, and headed toward the garden.

Along the way, he saw Serpent near some trees. Maybe he should talk to him, Mikael thought, and see if he could at least have some influence. He turned in that direction, but as he got closer, he realized this was not Serpent . . . it was Serpent's mate. Her coloring, while similar, was slightly different, more muted.

She looked up as he approached and smiled.

"Serpentess, I'm Mikael."

Serpentess nodded. "Yes, I recognize you. It's my pleasure to meet you."

"Oh, the pleasure is mine. I'm surprised we haven't met before this."

She smiled. "It's probably because I'm with the animals so much. They're quite needy." She chuckled. "But I'm not complaining. I love being with them." She bent down and picked up a small furry creature of some kind and stroked its fur as the tiny creature nestled closer to her causing her smile to broaden.

"And Serpent?"

Her smile vanished. "He isn't as enthusiastic." She quickly added, "Not yet, anyway." Her smile returned. "I'm working on him, though."

Mikael grinned. "I'm sure you can be quite persuasive. Yet . . ."

Serpentess cocked her head. "Yes?"

"Your mate can be quite persuasive as well."

Serpentess nodded. "Yes, that is a trait our Creator has given us. I use my innate ability to help the animals. My mate, unfortunately, has been persuaded by Lucifer to persuade others to yield to his side." She shook her head. "I'm sorry he is causing problems."

Mikael reached to touch her arm. "I'm sure you can reach him. Just keep trying."

She gave a weak smile and nodded. "Yes, that is my goal."

Mikael said goodbye and left her to her work. He shook his head in thought. *How could the two of them be so different?* Lucifer had evidently promised Serpent something. He quickened his pace to the garden, knowing Serpent was likely already there.

As he walked through the garden, he listened for voices but heard nothing. He strained to hear anyone talking as he continued to walk deeper into the garden. As he neared the center of the garden, he faintly heard someone talking. He walked toward the sounds and soon saw Isha and Serpent talking near the Tree of Life. He knew this couldn't be good, so he stood behind another nearby tree even though he knew he was likely invisible to them.

As Mikael listened in on their conversation, he noticed Adam. While not with Isha, he was sitting some distance away also listening. Mikael thought this odd. Why would Adam allow Serpent to talk to his mate without him being with her? Did he not know how crafty Serpent could be?

Isha picked one of the fruits from the Tree of Life and ate part of it.

Serpent spoke. "How does this fruit compare to the other fruit in the garden?"

Isha's eyes widened. "Oh, everything here is delicious. But there is something about this fruit. I can't say the taste is better than others I've tried, but this fruit definitely makes me feel better as I eat it."

"How interesting. I guess that helps explain the name the Creator gave this tree."

Isha nodded. "Yes, that makes sense."

Serpent then moved toward the tree nearest the Tree of Life. "What about this tree? How does its fruit taste?" he asked Isha.

"Oh, I have no idea. I've never eaten from this tree. Doing so is forbidden."

"Forbidden? How odd. Yahweh allows you to eat of every tree in the garden except for this one tree? Why?"

"Adam told me this is the Tree of Knowledge of Good and Evil. We are not to eat from it. Actually, we shouldn't be this close to it."

"So what would happen if you did eat from this tree?"

"Oh," Isha said, "we would surely die."

"Die!?" Serpent sounded shocked. "Why would he allow such a thing? After all, you are going to lead a kingdom. If he allowed you to die, who would then lead it?" He shook his head. "I'm not sure that is the reason he has forbidden you to eat from this tree."

Mikael's heartbeat quickened. Should he step in? No. Ruach had said to watch. But watching and listening to all of this and not acting was extremely difficult. He glanced at Adam. *Why isn't he stepping in?* Adam was no farther from them than he, so surely he could hear the conversation. Mikael's heart sank. Surely he wasn't buying Serpent's words. Isha was going on hearsay; Adam had heard the words from Yahweh himself.

Isha shook her head. "I don't understand why you would say that, Serpent. For what other possible reason would Yahweh say this?"

Serpent looked down and then slowly turned back to Isha. "Well, it seems what I told you before may be true. I'm sorry to say that, but . . . "

"You're saying he doesn't want us to know something?" She shook her head. "Wait. He's the Creator. Of course he knows more than we do. So your words aren't making sense."

Serpent gave her an expression, one nearly like the look Serpentess gave to the helpless creature in her arms a short while earlier. "If that was true, why would he give you something but then hold it back from you?"

"Well . . . "

It seemed Isha's defenses were crumbling.

Serpent patted the trunk of the tree. "Just think about the name he gave this tree. It's almost like a tease in and of itself: the Tree of Knowledge of Good and Evil. He's not protecting you from dying. He's holding back knowledge from you."

"What? What do you mean?"

"Think about it. Do you know the difference between good and evil?"

"Well, no. But the Creator does. Isn't that enough?"

"Ah," the Serpent said. "You said it right there. The Creator knows the difference. You don't. He knows if you eat of this tree you'll be just like him. You will know the difference. Your knowledge will be greater than it is now, more equal to his."

Mikael glanced at Adam. *Why is he just sitting there?! He's letting his mate be deceived!* That can't be what he wants, can it?

Serpent didn't pick the fruit, but he put his hand under one on the tree. "Look how succulent this fruit looks."

Isha nodded. "Yes, the fruit does look delicious." She shook her head. "But that is not a reason to eat something forbidden."

Serpent smiled. "No. No, of course not. Yet, becoming wiser would be a good reason."

Isha stroked her chin. "Wiser." She looked contemplative for some time. "Maybe the fruit would allow us to have better conversations with Yahweh. We would know more, so we could understand more, and then we could grasp more complex thoughts more readily. Our conversations could be deeper and more intimate."

Serpent pointed his finger at Isha. "Exactly. He will be so surprised at your increase in knowledge."

Isha smiled and slowly nodded. "He's done so much for us. It would be great to surprise him and show we are eager to learn what he knows."

Serpent smiled. "I can guarantee you he will be surprised."

Mikael couldn't believe what he was hearing. Serpent had turned this from being about disobedience to being something "positive" in which eating the fruit could presumably make them wiser and somehow please their Creator. How could this be happening? He looked at Adam.

Why is he just sitting there!?

Isha touched the fruit.

"No!" Mikael said to himself in a whisper.

She let go. Mikael breathed a sigh of relief. But just a couple of seconds later Isha pulled the limb lower and inhaled the fruit's aroma. She smiled. "It smells wonderful," she said, again inhaling deeply. "It must taste delicious."

Serpent nodded. "I'm sure it does."

Isha slowly reached up and took hold of the fruit. Mikael shook his head and whispered. "No, Isha, no!" He closed his eyes briefly and offered a short prayer. He wanted Adam to step in and save his mate. Otherwise . . . Mikael shuddered as to what would happen.

Isha pulled on the fruit; it snapped off the branch and now resided in her hand. Mikael gasped, eyes wide . . .

He buried his face in his palms as he saw her take a bite.

Disobedience had entered the garden.

"Mmm," Isha said. "It's really delicious." She chuckled as she wiped some juice from her chin. "So good." She looked around. "Adam?"

Adam stood and walked to where she was standing.

Mikael could not believe his eyes. *Had he wanted this? Surely he understood the ramifications.*

Isha smiled as she handed him some of the fruit. "Adam, you have to try this. It tastes so good."

Adam looked at Serpent. "I will see angels?"

Serpent nodded. "I would think so. A kingdom on your terms."

Adam nodded and took a bite. Mikael shook his head. *Deceit. Disobedience. Now rebellion.*

Actual rebellion.

Yet Adam's smile faded quickly after he swallowed. His gaze shot to Serpent.

"You lied."

The glow of Adam and Isha faded. They looked at each other in horror. Both ran into the thick brush, Isha sobbing while Adam yelled, "You liar!"

Serpent had a glib smile on his face as he headed out of the garden.

Mikael stood in disbelief. He thought back to his discussion with Ruach about everything appearing to unravel. He shook his head.

No, this was much worse than that.

Much, much worse.

CHAPTER 14

Rebellion

dam?"

Mikael heard Yahweh again. "Adam, where are you?"

Mikael knew this was a rhetorical question. The time had come for Adam to face his consequences.

Yahweh reached the Tree of Knowledge of Good and Evil and picked up a half-eaten piece of fruit. Mikael could see sadness in Yahweh's expression as he lifted his head and called, once more, "Adam. I asked, where are you?"

Adam came from the other side of a tree and stood behind one of the lower bushes so he would not be fully visible. "I am sorry, Yahweh. We heard you call, but knew we had to hide ourselves."

"And why would you feel you had to hide?"

Adam looked down as though he was ashamed, and then looked back up. His eyes were glistening, but tears had not yet formed. "We knew we were naked and did not want you to see us like this."

"Adam, you and Isha, come here."

Adam paused, but he took Isha's hand. They stepped from behind the shrubbery and faced their Creator. Both had their heads down and would not look at him. They had somehow taken some large fig leaves, used a type of vine as string to attach them, and used that to cover their intimate parts.

Yahweh had sympathy, love, and sorrow in his look toward them. "What is the meaning of the fig leaves?"

"Covering," Adam said.

"Why do you need them?"

"Isha and I were naked, and we needed some type of clothing."

"You have always been naked without being ashamed. Why are you now ashamed?"

"Our glow is gone. Our exposure is now too obvious."

Yahweh held out his hand with the half-eaten fruit. "Adam, what have you and Isha done?"

Adam's look went from one of shame to one of defensiveness. "Isha, who you made for me, gave me the fruit and I ate it."

A look of disbelief from Isha shot to Adam. She quickly let go of Adam's hand and crossed her arms across her midsection.

"Isha," Yahweh said in a low voice, "what have you done?"

The look on Isha's face went from one of hurt to, also, one of defensiveness. "Serpent deceived me. He twisted the words Adam told me. I . . . I only wanted to have more intelligent conversations with you."

Yahweh had a sorrowful look on his face. "And you thought disobedience would achieve that?"

Tears began trickling down Isha's face. "Serpent confused me. He deceived me into thinking such things."

"He is a liar," Adam interjected.

Yahweh looked at Adam but said nothing.

Yahweh turned. Mikael saw his gaze land straight upon his own. "Mikael."

Mikael stepped forward and genuflected. "Yes, Yahweh."

"Bring Serpent and Lucifer here."

"Yes, Creator. At once."

Mikael willed himself to be wherever Serpent was, and his body teleported there immediately. Both Serpent and Lucifer were sitting on a large rock next to a stream. He could hear them occasionally laughing.

Both looked up as Mikael approached.

Lucifer's eyebrows raised. "Anything wrong, Mikael?"

Mikael couldn't believe the audacity of the comment. "Yahweh has commanded your presence."

Lucifer put his hand to his chest. "Mine?"

"Both of you."

Serpent suddenly had a look of fright on his face as he glanced from Lucifer to Mikael. Before either could say anything, Mikael put his hand on the shoulder of each and teleported them back to the garden where Yahweh stood with Adam and Isha.

Yahweh looked at Serpent. "Explain yourself."

Serpent looked from Lucifer to Yahweh. There was fear on his face.

"Serpent, I created you for a special purpose. You have aligned yourself with Lucifer rather than me. Therefore, you will become part of his kingdom rather than mine. In doing so, you will become one of the most hated land creatures I have created. You will crawl on your belly and eat dust all of your life."

Serpent replied, "I am sorry. I am sorry. No, that is not what I wanted."

Yahweh shook his head. "You had a choice, and that choice was made. You choose your actions but not your consequence. And now you have tied your mate to your consequence as well."

"But she will be so disappointed." Serpent shook his head and muttered. "She doesn't deserve this. This is not what I wanted."

"You should have considered that in your choice. Choices affect many, not just one."

Serpent's upper body began to look like his lower body and his arms slowly, but surely, disappeared. His head became flatter to fit more in proportion to his serpentine body. His tongue now appeared forked.

"You will forever be associated with Lucifer and darkness," Yahweh pronounced. "You will have a forked tongue to show how you told Isha one thing but meant something completely different. You will be associated with Lucifer, deceit, and lying."

Mikael watched all this, stunned. For some reason, Lucifer had a smug look on his face.

Yahweh looked at Lucifer. "You believe you have won something?"

Lucifer shrugged. "Well, Adam here has given his kingdom over to me."

Adam's eyes grew very large. "That is not what Serpent said."

Lucifer raised his eyebrows. "You can see me and Mikael, as Serpent told you, correct?"

Adam slowly nodded.

"He didn't say how *long* you would be able to see angels," Lucifer said.

"But it was implied that . . . "

Lucifer laughed. "*Implied* is such an interesting word, isn't it?"

"Silence, Lucifer," Yahweh said emphatically.

Lucifer complied.

"From this point on, you will no longer be known as Lucifer, but as Satan, the Adversary. For indeed you have become an adversary to everyone you know: to your Creator, to Serpent, to his mate, and to humans. You will forever be known as a liar. That will be your legacy."

Lucifer stood and stared, seemingly unaffected by Yahweh's words.

"There will always be hostility between you and Isha, and between whomever you convince to follow you and those born through her who follow me. You will bruise the heel of the One to come, but he will eventually crush your head."

Lucifer sneered. "You and your riddles."

Yahweh looked at Isha. New tears cascaded down her cheeks. "I had given you and Adam the order of procreation. You will still fulfill this role, but with delivery will come pain. While you were created to be a helper by Adam's side, you will now desire to please him more than help him, and this will make him tempted to rule over you."

Yahweh then turned to Adam. The Creator had such sorrow on his face.

"Adam, you should have been the defender of Isha rather than being a willing participant in allowing her to be deceived. I had such great things in store for you. Although that will now not happen, remember all the things I have taught you here as you will need to use such wisdom on Earth. Yet your toiling to make the earth look like this garden will be impeded by thorns and thistles. Weeds will decrease your efforts for growing plants properly and increase your need for physical effort. You will produce food by hard labor and sweat.

"You were made from the components of the ground, and to the ground you will return when you die."

"Yahweh, I am so sorry," Adam began.

Yahweh held up his hand. "You wanted more than you thought I would give. Your trust in me to give you your heart's desire was not great enough to obey rather than disobey, and so you tried to achieve your desire a different way. As you see, Lucifer promised you things which he cannot deliver. My promises always come true. I hope you learn this lesson in your time on Earth. You have forfeited your kingdom to Lucifer, who is now the Adversary to both of us. Your offspring will now be born into his kingdom rather than into ours."

The sorrowful look on Adam's face was almost heart-wrenching.

"I told you a ruler knows the consequence that will elicit the most good for the offender. This will seem harsh, but this consequence is for your ultimate good. You must learn to trust me and teach your offspring to trust me as well. Although born into the Adversary's kingdom, you do not have to stay in his kingdom. I will provide a way." Yahweh gave a sincere smile. "I will not abandon you. I still love you—so much. Yet rebellion cannot be ignored. But as I stated, one will come who will make everything right in the end. One day, you will live in Eden again."

A look of hope came upon the face of both Adam and Isha.

Yahweh didn't hesitate. "But this will not be in your lifetime on Earth."

The eyes of both glistened with tears. Only the face of Isha became tear-stained, however.

"Adam, you will become the patriarch of many humans. The time has come to give your mate a proper name."

Adam looked at Isha. "I will call you Chavvah because you will be the life-giver, the Em, of all humans."

"Mikael, escort Adam, Chavvah, and Satan to the garden's entrance."

Mikael did so. As they looked back, cherubim blocked the way back into the garden entrance. The cherubim wielded swords whose blades were so bright they looked as though they were on fire.

Adam tried to comfort Chavvah, but she was distraught and bore fresh tears.

One of the cherubim spoke. "The way to the Tree of Life is blocked to each of you—until all Lucifer has done and hopes to do has been undone and prevented."

Mikael teleported both Adam and Chavvah to Earth.

CHAPTER 15

הHope

Yahweh appeared with Adam and Chavvah shortly after they arrived on Earth. Adam was still trying to console Chavvah, but with little success.

Yahweh put his hand on Chavvah's shoulder. The look of love in his eyes for her, rather than the look of condemnation she likely expected, seemed to provide enough comfort for her to stop crying and be able to focus.

Yahweh smiled. "There are still things to teach you before I leave. Yet I or one of my messengers will return periodically to provide guidance." He looked at Adam and then at Chavvah. "You and your descendants have continual choice. This is a gift I have not given to any other creature I have created."

The eyes of both of them grew larger. Adam spoke. "Why such a gift, Yahweh?"

"While things may look bleak now, you can make them better. Do not take the power of choice lightly. Before long, Earth will be filled with millions of people."

Both looked at each other almost in disbelief as to this coming reality—and it developing from just two people.

"There will be trillions of trillions of choices that can be made to change the destiny of this timeline in which I have now placed you," Yahweh said. "But rest assured, I can know, act, and be prepared for each decision that will be made."

Again they nodded.

"Now, the first thing is to provide clothing for you. This must come from sacrifice. Adam, your sin of rebellion will cause one of the creatures I have made to die for your preservation."

Adam glanced down, ashamed of what he had done.

"The body of this animal will be a burnt offering and a memorial for you."

Both looked at each other and then back at Yahweh. Adam shook his head. "We do not understand."

"Life is precious and should be respected," Yahweh said. "The death of the animal will be a reminder of the sin which has caused this need of death. The penalty for the sin of rebellion is always death. Remember this. The animal's body as a whole burnt offering is a memorial of you pledging yourself to live for me despite the kingdom in which you now live. The sacrifice is a memorial of your pledge now and a memorial of the One to come whose death will pay for the penalty of all rebellion, which is the meaning of sin, once and for all."

Yahweh had Adam build an altar from various nearby stones. He had Adam make a knife from a piece of stone and then use another to make the blade sharp. Adam did so but looked confused the entire time he was making the knife.

Nearby a small lamb lay resting, watching.

"Now take some young limber twigs and bind the feet of the lamb together," Yahweh said.

Chavvah found the twigs as Adam held the lamb in his arms. Adam then laid the animal on the ground. The lamb bleated and kicked, panic in its eyes. With eyes moistening, Adam bound the animal's legs as Chavvah stroked and calmed the creature, even as tears trickled down her checks. "Shh. Shh," she said between sniffles.

"Adam, take the knife and slice the throat of the lamb."

"Yahweh! You can't ask me to do such a thing." His voice quivered. "Please!"

"This is the way it has to be, Adam. Sin produces death. Only blood from death can atone sin. Only by this sacrifice can you be clothed."

Chavvah looked away as Adam thrust his knife.

"Chavvah," Yahweh said quietly but firmly.

She looked at him, her eyes moist.

"Do not look away. This is payment for your sin as well as Adam's. The act is ugly, yes. But this brutality is what will remind you to follow a different path."

After the life ebbed from the lamb—its blood pulsing into the grass underneath it—Chavvah watched Adam skin the lamb and then place the creature's entire body on the altar. Tears ran down Chavvah's cheeks. She did not wipe them away. Yahweh then ignited the lamb's carcass on the altar. As the animal's body burned, Yahweh made clothing for the two humans from the lamb's skin, which was not burned.

"Adam, this is an ordinance to you. Teach this to your offspring so they will teach this practice, and its meaning, to theirs. This is a memorial for you and your children and their children. Sustenance comes from the ground by the work you do. The payment for sin is death. Seeing the death of the animal brings remembrance that atonement for sin is needed. The sacrifice becomes a memorial for a future day when One will come to pay for sin in totality. Until that day, this must be done."

Adam and Chavvah nodded. "Yes, Yahweh, our Creator. This we will do, and this we will teach," Chavvah said.

"Remember all I taught you both here and in the garden. Apply them here. The techniques I taught you will no longer be easy. This Earth I had blessed to bring you abundance has now been cursed to produce resistance to your work so that abundance will only come through hardship. All these things will be a lesson for you and your future generations to teach obedience and the consequence of not obeying. The ultimate choice belongs to each individual."

Both nodded.

"Become the standard for all to follow."

Mikael looked around at the world in which they now lived. Earth had beauty, but this world was not as lush and as beautiful as the garden in which they had been trained. Much work and care were now needed to make this Earth like the Garden of Eden. Did they have the stamina and vision in them? Mikael guessed that only time would tell.

Yahweh put his hand on the shoulder of both Adam and Chavvah. "All I have taught you is still applicable. You are still the caretakers of this world. This Earth will still become lush and beautiful. Yet it will be difficult for you to maintain its beauty." He smiled. "But doing so is a challenge you can live up to, and achieving it will bring much satisfaction."

Both gave small smiles, then nodded. "Thank you, Yahweh," Adam said.

Yahweh held their gaze. "You now live in Lucifer's kingdom. He is now your Adversary, as he is mine." He gave a slight squeeze to each of their shoulders. "Yet he can be overcome. Resisting him will not be easy. In fact, doing so will be hard. Extremely hard. He will try to undo everything I have planned for you. Yet I will redeem both you and this world back to me."

Yahweh made sure both were looking directly at him. "Rest assured, I am in control. I planned for this contingency as I have planned the final outcome. You are in my time dimension. That means this world has an end, and in the end I will be victorious. Dark times will come, but don't lose sight, or hope."

Yahweh smiled. "Victory is assured. Trust in me. I do not lie, I do not change, and all my promises come true."

Both nodded.

"Teach this to your children and your descendants. They will become many and will need guidance and teaching. What you have learned in the Garden of Eden and what I have taught you today, you must teach. The Adversary will do all he can to teach otherwise. You must be diligent."

Yahweh gave Chavvah and Adam a final hug . . . and then disappeared.

His heart feeling a bit heavy, but also with renewed hope, Mikael teleported back to the angelic realm. He wondered what Adam and Chavvah were thinking now.

They had failed, but Yahweh had given them hope.

CHAPTER 16

שׂar

As soon as Mikael arrived in the angelic realm, he was immediately met by both Raphael and Gabriel. Their concerned looks had him worried. Each angel-warrior nearly had a look of panic. For angels of their caliber to appear like this, Mikael knew something terrible was happening.

Raphael spoke first. "He has gathered his army and is marching to the throne room."

"Yes," Gabriel said, "we need our commander to rally the angels on our side and take a stand against them."

Mikael held up his hands. "Whoa, whoa. Slow down. Who is marching against the throne room? You're talking about Lucifer?"

Raphael nodded. "And he has over a third of the angels on his side."

Mikael's eyes widened. "What? That many?"

Gabriel nodded. "Lucifer was far more charismatic than we gave him credit for."

Mikael felt stunned. Never in his wildest imagination would he think so many angels would turn against their Creator.

"They know their rebellion cannot be undone or forgiven, right?" Mikael asked.

Raphael shrugged. "I'm sure Lucifer forgot to mention that part."

Mikael put his hands on each of their shoulders. "Okay. You two go and get all those on our side at the entrance to the throne room. We'll rally from there."

Both nodded and disappeared. Mikael sighed. The time had come. He shook his head, his mind in nearly total disbelief. Lucifer was likely thinking that because he spoiled the Creator's plan and took Adam's kingdom from him, he could now take the Creator's kingdom as well. A look of determination came across Mikael's face. *We'll see about that!* With that thought, he teleported to the entrance of the throne room.

When Mikael arrived, several angels had already gathered at the entrance. Jahvan, one of the largest, was guarding the entrance.

"Jahvan, you remain here, just in case," Mikael told him. Jahvan nodded.

Mikael next turned to Azel and Uriel. "You both lead a legion. I'll have Raphael and Gabriel each lead a legion as well. Remember our training. We cannot allow Lucifer and his angels to win."

Each nodded and were off to rally the angels to set up a defensive perimeter.

Mikael flew to where Lucifer and his angels were advancing. All stopped as Mikael spread his wings and rose above them.

"Lucifer, what are you doing? Isn't one kingdom enough for you?"

Lucifer laughed. "Why stop there when I can have it all?"

"Your pride has no bounds."

"My *uniqueness* has no bounds," Lucifer shot back. "My followers are proof of that. We were *created* to serve. These here with me have chosen to serve. There is the difference."

Mikael held out his hands. "Angels, stop. Think about what you are doing." Mikael's gaze shot back to Lucifer. "Have you told them? Do they know?"

Lucifer looked irritated. "Told them what? That they have a mind of their own? That they have a choice to choose something better?" His eyes were full of hate. "Yes, they know this."

"No!" Mikael shouted. "Your words are only half-truths." He looked at the angels behind Lucifer and then raised his voice.

"You have choice, yes," Mikael said to the throng. "But it is a one-time choice. If this attempt fails, you will be banished forever. The Creator has no forgiveness for us. We were created to be his messengers. We are either with him or against him. We cannot vacillate in our allegiance."

"Semantics!" Lucifer shouted back at Mikael. "You and the Creator always speak in riddles. I speak in truth."

"Truth? Like you did to Adam and his mate? Like you did to Serpent, ruining the life his mate wanted?"

Mikael spread his wings to their maximum so he could look as commanding as possible, then refocused his attention on the throng behind Lucifer. "Lucifer told the humans half-truths, just like he's telling you. He tricked Adam to give up his kingdom on Earth to him. Probably just as he has tricked you into following him."

Lucifer's voice became hard and coarse. "I was made unique. No one else here, other than me, could leave their dimension and look at the Creator face to face. Now I will become the ultimate unique one."

"Aha!" Mikael said as he pointed to Lucifer and scanned the crowd of angels. "He admitted it. He was created, as were we all." His gaze panned the crowd again. "You are going against your Creator. Do you really think you can survive such an attack? Can those who are created be greater than their Creator?"

Mikael saw some of the angels doubting; it was obvious in their expressions. He wanted to press the moment to take advantage of their doubt.

"Angels, if you come to the Creator's side, you will be spared," Mikael said. "You have not yet rebelled. But beyond this point, there is no return. You are either for the Creator or forever against him."

Several hundred of the angels broke rank and came forward, placing themselves behind Mikael.

"Fools!" Lucifer yelled. "You are fools to listen to this Creator's pet."

Mikael was glad so many had come to their senses. Still, Lucifer had what looked like nearly a third of the angelic host behind him. This was going to be a difficult battle.

Gabriel, Raphael, Uriel, and Azel appeared next to Mikael.

"All are in position," Raphael said. The others nodded.

At that moment Ruach appeared next to them. Each bowed.

Mikael looked at Ruach. "Any further instructions?"

"Yes," Ruach said. "Those you defeat, teleport to Earth in the time dimension. We will prevent them from being able to teleport out of it."

Mikael and the others nodded. He knew angels could not be killed in the normal sense, not in the way he had seen the lamb die earlier. Yet if they could weaken the other angel enough and strike with what would be a fatal blow to an animal, or to a now-mortal human body, the angel would be incapacitated for a time. That should give them enough time to get the defeated angel to Earth before they recovered.

"Okay. We have our orders," Mikael told his commanders. "Spread the word, and let's let Lucifer know who is truly the ultimate unique one."

The sides drew up. All was silent for a brief time. There was a palpable sense of history about to be made. And then both sides began their charge . . .

From Mikael's vantage point, the view looked like two swarms rising and flying into each other. Chaos ensued. Mikael sighed, got a determined look on his face, and headed into the chaos.

The first angel he encountered was adept and able to defend himself fairly well, deflecting several of Mikael's attacks. Yet this angel tired easily, and as Mikael increased the fury of his attack, he found a weak spot and thrust his sword into the angel's chest. The angel at once became catatonic. In a flash, and before the angel could fall to the ground, Mikael teleported the angel to Earth and returned for the next fight.

As Mikael glanced around, he saw angels falling on either side. Yet since those on his side were not teleported anywhere, they eventually recovered and fought again. Yet there were only so many times an angel could be made incapacitated before he had no further strength to fight. At that point, he was merely an onlooker to the chaos above him.

Mikael kept on with his fight and continued teleporting defeated angels to the time dimension. He saw angels in all positions fighting, blade meeting blade causing sparks to fly. In one way, the display reminded him of the night he stayed on Earth and saw all the stars twinkling in the night sky. Yet the ambiance here was nowhere nearly as inviting. Mikael turned and took on the next angel before him. This one was more skilled than he had encountered before. He was a higher-ranking angel than the others he had defeated.

"Brother, why are you against us?" Mikael managed to say through breaths as he deflected a masterfully crafted lunge of the angel's sword. "Clearly, you were created special. Why are you against your Creator?"

"I could never be an archangel under the Creator," the angel said. "Lucifer can make me one."

The blows from this angel became more forceful.

Mikael had to concentrate carefully to be able to outmaneuver him. "Lucifer will use you and then discard you! He only cares about himself."

"We'll see about that." The angel descended with a hard blow. By staying calm, Mikael was able to see a weakness, even though slight, in the maneuver. Mikael blocked the strike, but then went in a circular motion before the angel had time to pull his sword back. The angel took a moment too long to recover from the unexpected force created from the event, which caused the angel to move his head backward but throw his lower body closer to Mikael. This allowed Mikael to give a downward slice of his sword in that split-second—into the angel's midsection. The angel was immediately incapacitated; he looked like a statue in a fighting stance. Mikael took a deep breath, grabbed the angel, and teleported him to Earth.

There were so many of these angels now on Earth that he had to be careful not to get attacked in that realm. Before he teleported back, he saw one of his own angels incapacitated. He fought his way to him, grabbed his arm, and teleported both back to the angelic realm. He placed him on the ground in that realm.

Mikael then realized his mistake in not ensuring the defeated angels' swords remained in the angelic realm before being teleported to Earth. He gathered several of those recovering from being incapacitated in the angelic realm.

"When you recover, teleport to Earth and gather all swords and bring them back to this realm. Spread this word!"

They nodded. Several teleported, and others ran to tell those recovering to let them know what to do before fighting again.

Mikael headed back to his fighting. He glanced toward the throne room and saw Jahvan fighting off a least a dozen of Lucifer's angels at once—and yet winning. *Jahvan. Such an amazing fighter.* Looking around, he saw Quentillious attending to the incapacitated angels in this realm. He yelled for Quentillious.

Quentillious quickly came his way and bowed. "Yes, my captain?"

"Go help Jahvan. He needs no help in fighting, but he needs help in teleporting those he incapacitates to the time dimension. Help him do that."

Quentillious nodded and turned. Mikael grabbed his arm. Quentillious turned back with raised eyebrows.

"Be *sure* to leave their swords in this dimension," Mikael said. "We want them as defenseless as possible in the time dimension."

Quentillious smiled and nodded. He took a step, disappeared, and then reappeared near Jahvan. Mikael saw Quentillious grab an incapacitated angel, pull the sword from his hands, and disappear. Jahvan looked up, locking his gaze with Mikael's. He lifted his hand quickly in thanks, gave a smile, and then went back to his fighting, incapacitating two with one massive blow.

Mikael smiled to himself. *Jahvan will make Quentillious work today.*

Azel flew to Mikael's position. "We should get Lucifer. If he falls, others will be demoralized and conquered more easily."

Mikael knew Lucifer would not be fighting alone. He would have others like the angel he just fought surrounding him. Yet Azel's idea was a strong one. "Okay. Go get the other leaders and have their seconds lead their battalions."

Azel nodded and flew swiftly to find Uriel, Raphael, and Gabriel. Mikael hoped those were enough as he needed the best for this next effort to be successful; these were his most skilled fighters. He looked around. Lucifer should not be hard to spot as his position would look like a ball of angels advancing forward.

Once spotted, Mikael flew swiftly in that direction, but he had to fight off several other angels along the way. He grabbed another of his angels and had him do the teleporting to Earth as he incapacitated the enemy along his path to Lucifer. He ensured each sword fell to the ground before the defeated angel was teleported to the time dimension.

He and Raphael arrived almost simultaneously and began fighting. Before long, Gabriel, Azel, and Uriel arrived.

Lucifer laughed. "How quaint. The Creator's pets banding together. You will find my angels quite formidable."

Mikael did not respond; he didn't want to get caught in a verbal parley. Yet Lucifer was not wrong. These were some of the most skilled angels he had encountered. It amazed him Lucifer could have such charisma to attract such quality of angels to his side. The battle raged on . . .

In short time, one by one, each of Lucifer's angels met their fate of incapacitation.

For once, Mikael began to see Lucifer having a tinge of doubt in his eyes.

After much more fighting, only Lucifer remained.

When Lucifer saw his last lieutenant fall, he stopped fighting and held up his sword in surrender.

Mikael pointed his sword directly at Lucifer's throat. "Surrender your sword and the battle."

Lucifer did, but he grinned while doing so.

Slowly, around them, Lucifer's remaining angels who were fighting realized what was happening and stopped their efforts. They watched.

Mikael shook his head. "I don't understand you, Lucifer. You had to have known you could not win this battle. Yet you took the war on anyway."

Lucifer laughed. "Yes, but look below you. Look how many of your angels fell."

Mikael looked. The ground was strewn with incapacitated angels. Both sorrow and anger filled him. "I see them, but all this was pointless. They will recover. And this was a pointless war."

"Oh, you may see it that way. But I see something totally different."

"Like what?"

Lucifer grinned. "If I just had a few more angels on my side, the tide would have turned. You see, if I can get this close, I can get closer next time. I will be the unique one before this is all over."

Mikael glared at Lucifer. "It *is* over. You have lost."

Lucifer laughed even harder. "Over? No. It's only just begun."

CHAPTER 17

Banished

Mikael looked around. The battle was over, but the cost had been extremely high. He shook his head as he looked at all the swords strewn across the ground. They were almost innumerable. His heart felt heavy. *Why? Why did this have to happen?*

Quentillious appeared. "My Captain. Where should we put all these swords?"

Quentillious looked exhausted, as did every angel. Mikael just shook his head. He was devoid of thought at the moment.

"There is a room off from the choir chamber that is empty. We can place them there," Quentillious said. He put his hands on his waist looking at all the swords, then turned for a three-sixty gaze around the battlefield. Somewhat weary, he sighed. "Maybe they'll all fit."

Mikael nodded and gave Quentillious a pat on his shoulder. "Thank you, my friend. Give that a try."

Quentillious nodded, gathered a few other angels to help, and got to work. They teleported and reappeared in rapid succession.

Mikael walked to the entrance to the throne room. Jahvan had returned to standing at his duty.

Jahvan gave a slight bow. "Azel and Uriel have Lucifer in custody inside. The Creator wanted a word with him before he is banished to Earth."

Mikael nodded. "And how are you, my friend?"

Jahvan gave a weary smile. "Probably as sprite as you."

Mikael chucked. "Indeed." He patted Jahvan's shoulder. "Indeed, my friend."

Mikael turned. "Speaking of our Lord, where is he?"

Jahvan shook his head. "I saw Ruach earlier, but I haven't seen Yahweh since the battle."

Mikael looked around, wondering where he would be. "If Ruach comes by again, tell him I am looking for Yahweh."

Jahvan smiled. This time he appeared a little amused. "I'm sure he already knows."

Mikael chuckled. "Probably so."

As Mikael walked away, he wondered why the Creator was often so mysterious. He . . . They . . . Trinity knew all, but often only told them in part. Trinity gave them missions to accomplish even when they were not really needed at all. He smiled. This was just one of the wonders of the Creator.

Mikael looked everywhere he knew to look in the angelic dimension, so he went to the creative dimension. While walking around and seeing everything on display was pleasant, he didn't see Yahweh, and that was his point in coming here. He did notice, however, that many of the creatures looked a little lost as well. He wondered if they were looking for Serpentess who was, unfortunately, no longer with them.

Mikael shook his head. *If only Serpent had been content. Pride is certainly a destroyer. Not only of one's self, but even of those one loves.*

The only other place Mikael knew to look was in the garden. Would he be allowed to enter? The cherubim were still on guard. He paused and looked at them. They really were awe-inspiring—in any dimension. He walked up to them, but they did not budge.

Mikael nodded as a greeting. "I am looking for Yahweh. Might I find him here?"

The cherubim did not speak, but separated, allowing him to enter. Mikael walked through, assuming their reaction to be equivalent to a confirmation that Yahweh was here.

Mikael walked deeper into the garden. All was quiet. Everything looked lush, but he heard no animals. While he did see animals and birds, they were strangely quiet. No birds sang, no animals frolicked.

All were still. They knew something was wrong.

In the distance, Mikael saw the Tree of Life and Tree of Knowledge of Good and Evil. Their bright colors were still in such contrast with the rest of the garden. Their glory made other beauty look almost plain. Noticing movement, he stopped and looked. Someone was there. Whoever it was, were they lying down?

Mikael approached slowly. *Is Yahweh on the ground?* He had never seen him look so vulnerable. *Is he weeping?*

"Yahweh?" Mikael said in a barely audible voice. "Are you all right?"

Yahweh slowly sat up, his cheeks tear-stained, and shook his head. "No, Mikael, I am not all right."

Mikael didn't know what to say. He felt uneasy not knowing what to do or say. "Are you disappointed and saddened, my Lord?"

Yahweh shook his head. "No, Mikael. I grieve, not from disappointment, but for what humans must now endure and the relationship with them that must be postponed." He looked up, gave a weak smile, and turned somber. "Choice is so glorious, and yet so painful. Knowing what could have been and will not be is painful, but not unexpected."

Mikael nodded. "Yes, my Lord." He tried to understand what Yahweh was saying. While he grasped some of his Creator's words, he was sure he did not grasp all with the intent in which they were meant.

Yahweh stood. "Contingencies were already in place before their decision was made. While I am never taken by surprise as I have a contingency for any decision to ensure my will continues, it does not change the grieving of poor decisions made."

"How long will their consequences last, my Lord?"

Yahweh looked at Mikael, then placed his hand on his shoulder. "Longer than anyone will ever think, yet shorter than some will imagine."

Mikael nodded, but really didn't understand. He assumed he would learn over time. He had to admit, Lucifer was right about one thing: sometimes the Creator spoke in riddles. Mikael smiled to himself. At the same time, he knew he loved this, and he loved attempting to figure them out.

"Lucifer, my Lord?"

Yahweh nodded. "Yes, my Adversary. How quickly things can change. Pride has arisen and will be hard to change in the hearts of many." He looked at Mikael. "Let us go and explain to him his limits."

Yahweh put his hand on Mikael's shoulder and teleported them both into the throne room. Mikael found himself standing next to Azel. He stood wide-eyed. No one had ever teleported him before. He looked up and saw Yahweh, now part of Trinity, above the expanse on the throne.

Azel nodded and turned sideways to speak to Mikael. "What happens now?" he said in a soft voice.

Mikael shrugged. "I think we're about to find out."

"Lucifer. Satan. Adversary." The Creator's voice was commanding, but matter of fact.

"So I get a new name?" Lucifer asked.

"No, you have earned it."

"So what happens now?"

Mikael was surprised how Lucifer could seem so nonchalant having lost the battle and now standing in the Creator's presence.

"You will be placed in the kingdom you stole."

"Well, it seems like we're back to semantics. Technically, Earth wasn't really occupied."

"Occupation does not determine ownership."

A smile crept across Lucifer's face. "But it helps."

"That you will find out all too soon. But remember where your kingdom lies: in a dimension of time. That means Earth will have an end. Your kingdom will most definitely come to an end."

Lucifer shrugged. "If you say."

"Lucifer, your pride will be your downfall. Now for the consequences of your actions. You will no longer be able to be in my presence unless summoned by me for you to give an account of your actions on Earth. I have a plan to redeem both humans and the earth. This you cannot thwart."

Lucifer gave a slight smile. "Time will tell."

"Yes, it shall."

Yahweh suddenly appeared before Lucifer and next to Mikael, Azel, and Uriel. His eyes, now looking as eyes of fire, were focused on Lucifer.

"To your kingdom you are banished."

And then, in a blink, Lucifer disappeared.

CHAPTER 18

The Gift of Choice

Mikael found himself standing outside the throne room with Azel and Uriel. They looked at each other dumbfounded.

"All over?" Jahvan asked.

Mikael turned and saw Jahvan at his post.

Mikael looked at Azel and Uriel, wide-eyed, as were they. He gave a slight nod to Jahvan. "Yes. Yes, I think so."

Jahvan smiled. "I guess your experience was something. All three of you look stunned."

Mikael rubbed the back of his neck. "That's putting it mildly. Yahweh sent Lucifer to the time dimension, and at the same time sent us out here."

"What do we do now?" Azel asked.

Mikael shook his head slowly. "I . . . don't know. Nothing, I presume. We wait for further instructions."

Both Azel and Uriel nodded, but they looked as lost as Mikael felt. They slowly disbanded and went their separate ways.

As Mikael walked, not anywhere in particular, he noticed the angels around him attempting to get back to their normal routines. Halayim scurried about getting his choir reassembled.

"No, Caylar. You cannot sing your part in B-flat," he heard the choir director exclaim.

Mikael chuckled just a bit as he heard the exasperation in Halayim's voice. He saw Caylar give a huff and return to his place in the choir rows.

"Captain!"

Mikael turned and saw Quentillious walking toward him. "Ah, Quentillious. Did they all fit?"

Quentillious gave a broad smile. "Indeed." He bobbled his head. "Well, I made them fit."

Mikael raised his eyebrows.

"Want to come see?"

Mikael didn't think seeing the swords was really necessary, but he nodded anyway, seeing the expectation on Quentillious's face. After all, he was the one who had told him to move all those many swords. He felt obligated to see his request through.

As they headed in the direction from where Quentillious had come, his fellow angel-warrior talked excitedly. "As I was putting the swords away, they just looked so junky being stuffed into a room. And for no good purpose! So I devised something different."

Mikael raised his eyebrows.

Quentillious raised his hands, patting the air. "Now, if you don't like what I've done, just say so, and I'll change the display." He developed a grin. "I like it, though."

Mikael patted his shoulder. "I'm sure what you've done is fine."

Quentillious nodded, then looked ahead and back to Mikael several times, still donning his grin.

Mikael didn't understand, but obviously Quentillious had done something he was extremely proud of. He just hoped he would like the display.

As they neared, Quentillious seemed to get even more excited. "I hope you don't mind, but I added clear doors to the room." He shook his head. "I just couldn't see putting something like this away for no one to see."

Likely seeing his squint of confusion, Quentillious added, "It wasn't just my opinion. Several other angels agreed with my decision."

Mikael gave a slow nod. He was now extremely curious, but also wary. Yet when he turned the corner, he gasped. "Quentillious! I . . . I don't know what to say."

Quentillious looked from the room to Mikael and back. "Is that a good thing?"

Mikael put his hand on Quentillious's shoulder and gave a pat. "My friend, this is spectacular."

Mikael stood in amazement as he took in the display Quentillious had created. The swords, arranged on the back wall of the room, with their blade tips touching, created a circle. Between each sword, with their blades facing toward each other, was another sword with its hilt between two swords and its blades facing in the opposite direction. He had repeated this pattern once more, and by doing so had three large circles composed of the swords' blades. Because the blades were in close proximity to each other, they resonated, causing color to emanate from hilt to tip in unison and thus creating three circular displays of morphing color.

Mikael looked at the spectacle for several moments before he could even speak. Above the sculpture of swords on the wall were these words in gold: *Out of chaos, beauty. Trinity transcends all.*

Mikael shook his head and turned to Quentillious. "I don't think any greater memorial to commemorate what happened here could have been created."

Quentillious's smile grew still wider. "Thank you, Captain. That means a great deal." He gave a slight bow.

"No, Quentillious. Thank you. Truly a job well done."

As Mikael continued to admire the work Quentillious had created, he received a message from Ruach to make his way to the Sacred Altar of Stones. He thanked Quentillious again, said his goodbye, and headed in that direction.

Mikael hoped he would receive some type of explanation of what happened in the throne room earlier. While Yahweh certainly owed him no explanation, Mikael truly wanted to understand.

As Mikael approached the altar of stones, he saw Yahweh sitting on the altar, seemingly waiting for him. Mikael bowed as he arrived. "My Lord?"

Yahweh smiled and patted the stone next to him. Mikael sat hesitantly. "Is something wrong, my Lord?"

Yahweh gave a slight smile with a sigh. "Unfortunately, Mikael, a lot will be wrong from now until all is made right again. I'm afraid your work has only begun."

Mikael squinted while trying hard to follow. "What would you have me do?" He gave a slight shrug. "I'm willing to do whatever is your bidding, my Lord."

Yahweh nodded. "I know you are."

There was silence between them for what Mikael felt was a long time. Yahweh seemed to stare straight ahead. Mikael was unsure if he was simply thinking or trying to find the words to help him understand.

Yahweh turned to him. "Did the silence between us make you uncomfortable?"

Mikael nodded, unsure of how else to respond.

"The pause was for you, Mikael. Sometimes a pause is needed to bring perspective. And clarity."

"Because of what has happened?" Michael glanced over Yahweh's face looking for the clarity of which he mentioned.

"Two wills now exist," Yahweh began, looking straight ahead but periodically glancing at Mikael. "Lucifer, now my Adversary, Satan, will lure Adam's descendants his way."

Mikael shook his head. "But not many, my Lord. Surely, not many?"

Yahweh locked gazes with Mikael, his eyes glistening. "Oh, so many, I'm afraid." He stared straight ahead again. "So, so many," he said in barely a whisper.

Mikael swallowed hard. He was unsure why his beloved Creator would allow such a thing. "My Lord, why?"

Yahweh slowly turned and looked at him, but didn't say a word.

"I mean, why allow Lucifer such sway? You can do *anything*, correct anything."

Yahweh gave a weak smile. "*How* I correct it is more important than being able to correct it."

Mikael tried hard to grasp his words but failed. He simply shook his head.

Yahweh put his hand on Mikael's upper arm. "It's all about choice, Mikael. I did something different with humans that I did not do with you angels. I have given them infinite choice."

Mikael stared at Yahweh, still desperately wanting to understand. "Infinite, my Lord?"

Yahweh nodded. "You were given a choice, and your fate was sealed." He smiled. "I'm happy with your choice, by the way."

Mikael smiled. "As am I, my Lord."

Yahweh looked straight ahead once more. "I have bestowed humans with a rich gift. They will be given multiple circumstances to choose between me and Satan. Many will not even recognize the gift given them, and Satan will try to blind them to it. Yet my gift remains."

Mikael could see he loved the humans very much. "How can I and my army help?"

Yahweh stood and Mikael did likewise. "Keep up the practice with the angels as you have started. Chavvah is pregnant. Satan has already planned his tactic of deceit. A grave choice is on their horizon. A choice leading to chaos, I'm afraid. You will need to help guard and protect those who make the right decisions."

With those words, Yahweh vanished. Mikael sat down again with a sigh. So many thoughts were going through his mind. He was unclear as to what was on his horizon. Yet he was determined to follow through with what his Creator expected of him.

He would prepare his army to meet whatever awaited them.

CHAPTER 19

Sheol

Mikael walked back from the practice field with Azel and Uriel.

"How long do we keep up the fighting simulations?" Azel asked.

Mikael gave him a side glance. "As long as necessary and as long as our Creator commands it."

"Speaking of our Creator," Uriel said, "I hear he goes to Earth quite often."

Mikael nodded. "Makes sense. Adam and Chavvah need guiding, especially now that they have children."

"First Kajin and now, just recently, Hebel," Azel said. "Curious, don't you think?"

Mikael stopped walking and looked at Azel. "How so?"

"Well, obviously Chavvah expects Kajin to be the destroyer of Satan since his name means spear."

Mikael sighed. "Yes, she likely does. I fear she will be disappointed."

"Why is that?" Uriel asked.

Mikael started walking again. "It's just a feeling I have based upon what Yahweh told me."

After a few minutes of silence, Azel spoke. "Well, our friend, tell us what he said."

Mikael chuckled. "Sorry. I got lost in thought. I don't have anything specific, but the way he said things leads me to believe this will be an exceptionally long ordeal and not something that can be accomplished quickly."

"What about Hebel?" Uriel asked. "Does he have a role in all of this?"

Azel shook his head. "Doubtful. It's obvious Chavvah believes him to just be an added blessing to their lives as his name, in a strict sense, means vanity."

Mikael nodded. "Yes, I think she is stating it is only Kajin who is tied to Yahweh's prophecy."

All three walked in silence for some time. Mikael noticed someone running toward them. He soon recognized the approaching angel as Raphael.

"Come quickly!" Raphael gasped as he neared their position. He didn't stay and explain, however. He turned and sprinted back the way he had come.

All three looked at each other wide-eyed and then began running after Raphael.

When they caught up with him, he was with a large number of angels who were in animated discussions.

Mikael grabbed Raphael's arm. "What's going on?"

"Our Creator is creating another dimension."

"What? Why?"

Raphael shook his head. "I don't know. Jahvan said the creation of this new dimension started right after the birth of Hebel."

Mikael knew that couldn't be a coincidence. As Azel and Uriel got caught up in all the discussions with the other angels, Mikael teleported to just outside the throne room. He had to find out what Jahvan knew.

"Hello, Mikael." Jahvan gave a large grin. "I guess you heard the news."

Mikael nodded. "Tell me what you know."

Jahvan's smile vanished. "Not much. Just that our Creator is creating another dimension. I don't know why, but I do know he is creating that dimension right now." Jahvan's smile returned. "I knew the news would bring you here."

As if on cue, Ruach appeared. "Mikael, come with me. There are things you need to see and hear."

Before he had time to say a word, Mikael found himself in an unfamiliar place. Beautiful, but a place he had not seen before.

"Is this the new dimension?"

Ruach nodded. "Part of it, at least."

Mikael cocked his head, but Ruach didn't explain. Mikael did a three-sixty to take in the view. This place almost looked like Eden—almost. There was something different about it, though. He couldn't put his finger on the difference. It looked lush and the colors were vibrant, but the feeling was just different. *Foreboding.* That was the nearest word he could think to describe it. Why would such a place have such a feeling?

As Mikael looked toward the horizon, it looked . . . hazy. Yet that wasn't quite the right word. No other word came to mind, though, to explain what he saw.

"Ruach, what is that on the horizon?"

"That is the barrier between the two sections of this dimension."

Mikael walked toward the horizon. "But what is the purpose of this barrier?" He turned another three-sixty as he continued walking. "What is the purpose of *all* of this? Why do you need another dimension?"

Yet when he looked toward Ruach for his answer, Ruach was no longer there.

Mikael shook his head, then chuckled. "There are better ways to end a conversation, you know."

Mikael continued toward the haze, or barrier, or whatever it was. He attempted to teleport there to make his trip faster, but found he could not. *Curious.*

Once he arrived, the barrier still looked hazy even though the impasse was directly in front of him, looking something like thick fog, but every so often would become almost transparent. He found this barrier impenetrable, feeling solid even though not looking solid at all. As his gaze went upward, there didn't seem to be an end to it. It was almost as if the entire sky was composed of this impenetrable material—whatever it was. Again he found he was unable to teleport. He found this a little disconcerting. So, without the help of Yahweh or Ruach, he would be trapped here. He looked around again. Beautiful surroundings, but confinement nonetheless. *Maybe that's why it feels so foreboding here.*

Just when the feeling started to become overwhelming, Mikael saw a shadow within the hazy barrier—as though it was coming toward him. He took a few steps back, not knowing what to expect. All these feelings were new to Mikael, and he found them unsettling.

Mikael breathed a sigh of relief when he saw Yahweh step from the hazy barrier into the place where he stood. "My Lord! I'm so glad to see you."

Yahweh gave a partial smile. "What were you feeling?"

"It was quite strange. I felt apprehension—a feeling I had never experienced before. While beautiful, this place is foreboding at the same time."

Yahweh gestured toward a couple of large rocks on which they could sit. As they did, several butterflies flitted away from some vibrant red flowers, and this caused both of them to smile.

"Mikael, this place is needed before death occurs on Earth."

Mikael jerked more upright. *Death?* He had not even thought of such a concept—at least not since the first time he watched the small lamb being slain. "Why death, my Lord?"

Yahweh looked solemn. "Death is always a by-product of disobedience. Though not immediate, death is nonetheless inevitable. Because of Adam's disobedience and rebellion, death is now a part of his life and all who follow him. Satan gained his kingdom, but it is a kingdom filled with disobedience and death."

Mikael shook his head. "Is there no other option for them, my Lord?"

Yahweh gestured toward all that was before them. "This, what I call Sheol, is part of the solution."

Mikael cocked his head. He so desperately wanted to understand, but he was failing at the task.

"No one of Adam's descendants needs to stay in Satan's kingdom," Yahweh said. "I have, and am, preparing a way for them to avoid a second death. Although all will die physically, they do not have to die spiritually."

Mikael nodded, but he knew he didn't fully understand. He knew these humans were different from himself and other angels. They had a different type of body. It made sense their bodies could not last forever in their current condition, but what was this second death?

"My Lord, could you explain a little more?"

"When humans die, their body will return to the ground from which it was formed. Yet their spirit will live on. This . . . " He gestured around him. "This is where they will reside until I make full restitution for their rebellion."

Mikael felt he understood a little better, but he still didn't understand the hazy barrier. Was this structure tied to all Yahweh was explaining to him?

"And the barrier, my Lord?"

Yahweh nodded in its direction. "Beyond the barrier is the antithesis of what is here."

The depth of his words impacted Mikael: no beauty, no light, no Creator. Mikael gasped involuntarily. "My Lord, I . . . I can't begin to comprehend being there."

Yahweh nodded. "And I do not want you to. It is necessary, though. There are those who will choose pride, just like the Adversary, over me. So I created a place where I am not. This other side of Sheol is not hidden from me but is a place where those who are there will not be able to experience me or what my love and creativity offer. Being there is most unpleasant—a place of spiritual unfulfillment until the time of second death."

Mikael slowly nodded as the realization dawned. A place for those who put their faith in his Creator waited for his promise to Chavvah to be fulfilled, and a place for those who do not put their faith in that promise also awaited. He glanced back at the barrier again: an impenetrable barrier which cannot be crossed.

As Mikael sat in thought, full realization hit. His eyes widened as he again gasped. "My Lord! There is only one way to save these humans. You . . . You . . . "

Yahweh nodded. "Must die."

Fear gripped Mikael. He had never felt such a feeling. How can this be? His thoughts froze. Could it even be? Was Yahweh's death even possible?

Yahweh put his hand on Mikael's shoulder. "It's okay, Mikael. This is all part of the contingency from the very beginning."

Mikael stared blankly at his Creator. "You can die?" His words were spoken in an awe of disbelief. "But . . . how?"

Yahweh gave a thin smile. "I will become human and die. Doing so is the only way. Humans are in a trap from which they cannot escape. Satan is counting on this dilemma for his success, but I have the solution. I am the solution."

Mikael's thoughts were whirling. Yes, he could see the Creator's plan would work, and it was the meaning of his promise to Chavvah. But . . . he looked around, remembering how he felt trapped here before Yahweh showed up. If Yahweh became human and died, he too would be trapped here.

Yahweh patted Mikael on his upper back, bringing him out of his thoughts. "Don't worry, Mikael. Everything will work out."

"But my Lord. You will be trapped here."

Yahweh smiled. "Yes, but only for a few days. Then I'll take all here to be with us in Paradise, in Eden, until all is fulfilled as I have promised."

Mikael nodded. He thought that wise because, in Eden, the foreboding feeling would be gone, and all would be only joy.

So that's why it feels so foreboding here, he thought. No one could feel comfortable and joyous without being in the presence of their Creator.

Yahweh stood. "Now come, Mikael. Let's go." He gave an intent look at his archangel. "Do you want to leave this place?"

Mikael stood in a flash. "Absolutely, my Lord."

Yahweh gave a light chuckle, placed his hand on Mikael's shoulder, and they disappeared.

CHAPTER 20

The Watchers

Mikael sat on a rock overlooking the nearby stream next to some gorgeous yellow flowers that swayed in the breeze. He always found being here relaxing. A butterfly approached. Or at least he initially thought the creature a butterfly as the delicate animal maneuvered in flight like one. Yet the more he looked, the more he realized this creature was something different entirely.

Mikael smiled. "Well, hello there. And what might you be?"

He found the creature's color magnificent. Its fragile wings shone a neon blue, but they also looked nearly transparent. He had never seen anything like this tiny, ethereal-looking creature. This was once again testimony to Yahweh's vast creativity. There was always something new to behold when Mikael came to the creative dimension. As he looked closer, he realized the creature's wings were curved, and this allowed it to hover and almost float downward onto the flower. He bent closer to get a better look. The delicate creature seemed to gather nectar like a butterfly, but when done, the creature gave one stroke of its wings to make its body shoot straight upward, startling

Mikael. He laughed and watched the creature travel across the stream to another patch of flowers. It took one stroke of its wings, propelled itself upward, and then floated downward slowly while using its wings in a nearly parachute-like fashion. Doing this repeated up-and-down process on the wind currents allowed the creature to reach its destination: some fuchsia-colored flowers near another boulder on the other side of the stream opposite where Mikael sat.

Mikael saw several others across the stream. The one he had just seen suddenly propelled itself upward to join them as they bounced on the current: first one, then another, then all of them simultaneously. Mikael found their movement mesmerizing. Everything here seemed to engender a sense of calmness and well-being.

Mikael leaned back with his hands behind him, propping himself up. If only Earth was this way now. Yet what was there now seemed to be almost the antithesis of what he was experiencing here . . .

Ever since the death of Hebel at the hand of his brother Kajin, who used one of Hebel's own spears making Kajin's name prophetic—but in a way the very antithesis of what Chavvah envisioned—life on Earth seemed to go from bad to worse. Evidently Satan was more influential on the humans than Mikael ever thought possible. While Adam had influence on some, as the population became more and more in number, his influence seemed localized to only those closest to him.

Several of his descendants, like Chanok, preached and prophesied to the people. Their words seemed to have only a marginal effect, though, falling mostly on deaf ears. He smiled remembering Chanok going for a walk just the other day and suddenly arriving in Sheol unexpectedly. Yahweh had allowed him, Mikael, to be the one to teleport Chanok there. Mikael smiled at the memory. Chanok was so confused at first, seeing family members who had died before him and now being among them! They all wept and laughed at the same time as they gave each other hugs.

Mikael suddenly felt a presence behind him. He quickly turned and saw Ruach. As Mikael watched Ruach come near, he felt something was amiss.

"Is anything wrong, Ruach?"

"I'm afraid so. Go to Earth and investigate the Watchers."

"Watchers?" Mikael shook his head. "I don't understand."

"Lucifer has had some of his angels begin to dwell among the people to better understand them."

Mikael thought about that. How did Lucifer accomplish such a feat? His doing so could not be good. At this point, Lucifer, or Satan, did not do things for altruistic reasons. He was gaining intelligence for something. And Mikael knew that something could not be good, or not good for the people of Earth.

Mikael bowed. "Very good. I will go there at once."

"Take Raphael with you. Traveling with a companion will be beneficial, I'm sure."

Mikael nodded and teleported back to the angelic realm to find Raphael. As he was looking for his friend, he saw someone approach. He stopped abruptly when he recognized the one approaching.

"Lucifer!"

The former angelic warrior grinned. "Hello, Mikael. Nice of you to still use my original name. I'm honored."

Mikael ignored his remark. "What are you *doing* here?"

"Well, the same as you. We come when summoned, don't we?"

"The Creator wanted to see *you*?" Mikael squinted. "Why?"

"I think that's a personal matter, don't you?" Lucifer's words were condescending, but he continued. "Yet if you must know, the Creator wanted information on my newest project."

"The Watchers."

Lucifer's eyes widened. "Well, good news does travel fast, I see." The dark angel smiled. "Want to come and see?"

"Raphael and I are coming."

"Oh, you were coming without an invitation? Not very polite of you."

"Ruach requested it."

Lucifer gave a slight bow, but his words were sarcastic. "Oh, then by all means. Whatever *Ruach* wants."

As he bowed, Mikael noticed Lucifer putting his hand on the hilt of his sword to keep it in place.

"How is it you have a sword?" Mikael asked.

Lucifer gave a slight smile. "Well, no need to worry. I didn't get mine from your little memorial over there." Lucifer pointed with his head in the direction of what Quentillious had built. "Impressive structure Quentillious made with *our* swords."

"Those swords were made by Yahweh, and you know it."

"Oh, of course," Lucifer said in a sing-song tone. "Yet this one is mine. I made it." Lucifer's tone then took on a tinge of regret. "Although this one doesn't resonate." The dark angel shrugged and gave a slight smile. "But it's almost as good."

"And the Creator is okay with all of this? All you're doing?"

Lucifer grinned. "Oh, it's all about choice, you know. I'm creating choice for my subjects."

"There is a fine line between choice and manipulation."

"Oh, such words of wisdom from one who no longer has choice." Lucifer laughed. "How does it feel?"

"It feels fine, thank you!" Mikael took a deep breath. He didn't want Lucifer to upset him any further. "It feels fine. Just fine."

Lucifer laughed. "If you say so."

"I do, and I'm coming down to see which side of the line you're standing on."

Lucifer's eyes narrowed, then returned to normal. "Oh, I'll always be on the right side of the line." He grinned again. "I may be close to it, but I'll be on the right side."

Lucifer walked on. Mikael could hear him saying, "Choice. Always about choice . . . " as he slowly walked farther into the distance.

Mikael shook his head in frustration. *Man, that angel can be infuriating,* he thought. He caught himself and laughed. That was probably why Ruach asked him to take Raphael with him. Two can work to help each other stay levelheaded.

Mikael realized Ruach knew he needed Raphael. He now had more sympathy for Chavvah and her original fall. Lucifer was adept at turning words around in a person's head and causing them to have an effect they would not otherwise have.

Yes, a level head would definitely be needed in this fight.

CHAPTER 21

Arakiba

Mikael and Raphael appeared in one of the human camps. Mikael had expected a peaceful-looking agrarian society. After all, Earth had been given enough time to become lush. The period was now a little more than a millennium since Adam and Chavvah first arrived here, and only a few "years"—humans had come to measure these periods as cycles of the planet moving completely around its sun—since Chanok had been teleported to the blessed side of Sheol.

But the sight here was not as Mikael had expected.

Raphael grabbed Mikael's arm. "Mikael, what's going on here?"

Mikael shook his head. "Something's definitely wrong." He turned when he heard arguing between two people.

"My Av warned everyone about you and your deeds," one of them yelled at the other. "You have led everyone astray! Yahweh is not pleased."

The other man, who had broad shoulders and looked twice as muscular as the first man, laughed. "Oh, and that concerns me . . . how?"

"Elohim will not put up with all of this." The man swung his arm wide, gesturing to everything around him. "You starve your people to feed *him*."

The other man tapped his index finger into the man's chest. "I'm within my rights. Your Av Chanok is gone." He threw his head back and laughed. "Good riddance."

"Yahweh blessed him by taking him to paradise so he would not see what he will do to this world," the first man said.

"Well, I don't care why he is gone. He was a pain to deal with."

Mikael realized the first man was Methushelach, Chanok's son. At that moment, a woman ran up to Methushelach and pulled on his arm. "We have to go. This Watcher's son will be here any minute."

The second man laughed. "Yes, he doesn't like you very much. Neither do I."

The woman turned to the man, her tone acidic. "You know the meaning of my husband's name, don't you?"

The man shot a look at Methushelach. "How dare you allow your woman to speak to me in such a tone." He turned to the woman. "Yes. 'His death will bring.'"

"Yes, something ominous," the woman said. "You had better prepare."

The man laughed. "Yes, his death will definitely bring something. Peace!" The man laughed still harder.

Methushelach put his arm around the woman's shoulders. "Come, my love. We've said our piece." He turned to the man. "Arakiba, this is not the last you will hear from us."

The man replied, sarcastically, "Oh, good. Come back anytime."

"Arakiba!" Mikael said in a whispered tone toward Raphael.

Raphael looked from Mikael to the man. "It can't be."

Mikael then saw the man glance around him and begin to turn to enter his tent. But he stopped when his gaze fell on Mikael.

Mikael gasped. "He can see us."

Other people had walked right by them, ignorant of their presence. To them, both he and Raphael were completely invisible. Yet they were very much visible to this man.

"There can be no doubt," Raphael said. "It has to be him."

Arakiba stared at them for several seconds and then motioned with his head for them to enter his tent. He held the tent flap open for them.

Once they entered, Arakiba closed the flap and stood stoically with wrists on hips. "What are you doing here?"

"Well, good to see you too, Arakiba," Mikael said, trying to break the tension. Yet Arakiba remained still.

"So, you're interfering again."

Mikael took a step forward. "Interfering? Who's the one invisible to these people?"

Arakiba turned in a huff and sat, not offering the same to Mikael and Raphael. "What do you want?"

"I want you to explain yourself."

"I don't have to explain anything to you."

"Yahweh sent me here. So, yes, you do."

"This is our realm, our rules."

"It is your master's kingdom, but not one you should be involved with so directly. And how did you even accomplish that? You're an angel. You should be invisible to these humans."

Arakiba smiled. "We've taken a more *personal* interest in their welfare."

Mikael turned in frustration. "*Their* welfare?" He pointed at the tent door. "That is not what I see outside. Where are all the trees? Why are the fields bare? Why do people look hungry, but you have a whole mound of food?"

"And most of the food is animal," Raphael exclaimed. "That's . . . that's despicable."

"You're here two seconds, and you're already the judge!" Arakiba said to them.

Mikael took a deep breath and tried to calm himself. "Okay. Let's just take it from the beginning. Why did that woman call you a Watcher?"

Arakiba, irritated, sighed. "Quite some time ago, we left our dimension and came into this one. We don't sleep, so we were given that name."

"We?" Mikael said. "Just how many of you are there?"

"Two hundred."

Mikael's eyes widened. "*What?* Why?"

Arakiba shrugged. "That's how many of us wanted to do this. Lucifer agreed."

Mikael turned again as he thought about this. Something else was going on here, and he needed to find out what.

A woman suddenly dashed into the tent. "My lord." She gasped for breath as she had apparently been running. She held her stomach, looking like she would burst any moment; she was in a very large state with carrying a child. "Nephel is coming."

Arakiba jumped to his feet. "Get everyone gathered. Make the food pile higher. We can't afford to displease him."

As Arakiba started to step through the door, Mikael grabbed his arm. "What's going on?"

Arakiba shot him a stern look. "My son is coming." He jerked his arm free of Mikael's grasp and walked out.

Mikael looked at Raphael, who simply shrugged.

As Mikael exited the tent, he watched in shock. People were scrambling everywhere, throwing all sorts of food stuffs onto the pile in the middle of the camp.

"What are they doing?" Raphael asked.

Mikael shook his head. At that moment, he felt the ground shake. At first he thought the shaking might be from an earthquake, but the people all gathered on one side of the large mound of food and bowed or genuflected.

Both Mikael and Raphael looked at each other with huge eyes. The shaking grew stronger. In the distance, Mikael saw movement of the trees. A man appeared, pushing trees out of his way, uprooting many like they were twigs.

Raphael grabbed Mikael's arm. "Mikael! He's massive. How . . . how is this possible?"

Mikael looked up; the man was taller than many of the trees. Most of the people were no taller than the man's shin. He noticed, although the man was massive, that he was very well proportioned and had handsome features.

While everyone else bowed or genuflected, Arakiba stood and walked toward the man, holding his arms wide. "Nephel, welcome!"

Nephel put his hand to the ground. Arakiba stepped onto his giant palm, and Nephel raised him to eye height. "Father, it's great to see you." He brought his father close to his face and Arakiba gave him a kiss on his cheek. Nephel then raised his hand further, allowing Arakiba to sit on his shoulder.

"My son, the people have prepared nourishment for you."

"It is so little, father."

Arakiba patted his son's cheek. "I know, my son. But the people have worked hard for this. Have mercy on them. If you do, they will serve you and worship you."

Nephel took several handfuls of food and stuffed them into his mouth. He then tossed two large cattle carcasses from the pile. "Prepare a feast for everyone!"

The people stood and shouted their thankfulness. A few men ran and gathered the beef and took both slabs away toward a large firepit. Nephel flicked several vegetables of different types from the pile and consumed the rest of the pile in only a few bites. Several of the children ran and gathered the vegetables and took them to the men who were now working to start a fire.

Arakiba stood on Nephel's shoulder and patted his son's cheek. "Well done, my son. You will be praised tonight."

"I'm still hungry, father."

"I know, my son. Did you scout the land as I asked?"

Nephel smiled and nodded. "There are two camps not far from here toward the north. Both have large granaries."

"And their Nephilim?"

Nephel's smile turned to a huge grin as he sat. "Still young. One is a female."

Arakiba laughed and hugged his son's neck. "Excellent. We can attack, and by this time next week, everyone will raise you to godlike status with our victory." Arakiba pushed on Nephel's chin with his fist. "Who knows? Maybe you will have a bride after tomorrow."

Nephel smiled broadly, but then turned serious. "They have defenses."

"What kind?"

"They have small killers."

Arakiba smiled. "They will be no match for the large, small-armed eaters you have raised. Their arms may be small, but they are massive." His smile broadened. "We've kept them hungry."

Nephel laughed. "Victory will certainly be ours."

Mikael looked at Raphael. "There is so much that is wrong here."

Raphael nodded. "We should talk to Methushelach."

"That may prove difficult," Mikael said. "But we can at least listen in."

CHAPTER 22

Diabolical Plot

"Calm down, Edna." Methushelach pulled his wife close and hugged her. "Yahweh will protect us."

The woman gave a couple of quick nods. "I know. I know. But that will not be true for everyone. Arakiba and his kind have destroyed our world."

Methushelach nodded. "I'm just glad Adam is not here to see this."

"But isn't he the cause of it?"

Methushelach pulled her from his embrace. "Edna! Yes, he sinned, but haven't we all? But no, he is not the reason for this. Everyone had a choice to make and almost everyone has chosen poorly." He kissed her forehead. "We are each responsible for our own actions and decisions."

Edna gave a small smile. "I'm sorry. Yes, you are right." She let go and took a seat. "It's just . . . " Her eyes became moist. "Our world has become such a horrible place."

He sat next to her. "No. Just the people. The world is still quite lovely. Except for where the Nephilim roam."

"Which is becoming almost everywhere!" She pointed. "If you go to the top of the ridge, you can see their devastation all around us." She stood and began to pace. "Most of the animals are becoming so afraid; most are coming into our domain. Soon we will become a target." She stopped and turned to Methushelach. "And what if the animals trained to kill come here?"

Methushelach stood and pulled her into himself again. "Shh. Elohim will protect us. Don't worry. Please don't worry."

Edna nodded, breathing in a staccato breath. "Yes, you are right."

A knock was heard at the door. Methushelach walked over and opened it.

"Noach!" He stepped back. "Please. Come in."

"Thank you, Saba. Sorry for the interruption."

Edna poured some wine and set the cup on the table. "No trouble," she said. "Please, sit and have a drink. Is Naamah with you?"

Noach shook his head and gave a weak smile. "Not this time." He sat and took a quick drink as Methushelach sat next to him.

"What's on your mind, my son?"

"I've heard Arakiba has planned a raid to the settlements north of here."

Methushelach sighed. "That doesn't surprise me. Keeping these Nephilim fed has become the reason for so much heartache, war, and death."

Noach nodded. "Not to mention the imbalance in the animal kingdom."

"The large creatures used to be so docile," Edna said. "Now one has to be careful wherever one goes. I used to think them majestic and was excited to see them when about." She shook her head. "Now I cringe when I hear them—not knowing if I need to flee or am able to admire."

Both Noach and Methushelach nodded in silence.

Edna sat. Both Noach and Methushelach raised their eyebrows. She went on. "Excuse me for speaking out of turn. But what is the Watchers' ultimate purpose?" She looked from Noach to Methushelach, who looked surprised. "I mean, they said they came to us to observe and guide us, but nothing but destruction has occurred in their wake."

Methushelach put his hand on Edna's. "Edna . . . "

Noach raised his hand. "No, it's fine. Savta speaks what everyone is wondering." He took another long swig from his cup. "I think the whole thing's a diabolical plan on their part."

Methushelach raised his eyebrows. "What do you mean?"

"Think about it, Saba. When they invade, who is in the front of their line? The pure-bloods. You know the Watchers are not entirely human."

"So, the rumors are true?" Methushelach asked.

"I do think so," Noach said. "There are not many of us pure-bloods left. The Watchers marry our women, have giants, who we then must feed in neglect of ourselves. These giants are too big to marry our women, but some of their offspring, while large, are not as gigantic in size and are able to intermarry with us. So many people practically worship these giants that they are happy to give their children to their offspring to intermarry."

Methushelach nodded. "They don't seem to understand the giants are the cause of their problems. Yet they treat them like their heroes."

"Our race has become contaminated," Noach said. "I fear Yahweh is not happy with this."

"I'm sure he isn't," Methushelach said. "But you are the answer to all of this."

"How is that?"

"Your name, Noach. We are in chaos now, but you will somehow bring rest to the world. Your very name means rest."

Noach shook his head. "Well, I hope you're right, but I don't really see how."

"First, you must keep your sons pure. Be careful of whom they marry."

Noach nodded. "That is on my mind constantly. It's not always easy to know who is pure and who is not anymore."

Edna put her hand on his shoulder. "Don't worry. Naamah and I will certainly help in that regard." She smiled. "Women can detect these things better than most men."

Noach laughed and winked at Methushelach. "I would not disagree with my Savta."

Methushelach laughed with him. "Lemek, my son, taught you well."

Edna pushed on Methushelach's shoulder. "And who do you think taught him?"

Methushelach took her hand and kissed it. "A very wise woman."

Edna laughed and kissed him on his cheek. "Indeed."

Noach stood. "Well, I need to get back. It will be dark soon, and it's not good to be out at night these days."

Methushelach went to the door and opened it. "Very true. Be well, Noach."

"You too, Saba."

He blew Edna a kiss and left.

Mikael looked at Raphael. "Well, that was enlightening."

Raphael nodded. "Lucifer has devised quite the plot."

Mikael nodded. "So devious. No one would have considered such a thing possible."

"Can he really achieve it?" Raphael asked.

"Well, he seems to be close to doing so. Bringing angel DNA into the human genome is quite diabolical."

Raphael cocked his head. "It's almost ingenious."

Mikael gave him a hard stare.

Raphael held up his hands. "I just mean, who else would even conceive of such a thing?"

Mikael nodded. "Yes, but since angels no longer have choice, this will put the Creator in a tough spot. How does he give choice to those who no longer have choice?"

"Surely the Creator has a plan for this."

Mikael thought about Raphael's statement. *Yes, surely he does. But what?*

He looked at Raphael. "I certainly hope so. I feel the outcome either way will be grim."

CHAPTER 23

Unnatural World

Both Mikael and Raphael went to the top of the ridge Edna had spoken about.

"Remember the first time we stood on Earth," Mikael said, "and watched the stars shine?"

Raphael nodded. "It was truly glorious." He looked up. "It still is."

Both angel-warriors sat for the longest time gazing at the stars. They were truly a beautiful site with their constant twinkling as the light of the stars penetrated through Earth's atmosphere. Occasionally they saw meteoroids being burned up in the atmosphere, and this caused a streak of light. Soon the moon rose. This night, the moon shone in full phase, producing enough light to adequately see all that was before them.

It was a shame the view before them was not beautiful to behold. The Nephilim had destroyed almost all the trees across the ravine from where they sat.

Raphael turned to Mikael. "Why do you think the giants destroy all the trees? It's not as though they actually do something productive with them. They seem to just uproot them because they're in their path, as if pulling a weed. Don't they know this destruction is causing havoc on their land—and to all the animals?"

Mikael shook his head. "I don't know. Our Creator wanted Adam and his descendants to be caretakers of this world. I can't see that they have taken any of his instructions to heart."

Both looked up as they heard a roar across the ravine in a sparsely foliaged area. A large beast, standing on two massive feet with small arms in front, was running full tilt toward a smaller creature, which was running on all fours.

Raphael stood. "Is that creature going to eat the other one?" He looked at Mikael wide-eyed. "That is not supposed to happen. I thought they were docile creatures!"

The size of Mikael's eyes matched those of Raphael's as he rose. "The last time we were here, they were. What has happened?"

They both watched in horror—and amazement—as they observed the large creature gain on the smaller and eventually step on its tail. The smaller animal cried out, clawing at the ground, trying to get away. The larger creature lifted its head, bellowed loudly, and then decapitated the smaller animal in one bite, chewing and swallowing. It then swallowed the remainder of the animal with its next.

The large animal walked on, giving another bellow. Mikael and Raphael noticed all the animals in the forest behind them running farther into the thicker parts of the brush. *Who could blame them?* Mikael thought.

"I would say Arakiba owes us an explanation about this," Mikael said. "When it's light, we should go see him."

Raphael looked at Mikael. "Why wait? He is a Watcher, after all. Apparently, he does not sleep."

Mikael nodded. "Good point. I had forgotten about that." He looked at Raphael. "Shall we?"

They teleported directly to Arakiba's camp. Both stood in place for a few seconds glancing right and left. All seemed quiet—mostly. They heard commotion in Arakiba's tent. A woman screamed in pain. They hurried to investigate.

As they entered the tent, two other women knelt while attending Arakiba's wife. She appeared to be in labor. Yet, evidently, all was not going well.

One woman applied cold compresses to the forehead of the woman in labor. "Shh, Rebkah. It's not yet time."

Rebkah groaned. "But I can't take the pain anymore. It's too big. Too big."

The woman looked at the other, who just stared back in shock. "Tima, it is only six months. How will she survive until term? She . . . she is so huge already."

Tima shook her head; she seemed to be deep in thought. "Maybe . . . maybe we can induce labor somehow."

The other woman looked around in fright. "But if the baby dies from a premature birth, Arakiba will have us killed."

Tima pointed at Rebkah. "You don't think a baby this size can live on its own? It's already twice the size of a normal full-term baby."

The woman wrung her hands. "I don't know. What do we do?"

Tima pursed her lips. "Go get the tincture we made with black licorice root and raspberry leaf tea."

The woman rose but looked conflicted—as if she should leave.

Tima waved her hand. "Go! Go! I'll take responsibility. We have to do something!"

The woman dashed from the tent—she almost ran directly into Mikael, who she couldn't see, but he moved at the last second—and returned a few moments later with a small bottle. Tima took the liquid and held up Rebkah's head. "Rebkah, here. Drink a few sips of this. I think this tincture will help."

Rebkah took a few swallows, then coughed and grimaced.

"I know the taste is bad," Tima said. "But this concoction should help. We need to get this baby out of you."

Rebkah laid her head back. She appeared to go to sleep. *Probably from exhaustion*, Mikael thought. Yet this was short-lived. Suddenly her eyes went wide and she screamed in pain. "It's coming! The baby's coming!" the woman screamed.

Tima lifted the woman's robe but shook her head. "Rebkah, you're not dilated. The baby can't come."

Rebkah rolled her head back and forth. "No! No, it's coming." Rebkah's stomach, already large, suddenly extended upward abnormally, like a hand pushing through a balloon. She again yelled in pain.

Both Tima and the other woman recoiled in shock. "What's going on?" the woman asked as she placed her hand over her mouth, her eyes now completely huge.

Tima shook her head. "I . . . I think the baby's coming out through the front."

The woman looked at Tima in horror. "What? How can it do that?"

"I've heard . . . " Tima stopped, her eyes wide, as Rebkah's screams became deafening.

Rebkah grabbed her stomach, screaming, "Help me! Help me!"

Suddenly a hand broke through her stomach as Rebkah kept screaming. Then another. The baby pushed the opening larger and pushed itself out. Rebkah's screams suddenly stopped.

Arakiba rushed into the tent. "Is the baby born? What is it?" Arakiba noticed Mikael and Raphael there, shot them an irritated look, and turned his attention back to Tima and the other woman.

Tima hurried and pulled the baby completely out of Rebkah, tied off the umbilical cord, cut it, and handed the baby to the other woman, who cleaned off the residual blood and vernix as quickly as she could. She then handed the baby to Arakiba.

"It's a boy," she said with a slight, nervous smile.

Tima turned to take care of Rebkah, but then stopped. Arakiba looked from the baby, giving it silly grins, to Tima. "How is she?"

Tima sat still, unmoving.

Arakiba suddenly seemed irritated. "Tima! How is she?"

She looked up at him, her cheeks already tearstained. "She's . . . dead."

Arakiba continued to bounce the baby, who was now cooing and no longer crying. He sighed.

"Understood," Arakiba said. "Prepare her for burial."

He quickly left the tent.

Mikael and Raphael started to follow Arakiba from the tent. Mikael definitely wanted answers, but he stopped when he heard the second woman speak to Tima.

"This is number five. How many other women have to die because of him?"

Tima waved her hand. "Shh! He may hear you." She pulled on her arm. "Now come. Help me. Rebkah at least deserves a decent burial."

Raphael looked at Mikael. *"Five?"*

Mikael shook his head. "Let's go find out."

They found Arakiba sitting outside, near a fire, bouncing the baby in his arms. This baby looked almost the size of a toddler. The baby smiled when they approached.

"Come meet Bakba," Arakiba said to the two. He set the baby on his leg, holding him up for them to see.

"This was number five?"

Arakiba stared at Mikael. "Yeah. So?"

Mikael's eyes grew wide. "Did they *all* die like Rebkah?"

Arakiba shrugged. "One survived—for a time, anyway."

Mikael put his hands on his head. "And none of this bothers you?"

Arakiba gave Mikael a hard stare. "Mind your own business. They're the ones who seduced *me*. I have a physique unequal to any human." He chuckled. "They can't resist me."

"And they're willing to die for you?"

Arakiba shrugged.

"Oh," Raphael said. "You don't tell them that part, is that right, Arakiba? At least until it's too late."

Arakiba stood, irritated. "Look. They're expendable, just like any other resource here. Like I said: they seduce *me*." He grinned. "I just give in." He repositioned the baby on his shoulder. "Now if you'll excuse me, I'm going to go show Nephel his brother."

They watched Arakiba walk away with a slight swagger in his step.

They could hear soft crying from inside the tent.

CHAPTER 24

Nephilim Battle

As dawn broke, Mikael witnessed activity beginning to increase. The people were preparing for war.

War, Mikael thought. *How has the world come to this?* The world was supposed to be peaceful with everyone in harmony worshipping Yahweh. Yet the world had become a violent place with so many atrocities taking place. Consideration of Yahweh resided in the hearts of only a few.

This thought made Mikael realize these few were indeed precious. He turned to Raphael. "You stay here and keep watch. I'm going to get permission from Ruach to bring angels here to help protect Noach and his family."

"That's a great idea."

Mikael turned with a start. There was Ruach.

"Ruach! You startled me." Mikael squinted. "Why are you here?"

Ruach put his hand on Mikael's shoulder. "You know I'm everywhere."

Mikael nodded. "Yes, of course." He shook his head. "I only meant . . ."

"How did I allow all of this to happen?"

"Well, yes." Mikael looked at the people walking by. He pointed to several. "The people here are all about surface things. The women put color on their face and lips to look more desirable, only to be taken by the men without marriage. The men are driven by their lust and not their reasoning. On top of that, Arakiba and his fellow Watchers fuel the aggression in all of them. Not to mention the Nephilim, who have brought destruction to this planet and its inhabitants. Yet the people don't even realize they're duped. They see these giants almost like gods, who they worship. They follow their every bidding, gladly giving their own children to the Nephilim's offspring."

He turned back to Ruach. "You can't be pleased with this."

Ruach shook his head. "No, Mikael. No, we are certainly not pleased."

"Then why allow it?"

"It's about choice, Mikael. We made these humans with the capacity to choose. Unfortunately, they have chosen poorly. Lucifer has taken advantage of their propensity to sin and has led them down this dark road. Adam and several of his descendants, like Chanok, have tried to warn them of the path they are on. It is hard for people to see the possibility of something better when that possibility is so different from what they know as ordinary. The possibility seems almost unattainable to them. They can believe in a better future, but not that such a future can occur within their lifetime."

"Then what do we do?"

"Gather your angels and protect Noach and his family. As you have already surmised, that is important. He is the hope of mankind."

Raphael got Mikael's attention. "Let me do that for you, Mikael." He looked around. "I think you need to be here for what happens this morning."

Mikael looked back to get Ruach's opinion, but he was gone. Mikael shook his head and looked back at Raphael. "Yes, go ahead. You are probably right."

With that, Raphael disappeared. Mikael heard a creature roar and went to investigate.

Several people were scurrying away from the direction where the creature came. Many children tried to go toward the sound, but the adults grabbed their hands and pulled them back.

"Aw, Ima," one of the lads said. "Nephel is going to get his pets. I want to see."

The woman pulled her son farther away. "Not until they have eaten something. I don't want you to be their morning snack."

"Nephel wouldn't let that happen."

The woman shook her head. "I know he wouldn't want anything to happen to you, but those creatures are unpredictable. Just because he raised them doesn't mean they are tame."

Mikael continued to go against the flow of the people. Extremely far back from the camp, he found Nephel and Arakiba with two large creatures; their height was only up to Nephel's waist. These creatures would, Mikael reasoned, be several times higher than most of the humans. While he knew the creatures were made to be docile and eat plants, they now looked very menacing. They had thick, sturdy legs, thick bodies, and huge jaws with jagged teeth. Yet their upper arms were tiny compared to their overall body size. It was their eyes, though, that disturbed Mikael most. They exuded hate in their look. He shook his head. This was not the way the

Creator had made these animals. Somehow, the Nephilim had changed their demeanor.

"What have you done, Arakiba?"

Arakiba quickly turned, then sighed. "Oh, it's you." He gave a fake grin. "Come to see what Nephel has done?"

Nephel looked down at his father. "You say something, Father?"

Arakiba shook his head. "No, son. I'm just talking to one of the angels."

Nephel nodded and went back to petting the large creatures he had caged in front of a large cave using what looked like tree trunks jammed in the ground. Apparently, Arakiba talked to his fellow angels often enough for this to not be a surprise to Nephel.

Mikael came closer. "And just what has he done, Arakiba? He has turned docile creatures into menacing ones."

"Yes," Arakiba said with great pride in his tone. "These will allow us to conquer the clans to the north and provide us with enough food to last for quite a while."

Mikael pinched the bridge of his nose, slightly shaking his head. "Is that really necessary? Why not just plant crops and thereby feed everyone?"

"The ground is not rich enough to sustain enough crops for all of us."

"Well, if the Nephilim wouldn't uproot all the trees and would rotate crops as Adam, I'm sure, taught you, the earth would definitely sustain everyone."

Arakiba turned to Mikael with irritation in his voice. "It's too late for that now. Besides, this is easier. Plus . . . " He looked up at the creatures. "The odds are on our side. Today, victory will be ours."

Mikael couldn't believe what he was hearing. "While you may win this battle, do you really win the war?"

"And what is that supposed to mean? You sound like Yahweh with his riddles."

Mikael paced while trying to think of what might make a difference with Arakiba. "You don't care about anyone but yourself. Do you even care if those in his village die?"

"Oh, grow up, Mikael. They all eventually die. What does it matter if they die sooner or later?"

Mikael's eyes widened. "These people adore and worship Nephel. I see their adoration is not reciprocated." Mikael pointed his finger at Arakiba. "Yahweh would never treat *anyone* like this."

Arakiba's eyes flashed with hate. "Are we not *anyone*? That is exactly what Yahweh did to us. He abandoned us and then banished us." He shook his head. "Don't deny it. I was there. Remember?"

"As was I, Arakiba. Our Creator gave you a choice. You chose Lucifer. This is your consequence. You are now just on a path of vengeance. Don't expect me to pity you now after what you did in the past and what you are doing now."

"Whatever." Arakiba turned his back on Mikael. "The die is cast. So be it."

"Arakiba."

He did not acknowledge Mikael but turned to Nephel.

"Nephel, are the creatures ready?"

Nephel looked down and smiled. "We are." He reached down and put Arakiba on his shoulder. "Shall we go?"

Arakiba patted Nephel's neck. "They'll never know what hit them."

Nephel laughed loudly. This caused the creatures to throw their heads back and bellow just as loudly. They became more excited as Nephel took out several of the tree trunks and threw them aside. They followed Nephel and Arakiba as they walked back toward the camp. Each of their steps caused the ground to quake. Mikael knew if he found the quaking unnerving, the humans most definitely did.

When they reached the camp, Nephel put his father down. As Mikael predicted, the humans were cowering behind whatever they could find. Arakiba pushed them out into the opening and arranged them in rows. It was clear he was giving them no choice but to take part in this war. He had Nephel and the creatures in front, then the pure-bloods, and then the hybrids arranged by size.

Before they headed out, he went to Tima. "You be sure and see to the needs of Bakba. We'll be back with nourishment for him as well as everyone else."

She nodded but did not look convinced. Mikael couldn't tell if she wanted them to return or if she hoped they would never return. Apparently, Arakiba felt she wished the former as he kissed Bakba on his forehead and then commanded the people to proceed. While the pace was a slow walk for Nephel and his creatures, their stride made the trek almost a jog for everyone else. As usual, Nephel and the creatures pushed trees out of their way rather than walking around any of them.

Mikael sighed and shook his head. *They never seem to learn.* Rather than walking with them, he teleported to the top of the ridge and watched from there. Following their path was easy as the advancement was evidenced by trees falling before them. Mikael then teleported to the first village.

At first everything looked normal; everyone was going about their daily activities. As Nephel and his creatures got closer, Mikael could feel the ground begin to quake. At first this did not unnerve the villagers. Yet as the ground moved more, the more agitated the villagers became. Soon all were in a panic. Their giant came running into the midst of the camp rallying everyone to prepare for battle. Yet he looked to be about half the height of Nephel. This giant was evidently very young.

Mikael had a bad feeling about the coming encounter.

Mikael knew the pace of Nephel and his creatures' advancement had increased; he could feel the intensity of the vibrations through the earth. In virtually no time they were on the outskirts of the village . . .

The villagers released their creatures. While these creatures were only shoulder height to the humans, they were numerous and looked menacing.

The village giant commanded they attack, and they did so with a vengeance.

The creatures first went after the large creatures with Nephel and against Nephel himself. Stunningly, these creatures became ready snacks for Nephel's mighty animals. While some managed to get on the back of Nephel's large creatures and tear into their flesh, Nephel picked them off and flung them into the villagers, quickly causing still more deaths.

It seemed these creatures learned quickly and soon abandoned their initial attack to turn their attention to the humans. The pure-bloods were the first to be attacked. Mikael cringed in horror as these small creatures tore into the flesh of the humans and literally tore them limb from limb. The humans had to work together to take down just one of the creatures . . .

Eventually, the humans and hybrids worked together in their attack against these creatures and won. Yet there was a trail of blood and body parts in their wake.

Mikael heard a large boom. When he turned he saw Nephel engaged in battle with the other giant. Being smaller, the village giant was able to maneuver quickly. He felled Nephel by knocking his legs from under him. Yet one of Nephel's creatures bit into this giant's shoulder causing him to yelp in pain. This giant grabbed the large creature's neck and was able to flip the beast over him and onto the creature's back. The ground shook, causing several people to lose their balance in their own fights. Before this giant could stand up again, Nephel grasped the giant by his feet, swung him over his head, and plummeted him into the ground. Again the ground shook; the giant groaned but was able to grab Nephel's ankles, causing him to trip and fall. But before the village giant could stand again, one of Nephel's creatures bit hard into the giant's neck, nicking a major artery. The giant attempted to rise but was bleeding out too quickly. This incited Nephel's creatures, and two of them devoured him in only a few bites.

Mikael stood, aghast at the scene. He could not believe this was happening on the world his Creator had made. The scene was visually and emotionally too surreal, even for an angel.

Before he could rationalize what had happened, Mikael saw another giant break into the clearing along with more of these smaller deadly creatures. Before Nephel could stand, several of these creatures were on him, biting and tearing his flesh. Nephel stood and pulled them off. He then took one of them and used the creature as a weapon, hitting several of the creatures, causing them to fling high into the trees in the distance.

His creatures headed for the other giant. "No!" he said. "Heel!" They obeyed but looked irritated. Nephel pointed to the humans and hybrids now pouring into the village. "Attack!" The creatures did so, beheading, or cutting in half, several as they ran through the crowd of people. The humans fled in all directions, screaming as they fled.

Nephel then turned to attack this latest attacking giant. Although female, she proved quite the opponent. Mikael could tell Nephel was being more careful in his attack on this particular Nephilim than he had with the other male giant. Yet this giant woman was holding nothing back in her approach. She felled Nephel several times, but eventually he had her pinned; she could not move or get him off.

"Do you yield?" Nephel asked.

"Never! I will never yield to you!"

Nephel laughed. "If you yield, I will spare the rest of your people."

She struggled to free herself, but again was unsuccessful.

"Look!" Nephel said, turning her head to force her to see her people being devoured by his two largest creatures. "You cannot win. You must yield."

The woman closed her eyes and slowly nodded. "I yield."

"You swear?"

The woman nodded. "Yes, I swear. We yield. Now call off your creatures."

Nephel looked over and yelled, "Heel!"

The creatures acted as if they did not hear. *"Heel!"* Nephel bellowed again.

His creatures stopped and turned toward him. Nephel stood and helped the female giant to her feet. Her height was only to his shoulders. She dusted herself off.

Nephel looked at his father. "Assess who remains."

Arakiba nodded and went through the crowd placing people into ranks.

Nephel turned to the woman. "I'm Nephel."

The woman stopped dusting herself off and glanced his way. "Artel."

Nephel smiled. "It is nice to meet you."

The woman took off her helmet and shook her long blonde hair, brushing her thick locks behind her shoulder. "Yeah, I bet."

Nephel laughed. "Playing hard to get, huh?"

"Oh, you think you have me, do you?"

Nephel gave a smirk. "Well, you did swear."

Artel pushed on his shoulder and walked toward Arakiba. "Just because I surrender doesn't mean you have me."

Nephel laughed again. "We'll see about that."

Artel looked at him over her shoulder. To Mikael, there seemed to be almost the hint of a smile. She focused on Arakiba. "How many of my people are left?"

Arakiba shrugged. "Hard to tell. I'd say about one-third."

Nephel walked toward them. "And how many of ours?"

"About half, I would guess."

Nephel nodded as if he was fine with that report.

Mikael was having an extremely hard time processing all of this. The giants seemed to have no regard for human life. Humans were just a resource meant to be used for their own purpose and agenda.

"Let's get everyone back to our camp," Nephel said. "I'll come back with Artel and get all the granaries and other food stuffs transported."

Arakiba nodded and led the people back through the forest—or what was once a forest before their raid.

Nephel glanced at his creatures, who were standing still but salivating. He laughed. "Go ahead. Go ahead and clean up."

The creatures immediately started gulping up the remains of the other creatures and human bodies strewn throughout the village.

Before long the scene was quiet, empty. Mikael had never been sick before, but if feeling sick felt anything like he was

experiencing at this moment, he now had a better apprecia-
tion of human feelings.

At that moment Raphael returned. His eyes went wide.
"Mikael! What happened?"

Mikael took Raphael's shoulder. "Let's just go, Raphael. I'll
explain. But I can't take the sight of this anymore."

Both disappeared.

CHAPTER 25

Plot Revealed

Mikael sat with his back against a large tree. Raphael sat near him. They had both sat quietly, not speaking, for nearly the entire night. Mikael kept thinking about the events of the previous day. The whole ordeal seemed like such a waste.

Raphael leaned forward. "Mikael, want to talk about it?"

Mikael shook his head. "No, not really." He glanced at Raphael. "I'm not sure how to even describe what I saw. I don't know if I could have ever imagined anything like it."

"So, what do you think is the Watchers' overarching agenda?"

Mikael looked at Raphael. "Overarching agenda? Producing chaos, I imagine, just to be spiteful." Mikael shook his head. "And doing a good job at it, so it seems."

Raphael rubbed his chin. "You don't think there's more to it?"

Mikael gave Raphael a blank stare. He didn't understand what Raphael was driving at.

"I wonder if their actions are tied to Lucifer's interest in Noach?"

Mikael sat up straighter. He had forgotten about Raphael going back and getting other angels to come to Earth to protect Noach and his family.

"Oh, Raphael. My apologies. I had forgotten about your mission. How did everything go?"

Raphael nodded with a slight shrug. "It went fine. Many were anxious and willing to come help. When we went to Noach's village, many of Lucifer's angels had surrounded the camp, but they appeared to just be watching. Likely sending back intelligence to their leader."

Mikael's eyes widened. "What happened when you arrived?"

Raphael chuckled. "Nothing. When they saw us, they left."

Mikael tilted his head. "Really? Why is that, do you think?"

Raphael shrugged. "Don't know. But I'm happy they did. I don't think that's the last we'll see of them, though."

Mikael nodded. "Likely not." Mikael paused and looked back at Raphael. "And you think there's a connection?"

Raphael stood and stretched. He looked over the valley below them and turned back to Mikael. "There has to be. You know Lucifer is manipulative. He's doing all of this for a reason. Arakiba and the other Watchers are fulfilling some type of plan. I'm sure of it."

Mikael looked up at Raphael. "Well, let's go find out." He stood. "I think Arakiba owes us an explanation. Maybe he'll leak something if we goad him enough."

Raphael grinned. "Feeling crafty, are we?"

Mikael laughed. "Well, he seems as full of pride as Lucifer. That makes him overconfident. And that, my friend . . . " He patted Raphael on his shoulder. "That makes him vulnerable to leaking information he otherwise would not."

With that, both teleported into Arakiba's village. Evidently, everyone was still asleep. But Mikael noticed new granaries were already erected as were several water towers. Mikael pointed them out to Raphael. "These are from the other two villages they defeated." Mikael lifted his eyebrows. "I think Arakiba will be feeling very overconfident."

Raphael nodded and smiled in return.

Without announcing themselves, both entered Arakiba's tent. He was sitting, holding Bakba, as Tima fed the giant infant some kind of fruit pulp. Arakiba's head jerked around when they entered; a scowl came across his face.

Arakiba handed Bakba to Tima, kissing the baby's forehead. "Please finish feeding Bakba in your tent."

Tima gave Arakiba a strange stare but obeyed, stepping from the tent.

When Tima left, Arakiba stood. "And to what do I owe the pleasure?"

"Ah, so you're starting to like our visits?" Mikael couldn't resist this response.

"Oh, as much as I love stubbing my big toe."

Mikael smiled. "Well, this may be a painful visit."

Arakiba forced a smile. "I think may is the wrong word."

Mikael gave a forced smile in return. "Arakiba, what are you really doing?"

Arakiba smacked his cheek with his palm and shook his head. "No riddles this early in the morning, please."

Mikael shook his head. "No riddles. I want to know what you're really up to."

Arakiba shrugged. "Just making a life for myself, my children, and my people."

Mikael cocked his head. "But you just witnessed the demise of one of your people yesterday. Why?"

Arakiba squinted. "*What* are you talking about?" He shook his head. "You said no riddles, remember?"

"That other giant. Nephel killed him. Why?"

Arakiba tilted his head, apparently confused. "Because we needed the food they had stored. Why is that difficult to understand?"

"But isn't he one of your people?"

Arakiba shook his head. "No. My other children are south of here. I wouldn't attack one of their villages."

Now it was Mikael who felt confused. "Yes, but all the giants are still part of *your* people, aren't they?"

Arakiba laughed. "We don't have your sense of morality. He was the son of another Watcher."

"And you don't respect each other?"

Arakiba shrugged. "Not all."

Mikael shook his head. "I don't understand."

Arakiba gave a huff. "And I should care about that?" He turned and sat. "I don't care what *you* don't understand."

Raphael nodded. "So, Lucifer's agenda goes higher than even the lives of your offspring."

Hearing this, Arakiba gave a hearty laugh. He pointed at Mikael. "You know, you may have to actually promote this one."

Mikael turned to Raphael with eyes wide, giving a slight nod. Raphael had hit a very important point. One he had not considered before now.

Mikael pointed at Arakiba. "You're against Noach and his family."

Arakiba now turned to address Raphael. "He's starting to catch up with you." Arakiba then looked at Mikael. "And what of it?"

"Only those of Nephilim descent are your people. That's why you put the pure-bloods in front of the line of defense yesterday. You hoped they would all get killed."

Arakiba smiled, but his smile now looked evil. "So you're not as incompetent as you look. My people, as you put it, become more my people with each generation."

Mikael and Raphael gasped simultaneously, realization hitting them both. They looked at each other, mouths slightly open.

"Lucifer really is trying to follow in the Creator's footsteps," Mikael said.

Arakiba once again gave a hard laugh. He shook his head. "There is no *try* here. The Creator took the first step. Lucifer has taken the next step. Soon his kingdom will be entirely in his image."

Mikael now realized that bringing the other angels here was more important than ever. Lucifer had almost accomplished what no one would have thought possible. If all humans had angel DNA incorporated into the human genome, after a few generations all would be like Arakiba, with no human DNA left—or very, very little of it. The Creator's design of humans would no longer be of his design. All his plans would be null and void. *Could* that happen? Would the Creator let such a thing happen?

He suddenly understood this was why Ruach had him come here: to understand this revelation.

Mikael turned to Raphael. "Come, Raphael. We must go."

"Oh, don't leave on my account," Arakiba said. "We have another human village to conquer." Arakiba gave another wicked laugh.

Mikael and Raphael disappeared.

CHAPTER 26

The Challenge

Mikael and Raphael reappeared at the ridge where they had been previously. Mikael began to pace.

"Raphael, I can't believe this is happening." He stopped and looked at his fellow angel. "I know Lucifer can be manipulative, but this . . . " His voice trailed off as he became lost in thought.

What can I do? The thought kept swirling in his head.

"Mikael?"

Mikael looked at Raphael. "Sorry. I was thinking."

"Obviously."

Mikael chuckled. "Well, I'm just trying to process all of this. Figure out what to do next."

Raphael laid his hand on Mikael's shoulder. "Don't feel you have to solve this, Mikael. Remember, we're just messengers. Our Creator, I'm sure, is on top of this. We just have to do his bidding."

Mikael suddenly felt relief flowing through him. Yes, Raphael was correct. Ruach didn't send him here to solve this problem, but to understand it. He now definitely understood it, and this was a very big problem. But it was not something that he, Mikael, had to solve.

Mikael nodded. "You're right, Raphael." He smiled. "I'm afraid I was getting caught up in trying to decide how to rectify this dilemma."

Raphael chuckled. "That's what I thought. We can't out-think our Creator."

"Definitely not."

"Let's go to Noach's village and see how the others are doing."

Mikael nodded. "Good idea."

In a matter of seconds, they were on the outskirts of Noach's village. Mikael turned and saw Gabriel standing nearby.

"Gabriel, how are things here?"

Gabriel clasped forearms with Mikael. "All is quiet so far. How are things elsewhere?"

Mikael shook his head. "Not good. I have never seen so much violence and gore."

Gabriel gave Mikael a quizzical look. As Mikael told of his experience the previous day, Gabriel's eyes grew wider and his jaw slacker the more Mikael told.

Gabriel shook his head. "Mikael, if I didn't know you aren't prone to exaggeration, I would question if I believe you. It's just hard to grasp all you said."

"I know. I know. I can hardly believe what I said myself—and I witnessed it."

"Now I see the gravity of us being here," Gabriel said. He looked toward the village. "The people in this village are now extremely rare and must be protected."

Mikael nodded. "At all costs."

"After what you said, how does this village compare to the one you were just in?"

Mikael walked through the village with Gabriel. He slowly took the measure of things while looking side to side. "In many aspects this village is similar in regard to abodes, grain storage, herds. Yet the other village had a sense of chaos to it, where this one does not. This place almost feels calm."

Raphael pointed to an altar. "Did the other village have this?"

Mikael nodded. "Yes. But the people would become drunk and disorderly as they ate the flesh of the animal." Mikael shook his head. "Please don't tell me that goes on here as well."

Raphael's eyes widened. "Oh, no. Not at all. The animal becomes a sacrifice, a whole burnt offering. The entire animal is consumed by fire on the altar to show obedience to our Creator and a devotion of the people to him. After sacrificing, they typically sing songs of praise to Yahweh."

Mikael smiled. "That is so good to hear. I was beginning to think all was lost."

Gabriel cocked his head. "I don't think Yahweh would allow complete loss of hope."

Mikael nodded. "Yes, but one can get lost in that thought when surrounded by so much chaos. It's important for one to maintain perspective. I'm glad I have you and Raphael to provide that for me."

Gabriel patted Mikael's upper arm. "We're in this together."

"So what do you think Yahweh will do about all of this?" Mikael asked.

Before Gabriel had time to begin an answer, Ruach appeared.

"I need both of you, Raphael, and Uriel to come with me," the Spirit said.

"What's wrong?" Mikael asked.

190

"All will be revealed in time. Yahweh has requested the presence of all top-ranking angels."

Mikael nodded and waved Raphael over. Gabriel did the same to Uriel. Both angels had raised eyebrows as if wondering what was being asked of them.

"Ruach needs all four of us to go with him for a time," Gabriel said. "Who do you recommend to stand guard here with the others?"

Both Raphael and Uriel looked at each other, turned back, and said, simultaneously, "Quentillious."

Mikael nodded. "Very good. Uriel, go inform him and tell him we'll return as soon as we can. Then meet us . . . " He looked at Ruach for a destination.

"And then report to Jahvan," Ruach said.

Uriel's eyebrows went up as he glanced at Mikael. He could only shrug; he had no idea what Ruach was thinking. Uriel simply nodded and headed toward the other angels to inform Quentillious of his new orders. The three of them then teleported with Ruach . . .

They discovered themselves at the Sacred Altar of Stones. In a matter of minutes other high-ranking angels teleported in. Mikael turned when he heard gasps behind him. Mikael's eyes widened. He poked Gabriel with his elbow.

Gabriel turned and gasped. "What is he doing here?"

Mikael could only shake his head. Words failed him.

Coming up through the angels, as each stepped aside upon seeing him, was Lucifer.

Lucifer grinned when he stopped next to Mikael. "Surprised to see me, I see."

"That's an understatement," Mikael said. "What are you *doing* here?"

"Oh, the same as you, I suppose." He shrugged. "Who can resist the charm of Ruach and his requests?"

Mikael's eyes widened. "He . . . asked you to come?"

Lucifer shot him a look of disgust. "And why else would I be here? I didn't come to see my friends." He looked around and then gave a wry smile. "Even though I can see they are thrilled to see me."

Jahvan, Azel, and Uriel appeared next to the altar with their swords raised. Mikael smiled, now realizing why Ruach had told Uriel to report to Jahvan. The swords of these three around the altar of stones began to resonate; color went from hilt to tip and then shot straight into the air. At that moment Yahweh descended as the color receded with his movement. When Yahweh's feet touched the altar, there was a bright flash of light, which then vanished.

Jahvan, Azel, and Uriel turned and sheathed their swords.

Mikael heard Lucifer mumble under his breath, "Show-off."

Mikael gave him an incredulous stare. Lucifer returned the same—with a smile.

"My angels," Yahweh said.

Mikael turned his attention back to his Creator.

"I have called you here because things are about to change on my Earth."

"*My* Earth," Lucifer interjected.

Yahweh looked at Lucifer and said, matter-of-factly, "Your kingdom. *My* Earth."

Lucifer shrugged.

"When you can create a world, then we'll discuss who owns it," Yahweh said.

Lucifer remained quiet. Mikael noticed he still looked smug, though. That greatly irritated him.

"As a number of you know," Yahweh continued, "Earth is no longer as originally designed."

Mikael heard murmuring behind him. What he knew had not yet spread to everyone.

Yahweh turned to Lucifer. "You will not win."

"Oh, I'm not in competition," Lucifer said as he smiled. "It's really the highest form of flattery."

Mikael gave him a hard stare. Lucifer couldn't be serious, he thought.

Lucifer gestured to Yahweh. "You created man in *your* image. Adam and Chavvah populated Earth after their image. Now I'm *re*populating Earth after *my* image."

Mikael shook his head. Lucifer glanced at him but ignored him.

"After all, if it's my kingdom, then shouldn't they be after *my* image?"

"You're destroying everything our Lord has created," Mikael said, inserting himself into the moment.

Lucifer turned to Mikael. "That's *your* opinion. What I am really doing is redefining what has been given to me."

Yahweh looked at Lucifer. "Quiet! Listen."

Lucifer turned and looked at Yahweh, seemingly unphased.

"Your plan will fail. I have just returned from Noach, who is even now carrying out my instructions for the salvation of his family. I will extend my longsuffering to the rest of those on Earth for one hundred and twenty years. If you love your people, you will heed Noach's words."

"Noach and his few descendants are no threat to me."

"Threat?" Mikael couldn't believe Lucifer's audacity. This dark angel's ego knew no bounds. Mikael didn't say anything further; Yahweh held up his hand toward him.

Surprisingly, Yahweh gave a smile, a genuine smile. "Lucifer, I don't threaten. I offer opportunity. This is an opportunity for all peoples on Earth to live and survive. The choice, however, is yours."

"You and choice. That seems to be your mantra. What's the real choice? It's either your way or no way. Is that really choice?"

"Choice is provided by the one who defines the opportunity. There is consequence for any decision made. The opportunity defines the consequence."

"Perish or comply. Is that it?"

Yahweh nodded. "I'm afraid so. But realize, you helped shape both the opportunity and the consequence. Each choice you have made has helped shaped the next opportunity and the next consequence. You have a play in what has been offered to you."

Lucifer shook his head and gave a chuckled sigh. "You love your riddles, don't you?" He looked directly at Yahweh and turned solemn. "You're giving me an opportunity? Well, I'm giving you one as well."

Mikael's eyes went wide. "You can't be serious. You're going to challenge Yahweh, your Creator?"

Yahweh held up a hand. Mikael backed down and looked to Yahweh. He couldn't wait to hear what would be said to Lucifer next.

Yahweh stepped from the Sacred Altar of Stones and faced Lucifer. "You were my first, and one who could have been my triumph. Great things were possible for us together. I know in your heart what you want." He shook his head as his tone became sad. "It will never happen, Lucifer. It can never happen."

Mikael saw Lucifer's body stiffen as he took a step backward. "We'll just have to see about that, won't we?"

Lucifer disappeared. Yahweh shook his head and sighed.

Yahweh looked up and addressed every angel in attendance.

"My angels, prepare yourselves. There is a battle approaching. Lucifer has determined to win this war for his gain. His success will not happen, and I will let you be part of my victory. Yet this will not be easy for you. He has become more determined and will fight even harder than last time."

Yahweh then disappeared. All the angels turned to Mikael. He knew all of them would look to him for guidance. He needed to be sure they were ready.

"Assemble at the practice field," Mikael told them. "I have some news to tell you that will be sobering. Yet you need to know what we will be up against."

In ones, twos, and threes, the angels disappeared. Before he disappeared, Gabriel took his arm.

"You have a job to do here, Mikael. I'll lead the charge at Noach's village. I feel Ruach has given me that responsibility."

Mikael nodded. "That's the sense I received as well. Elohim's speed to you, Gabriel."

"And to you, Mikael."

Gabriel disappeared. Mikael took a deep breath and let it out slowly. Interesting days were ahead.

CHAPTER 27

The Ark

Mikael appeared with a legion of his angels. He looked over and saw Raphael approaching. "How are things here, Raphael?"

"Quiet right now." Raphael positioned his head to allow the wind to blow hair out of his eyes. "It's uncanny how Noach and his family have been praying more at this time, which has helped energize us for the three attacks that occurred since you last left."

Mikael nodded. "Ruach did tell me how he has instituted this spiritual connection between the earthly dimension and ours. I see now why he did so."

"Arakiba has been working with the other Watchers. They have started making alliances rather than being against each other. We don't let any of Noach's family walk alone anymore. The risk is too great."

Mikael nodded as he looked around Noach's village. He didn't see any of the other angels. "So, where are your other angels?"

"They're with Noach and the rest of his family. Naamah and her daughters-in-law are preparing food for their husbands."

At that moment four women stepped from their abode, each carrying a basket in each hand and a wineskin draped across their shoulder.

"Do we have everything?" Naamah asked. "Rayneh, are you okay? It looks like you're straining."

"Really, Ima," Rayneh said. "I'm not straining any more than anyone else. I'm fine."

Naamah looked at the others. "Ar'yel, Kezia. Are you okay with the weight?"

Ar'yel laughed, nodding her head. "Yes, Ima, we're fine as well, but won't be for long if we don't hurry and get these supplies to our husbands. It's a short journey, but a difficult one."

Naamah nodded and headed down the road with the other women following. Mikael sent half the angels with him ahead to join the others. Then he, Raphael, and the other angels followed. Each angel looked right and left, watchful of whatever might happen.

A bit later, as they passed a stream, Naamah placed her baskets near a boulder and sat. She motioned for the other women to do the same. "Rest, my daughters. Rest."

Kezia took a gourd cup out of her basket and went to the stream, filling the vessel with water. She took a long drink. "Ahh, that hits the spot," she said. Putting her hand on the back of her hip, she stretched, then walked to the others, handing the cup to Naamah. "We're about halfway, right?"

Naamah nodded after she took her drink and then passed the cup to Ar'yel, who passed the cup to Rayneh after she took a drink. Rayneh took a long drink, repacked the gourd cup, and stood. "Let's get going, then."

The women crossed the small stream and continued their journey, sometimes stumbling over the rocky terrain but always managing to keep their balance without spilling anything. They seemed to keep a good disposition about the whole thing and would laugh and gently chide each other.

Once when Naamah stumbled, Rayneh quickly set down a basket and took her arm. "Are you all right?"

Naamah laughed and nodded. "Yes, for goodness sake. I'm fine. I'm only five hundred, after all."

The other women looked at each other and burst out laughing.

"Oh," Ar'yel said, then grinned. "Maybe your wineskin is no longer as full as when we started."

They all laughed as Naamah poked her tongue out at Ar'yel.

"Ooh," Kezia said, looking at Ar'yel. "You've been scolded."

All four women laughed again.

Mikael laughed at the women's light banter. He could tell they were becoming a tightknit family. That was good, and it was very much needed during this time. There were undoubtedly rough times ahead.

As they rounded a bend and crested a hill, the women set their baskets down and looked at the view before them.

Kezia shook her head. "I still don't understand what our men are doing. Everyone is calling them crazy."

Naamah rubbed Kezia's upper back. "Keep the faith, Kezia. Yahweh has given my husband a vision of what must be created." She pointed. "And it's coming together quite nicely."

"It's so big," Ar'yel said. "Why does the ark have to be so big?"

Naamah shook her head. "I don't know how, but Yahweh is going to save the world in this ark." She picked up her baskets and continued. The other women sighed and followed with theirs.

As they approached, Mikael saw about one hundred men working on various things: some hauling logs from the forest, some chopping, some soaking wood, others forming the wood to a curved shape, and others on scaffolding building the ark itself. The activity reminded him of bees in a hive. All looked chaotic from a distance, but one could see the harmonic detail as he got closer.

When Noach saw the women, he waved and patted Jepheth on his shoulder. His son turned and grinned.

Mikael's eyes widened as he saw Noach, like a giant ape, bound down the scaffolding, swinging and jumping like he was half his age.

Jepheth laughed. "Shem. Cham." They turned and he pointed.

Each then followed their father down, making similar moves, but not with quite the same abandon.

The women had the food out and prepared by the time the men arrived. Each kissed their wives and sat on the ground in pairs eating their meal after giving a quiet blessing.

"It looks like you're making good progress," Naamah said.

Noach nodded as he took a long drink of wine.

"Yes," Cham interjected. "But work could go a lot faster if we had support from at least one of the giants. They could get the trees here in record time."

Shem shook his head. "No, I don't trust them. Besides, they're the reason Yahweh told Aba to do this in the first place."

Ar'yel looked around. "I don't trust anyone here other than us." She gave a slight shudder as she watched the other men eating not far from them. "Why did you hire that cook for the others, anyway? He's cooking . . . meat . . . for them to eat."

Shem rubbed her back. "Don't worry, honey. If they're content, they will be fine."

Noach nodded. "I don't like the way they live any more than you, but we need their help, and this was the only way." He made eye contact with each of them. "Also, they get paid today, so it's best to stay in our village tonight and tomorrow. They get a little . . . wild when they have the resources to do so."

Naamah nodded. "Yes, I think that is very wise."

"Aw," Rayneh said, "I wanted to go see the wares of the new vendor in the next village over tomorrow."

"I know," Jepheth said. "It's disappointing, but better safe than sorry."

Rayneh sighed. "It's dangerous at night because of the animals they have trained and bred to be hungry for the blood of humans. Now it's dangerous even in the daytime because of their greed and lust." She shook her head. "Our safe world has shrunk to only a few acres of land."

"I can't argue with you there," Noach said. He looked behind him. "But this ark will be the answer to all of that."

"Why is the structure so massive?" Kezia asked. "How many people are you planning to save?"

"Kezia," Cham said. "We've talked about this. This ark may be just for the eight of us. I don't think the Watchers are going to let others join us."

Kezia's eyes widened. "So, you're making the ark so big just in case?"

Noach shook his head. "No, my dear. While the ark will be able to accommodate others, the main purpose for its size is to save the animals."

"Why?" Kezia asked. "My Av says the animals can take care of themselves. He's asking me to come back home."

"Do you want to do that?" Cham looked crushed that she had said those words.

She put her hand on Cham's upper arm. "Oh, no. Not at all. And I told him so."

Cham gave a small smile upon hearing those words; he kissed her cheek. "Good."

"I'm just trying to understand." Kezia shrugged. "Why can't the animals take care of themselves? How can water from the sky be so bad? I can't imagine water coming from the sky anyway. Such a thing has never occurred before. What makes you think it will now?"

"Because Yahweh has said so," Noach replied. "His words are truth; they are reliable."

Mikael looked at the horizon. Lucifer's angels surrounded the area, but they were far in the distance, and they only seemed to be watching. Hopefully, them seeing he had brought reinforcements would make them think twice about attacking.

"Raphael, have Lucifer's angels attacked here before, or just at Noach's village?"

"Just at the village so far." He gazed at their presence in the distance. "They come here and watch but have not attacked. My guess is they won't do that until the project is complete or almost complete."

"Why so?"

"Well, that seems to be their nature. They try to confuse at the critical times. Currently, the folks here are happy as long as they are paid on time and can feed their families. Once the job is complete, that is when they'll think about how to continue to feed their families, and that is when the unrest will likely escalate."

Mikael nodded. Raphael made sense. Noach's project was likely not a threat until the ark was completed.

Noach and his family were the continued threat.

Noach stood. "Well, boys, let's get back to work." He helped Naamah to her feet. "I'll see you later this evening." He gave her a kiss as his sons did the same with their wives.

Naamah looked over at the men who were starting to get back to work as well. "It's a good thing I water down their wine, or you would likely get no work out of them in the afternoons."

Noach grinned. "You have always been very wise."

She slapped his arm lightly. "Now, don't you start."

Noach laughed. "Honey, I'm agreeing with you."

"You'd better." She kissed his cheek. "Because I married a wise man."

Noach laughed even harder. "Indeed."

As the women packed up and left, Mikael had two-thirds of the angels return with them; a third stayed at the work site. Since the attacks had so far occurred at the village, he thought it best to have most of them there.

He just hoped this pattern remained. He didn't want to be caught off guard.

CHAPTER 28

The Nephilim Plot

Mikael walked next to Raphael as they followed the women from their village to the clearing where Noach was building his ark.

Mikael looked at Raphael. "It's been a little over four Earth years now without any type of incident. It's making me wary."

As they came over the crest of the hill with the women, Raphael pointed. "Noach and his family are so close to finishing now. I do predict conflict within the next few months."

Mikael looked at the scene before them. The ark had taken shape and was nearly complete. The massive structure seemed to fill the valley, dwarfing everything surrounding it.

Naamah stopped and stared at the structure. "Look, girls! They're nearing completion."

Rayneh nodded. "Jepheth says when he's on top he can see beyond all hills around here. He can even see far into the forest." She shrugged. "Or what's left of it."

Ar'yel chuckled. "It's the only time the Nephilim have come in handy. They had toppled so many trees, Shem said, that it saved the men a lot of time not having to fell them."

Naamah picked up her baskets again. "Come along, girls. We won't have to do this for too much longer."

Kezia laughed. "We've done this for so long, I'm not sure I'd know what to do with myself."

Ar'yel bumped shoulders with her. "Well, I'd certainly like to try."

"Amen," both Rayneh and Naamah said almost simultaneously. They all looked at each other and laughed in unison.

As the women headed toward the ark, Mikael took Raphael's arm. "Let's go see Arakiba."

Raphael turned up his brow. "Why?"

"Maybe we can glean what will soon happen."

"You think he will give anything away?"

Mikael shrugged. "Perhaps. It's worth a try, anyway. I think we have plenty of other angels here."

Mikael first teleported to Quentillious's position and put him in charge for the time being. Then he and Raphael teleported to Arakiba's village . . .

Mikael sensed something different from the last time he was here. People were scurrying everywhere trying to pacify what looked to be a man sitting near the communal altar. Mikael assumed the person to be a man as he looked mature in facial and musculature development, yet he was acting very childish and nearly in the middle of a tantrum.

A woman ran frantically here and there calling, "Arbel! Arbel!"

A woman stepped from Arakiba's tent along with Arakiba. The other woman looked frustrated and ran over to the woman who had just left the tent. "Arbel, I've been calling for you!" She pointed back at the man . . . child? "You know how upset he gets when he can't find you."

"I'm coming. I'm coming," Arbel said as she scurried across the compound. The man stopped his tantrum as soon as he saw her, holding out his arms toward her. Arbel ran into his arms, hugging him and stroking his hair.

Mikael found it curious that this man—or child—was as tall as Arbel herself even while seated. Mikael and Raphael walked over to engage Arakiba.

Arakiba gave the two angel-warriors a disdainful look and a sigh. "You always show up at the most inopportune time. What do you want this time?"

Mikael gave a pleasant smile. "Oh, we're just here to visit a comrade angel—or used to be an angel."

Arakiba rolled his eyes. "Oh, please." He turned and went into his tent. Mikael and Raphael followed.

Arakiba took a seat. As usual, he didn't offer one to his visitors. "So, what really brings you here?"

Mikael pointed behind him. "Who is that out there?"

Arakiba smiled and sat up straighter. "Oh, that's my grandson, Kilion. The first son of Nephel and Artel."

"First?" Mikael knew the time lapse had been almost a century since the two of them had become mates. He was also pretty sure they never had a marriage ceremony: another bad habit taught to humans by the Watchers and their children.

"Yes, they've had several children over the years—all girls." Arakiba smiled broadly. "Until now."

"And where are they?" Raphael asked.

"Oh, they have all started their own villages." He laughed. "These humans treat all of us like gods. We do them little favors, protect them from their enemies, and they reward us with devotion. Quite the symbiotic relationship, don't you think?"

Mikael's eyes widened. "*Protect* them?" He couldn't believe what he was hearing. "You're practically destroying them."

Arakiba laughed. "Well, clearly you don't see things the way we do. We love our pets. We're just . . . improving them, making them a better breed."

"They're not *cattle*," Raphael said emphatically. "They are the Creator's highest earthly creation. You can't improve upon that."

Arakiba's eyebrows went up. "Oh, I think that's where we disagree. My lord feels otherwise."

"Yes, I guess Lucifer would," Mikael said. He paused, sighed. "And just what was that going on outside?"

Arakiba shrugged. "Kilion got upset, and I sent Arbel out to comfort him. He met her when scoping out another village. She really does adore him, you know. I bet they mate before too long." He next acted as though he was talking to himself. "I really need to encourage their union before Kilion gets too large to enjoy her."

Mikael looked at Raphael and back to Arakiba. He found this disturbing. "And just how old is Kilion?"

Arakiba tapped his lips. "Let me see. I guess about eleven or twelve." When he looked back at them, he laughed. "Oh, wipe that astonished look off your faces. Our offspring mature very quickly."

"And I assume she's a pure-blood," Mikael said with sarcasm. "How could her Av allow such a thing?"

Arakiba got a sad look. "Oh, unfortunately he was killed in a recent raid his god led on another village."

"Oh, how convenient." Mikael was irritated Arakiba called this Nephilim a god, but that was not the main point to address right now.

Arakiba cocked his head. "Yes, isn't it?" He smiled. "Very fortunate for Kilion. And for Arbel. They can now be together unencumbered."

Mikael turned in frustration. "You think you're doing something wonderful here, but can't you see what the end will be?"

"Oh, I most certainly can, I assure you."

Mikael shook his head. "No, I don't think you do. So even if you get rid of all the pure-bloods and you have your own race, how will you be able to sustain yourselves? Your descendants feed off the contributions of others and their conquests. How is that sustainable when they at the same time destroy the trees and other vegetation? You're destroying the very thing our Creator gave to sustain life."

Arakiba laughed. "You just don't get it, do you?"

Mikael and Raphael looked at each other and then back at Arakiba, slightly shaking their heads.

"The goal is not to sustain." He shrugged. "Although that would be nice." He gave them both a hard stare. "No, the goal is to have *no more* pure-bloods. That's the goal, and . . . " He shot a devious grin. "It's almost achieved. Only Noach stands in the way now."

Mikael's eyebrows raised; he understood the implication of Arakiba's statement. "Oh, that's not going to happen."

Arakiba leaned back, placing the fingers from each hand together and producing a bright smile. "We'll see."

Mikael took a step forward. "What is that supposed to mean? What are you up to, Arakiba?"

Arakiba suddenly displayed a cavalier attitude. "Oh, not me. Well, I may have suggested the plan, but Nephel and Artel are off to achieve it."

"Achieve what?" Raphael asked.

Arakiba now displayed a smile that was nearly impish. "Unity."

"Unity?" Mikael almost shouted the response. He laughed.

Arakiba squinted. "What? You don't think that's possible?"

"You've had, what, five children?"

Arakiba nodded. "And what of it?"

"Where are they?"

"They have their own villages."

Mikael pointed at Arakiba. "Exactly. Because they can't get along."

"That's changing," Arakiba said with a tone of defensiveness. He leaned forward. "Nephel and Artel are gathering them now." He smiled. "Noach and his precious ark don't stand a chance. Our lord will not allow either to survive."

Raphael laughed. "You think they're against Noach." He shook his head. "No, they will be against our Creator. It is you, Arakiba, who doesn't stand a chance."

"Plus," Mikael said, "how will they even unite the Nephilim? They're too selfish to work together. Their pride will do them in, just as it did for Lucifer."

Arakiba jumped to his feet. "How dare you degrade my master that way! Ever heard of 'the enemy of my enemy is my friend'? That is the message Nephel and Artel will teach. All Nephilim know the removal of all pure-bloods is a greater objective than selfish ambition."

Mikael shook his head. "Lucifer is the one who should know pride does not follow reasoning. Their message will just incite ire, not ideology."

Arakiba pushed between the two of them to leave the tent. "What do you know?"

They followed Arakiba outside. Arakiba kept walking, then turned. "Just leave. And take your rhetoric with you."

They watched as Arakiba walked over to where Kilion and Arbel were in a tight embrace. Mikael couldn't tell what Arakiba said to them, but Kilion took Arbel in his arms, stood, and walked into a nearby tent.

"Come on, Raphael," Mikael said. "I think we've seen enough here."

Raphael nodded. "We should prepare everyone for what might happen."

Mikael nodded. Both angels disappeared.

CHAPTER 29

Demise of the Nephilim

The next few months went the same as those before. Noach and his sons went to work on the ark each morning, and their wives delivered them food midday. Yet Mikael noticed the number of other workers dwindling with time.

This day, as the women prepared to serve their husbands their midday meal, only Noach and his sons could be seen.

After Noach prayed, Naamah looked around. "Where are your workers, Noach?"

Noach sat down, took a bite of bread, and shrugged. "No one showed up today."

Naamah sat next to him. "Why?"

"I'm surprised they lasted this long," Shem said. "I heard some of them talking. They had a lot of peer pressure and resistance from the Watchers."

"It's no matter now," Cham said. "We can complete the task. The work may take longer, but it's just finishing touches now."

Noach nodded. "True. Mainly just coating everything with tar pitch to make the ark waterproof."

Naamah shook her head as she stared at the ark. "It's almost beyond my comprehension how such a large structure could float. And we're so far from water here."

Noach chuckled and leaned over to give her a kiss on her cheek. "No worries, my dear. Yahweh will supply the water—and lots of it."

Naamah gave a slight nod. "I know his words are truth. Yet they are still hard to comprehend."

With a few large reverberations pounding the air, everyone suddenly got wide-eyed. Kezia was the first to speak. "What was that?"

Shem stood. "I don't know. But from the vibrations in the ground, it feels like Nephilim approaching."

"Here?" Naamah said with a worried look. "They've never come this far before."

Jepheth stood and tapped Shem's arm. "Let's go look."

Both ran to the ark and scurried up the scaffolding to reach the large structure's top. Everyone else ran toward the ark behind them.

"What do you see?" Noach yelled up to them when he reached the ark's base.

Jepheth yelled back, "It looks to be hundreds of them."

Noach's eyes widened. "What?"

Naamah grabbed Noach's arm, fear in her eyes. "What do we do?"

Noach patted her hand. "Don't worry, my dear. Yahweh will protect us."

He and Cham then led the women into the ark and up the ramps for easier access to the ark's roof. Once they arrived, Jepheth and Shem helped them onto the topmost roof of the ark, where they were standing.

"Wow," Ar'yel said. "You can see almost forever from here." She turned and gasped, seeing what everyone else saw. "I've never heard of so many being together before."

"Neither have I," Noach said. "I didn't think that was even possible."

Rayneh held onto Jepheth's arm as she pointed. "What are those other creatures? They don't even look human."

"Those, my dear, are the Watchers' experiments," Noach said. He shook his head. "They had the audacity to try and alter Yahweh's reproductive processes producing what the Watchers call chimeras—part man, part animal."

Rayneh's eyes practically bulged. "But . . . why? Why would anyone even conceive such a thing, much less actually carry it out?"

Noach just shook his head. "Our world has turned into a pretty mixed-up place. What is evil is taught as good and good as evil." He sighed. "I'm glad Adam is not here to see this. This scene would break his heart. Having so many descendants not following after Yahweh was heartbreaking enough, but this . . ." He shook his head again. "This would be beyond heartbreak."

Naamah took his arm. "It is beyond heartbreak. What has our world become?"

Shem pointed. "Look! They've stopped approaching—and seem to be fighting among themselves."

Mikael gave commands to many of his legion; he had them form a shield between the ark and the Nephilim and their army.

Raphael looked at Mikael. "How is it possible to even have chimera? If I understood what Gabriel said, humans can't reproduce outside their kind."

Mikael shrugged. "Well, we're talking about infused angel DNA. The combination likely makes this possible." He shook his head. "It is diabolical, though."

He and Raphael went for a closer look. Mikael found what he saw and heard hard to believe.

Nephel and Artel were giving commands to attempt to get his army into some semblance of structure and order, but Nephel was having little success.

Nephel got Artel's attention. "Go and get the group from the north to flank on the left."

Artel attempted to do so, but another female Nephilim refused to follow her command. "You go back to your husband. I don't have to take orders from you. I can lead myself." She shoved Artel to the ground, Artel coming down with a large crash.

"Hey!" Nephel said to the woman as he lifted Artel to her feet. "We have to get organized or we will not be successful. Remember what the Watchers, our fathers, told us."

"Yeah, yeah, yeah," the other female Nephilim said. "The enemy of my enemy is my friend." She pointed at Artel. "But you are not my friend, so don't even try. And you will never be my leader."

Nephel held up his hands. "Whoa, whoa! We're all here for the same reason. We need to work together."

The female Nephilim then turned to him. "And who put you in charge?"

"I'm the one—"

This female slugged him square on his jaw, knocking him to his knees. "You don't speak for me."

"Yeah," another Nephilim said. "Follow me!"

"I don't follow you, either," the female said. She then sent one of her chimeras onto him. Yet this Nephilim quickly took his club and killed the creature. This angered her and she had her largest creature, one with thick, sturdy legs, a thick body, and huge jaws with jagged teeth, attack. Before this Nephilim could get to his feet, the large creature had decapitated him. The blood then incited the creature to attack others. One of the other Nephilim then killed this creature, which incensed the female Nephilim, who began attacking at random.

Nephel held up his hands. "Order! Order! We need to unite!"

Before he could do anything more, another Nephilim slugged him, causing him to stagger backward and fall. "Here's what I think of your superior attitude." He then had his deadly creatures attack Nephel. They rolled over the ground several times, but Nephel eventually prevailed.

Still, as Nephel stood, another Nephilim hit his head with a ferocious blow with a club, spraying blood on those nearby. The fresh blood incited other creatures causing them to attack the blood scent, adding more chaos to the fray.

Artel ran to Nephel and cradled him in her arms, tears streaming down her face, his blood pooling in her lap.

"This is not how it was supposed to happen." She then screamed, "Arakiba, I blame you!"

The dominant female Nephilim then ran her through with a spear.

"Oh, stop your whining," the dominant female said.

But before she could even remove her spear, someone else pierced her through as well, and she fell across Artel.

The chaos continued until all the Nephilim, their chimera, and many of their deadly creatures had fallen. The flesh-eating creatures they had raised became so incensed with the blood that they ate their fill, and each killed many of the others fighting over the bloody corpses even though there was enough for all of them to eat.

Mikael, Raphael, and other angels hovered above all the chaos not believing their eyes. There was no one for them to fight against.

The Nephilim had done themselves in.

Mikael motioned for his angels to return to the ark.

Once back, Raphael asked, "Mikael, what did we just witness?"

"I think we just witnessed what pride and arrogance lead to. These Nephilim never had to follow anyone else. Their every desire had been granted them. They never learned to work together for a common goal. Their lives had always been about them. I'm afraid that was their very downfall. Arakiba using Nephel and Artel to gather them was one thing, but to get them to work in unison was something entirely different. Each wanted to be the leader they had always been."

"So, is Noach and his family finally safe?"

Mikael cocked his head. "For now. Yet I'm sure the Watchers will come up with something else."

"Like what?"

Mikael shrugged. "I don't know. But knowing how shrewd Arakiba is, Samyaza, the leader of the Watchers, is probably even more so."

Raphael's eyes widened. "More? I can't even comprehend."

Mikael nodded. "I know. We need to remain vigilant."

CHAPTER 30

Methushelach

W hen Mikael and Raphael returned to the ark, they found Noach and his family embracing with tears of joy.

"Yahweh has saved us," Naamah exclaimed. "Praise his name."

Noach nodded. "That is exactly what we should do. When we return to the village this evening, we will offer a burnt offering to him."

Naamah frowned. "Village? It's just us now, I'm afraid, so I don't know why you still call our camp a village. I can't believe everyone else was pulled into the deceit of these Watchers."

Noach gave her a hug. "I know, my dear." He looked deeply into her eyes. "But it's not just us."

She cocked her head.

"There is Saba and Savta." He smiled. "And Eldad."

She looked at him and chuckled, placing her head on his chest. "That's why I love you." She looked back into his eyes. "Always the optimist."

The women stayed at the ark for the rest of the day helping prepare tarry pitch which Noach and his sons applied to the ark to make the structure waterproof. Everyone remained in a joyous mood through the rest of the day.

Mikael had his angels stand guard around the ark as Noach and his family worked. He had no idea what Arakiba or Samyaza might do once they heard all the Nephilim had destroyed each other. Their hatred was likely building.

Still, for now they were all enjoying the levity Noach and his family exhibited this afternoon. Many of the angels would look at them and then at each other and smile. It was good to see joy could still exist in such a world, one the Watchers had created.

Their levity was suddenly broken by the shout of someone running toward the ark. "Noach! Noach!"

Noach turned from his spot on the scaffolding. The others turned as well.

"Is that Eldad?" Naamah asked. She glanced up at Noach. "Something must be wrong."

Noach, as well as his sons, scurried down from the scaffolding and ran toward the lad. The women followed.

Once Eldad reached them, he was out of breath and had a difficult time speaking. "Come . . . you . . . have to . . . come."

Noach went to one knee, patting the boy on his upper back. "Get your breath, my son."

The boy breathed in and out laboriously for a minute. Finally, he shook his head.

"So what's the trouble?" Noach asked.

"It's Saba Methushelach, my lord. He's extremely ill." He took a few more breaths. "Savta Edna asked me to get you."

217

Naamah put her hand on Noach's shoulder, the other over her mouth. "Poor Edna. We should go to them. Now."

Noach nodded. He glanced at his sons.

Shem waved a hand at his father. "Go, Aba. Jepheth, Cham, and I will get things cleaned up here and then come." He looked at Ar'yel. "You and the others go with them." He gave her a hug. "We'll follow as soon as we can."

Mikael and Raphael followed Noach, Eldad, and the women as the other angels stayed to protect the ark.

"So, Eldad," Naamah said. "Tell us what happened."

Eldad shook his head. "I'm not really sure. Apparently, Saba Methushelach took his normal walk as he does each morning. Savta became concerned when he did not return at his normal time, so she sent me to find him."

Naamah nodded. "Yes. And?"

"I found him sitting on the side of the road. He was pale and out of breath. Of course, he said he was fine, but I knew otherwise."

Noach chuckled. "Sounds like Saba."

Naamah pushed on Noach's shoulder. "You men. Really."

Noach grinned, then turned solemn as Eldad continued.

"I was able to help him get back to Savta, but he's now in bed and doesn't look good. That's why I came to get you." He gave a nervous look at Noach. "I . . . I don't know if he has much longer to be alive."

Noach nodded; he was now frowning. Naamah gave his shoulder a squeeze.

"He has had a long life," Ar'yel said. "Longer than anyone else."

"That's true," Noach said. "But one's life always feels short when one gets to the end of it."

"You know what this means," Raphael said as he glanced at Mikael.

Mikael nodded. "His death shall bring."

"If he dies," Raphael said, "the flood will come this year."

Mikael rubbed his chin. "Maybe we should evenly split the angels between the village and the ark. I don't trust the Watchers. They could attack either place."

Raphael nodded. "Yes, they are likely getting desperate. Hearing that their Nephilim killed each other, and then hearing that Methushelach is dying, might just push them over the edge in their demented thinking."

When they entered Methushelach's dwelling, Edna stood; there was some relief on her face. "Oh, thank you for coming." She gave both Naamah and Noach a hug.

"How is he?" Noach asked.

She gestured toward the bed in the corner. "He has been asking for you."

Naamah rubbed Edna's arm. "And how are you?"

Edna gave a shaky smile. "Concerned." She glanced toward Methushelach and back, her eyes wet. "Frightened."

Ar'yel pulled out a chair from the table. "Here, Savta, sit here."

"I'll make some broth for Saba," Kezia said.

"Great idea," Rayneh said. "I'll help."

As the women did their preparing, Noach went to Methushelach's bedside, sat next to him, and took his hand. "Hello, Saba. You were asking for me?"

Methushelach gave a weak smile, then patted Noach's hand. "Yes, my son. The time is almost upon us."

"Now, now, Saba. You have many years left, I am sure. Yahweh is not done with you."

Methushelach slowly shook his head. "No, my son. I will soon be in Sheol with Adam, Sheth, Chanok, and the others. "My time on Earth is almost over." He pulled Noach closer and looked directly into his eyes. "It is time for you to prepare and be ready. Yahweh has called you to a mission you and your family must fulfill. The fate of mankind is with you."

Noach swallowed hard. "Yes, Saba. I know. But you have always been my strength."

Methushelach slowly shook his head. "No, my son. Yahweh has always been your strength. I have just been cheering you on. Now you must rise to the task for which you have been born. I have fulfilled my duty. Now you must fulfill yours." He grabbed Noach's arm. "Are you willing?"

Noach nodded. "Yes, Saba. I am willing."

"We should have prayer tonight."

Noach smiled. "That was what I had already planned. Yahweh has saved us from the Nephilim."

Methushelach smiled. "Really? Praise Yahweh. He is always faithful. May we be also."

Kezia came over with some broth. Noach helped his grandfather sit up in bed and then gave up his seat so Kezia could feed Methushelach. He went outside to prepare the altar.

When the sun set, Noach lit the burnt offering. They held hands, Noach prayed, and they sang songs. Mikael was impressed they sang with such conviction.

He turned to Raphael. "Since the time of Earth's creation, there are only ten who still remain faithful."

Raphael nodded, then stopped. "Wait. Mikael, I count eleven."

"The boy."

"How does he fit into all of this?" Raphael asked.

Mikael shook his head. "I don't know."

The scene was curious. Eldad was singing with just as much gusto as the others. Yet Mikael was quite sure Eldad's bloodline was not pure.

CHAPTER 31

Eldad

Over the next several weeks Methushelach became weaker, so Noach and his family put more time and effort into getting the ark completed. While Eldad's family would not let him help Noach at the ark site, he was allowed to help Edna take care of Methushelach. For that, Noach was grateful, as he hated to leave Methushelach and Edna alone while everyone else worked so long and hard on the ark.

Working one late afternoon, Noach dropped his pitch brush into the gourd bucket, wiped his brow, and smiled.

"Finished," he said with much satisfaction in his voice.

Shem smiled, wiping sweat from his own brow. "At last."

Naamah grinned. "The girls have a meal prepared. Come, eat."

Noach wrapped his arm around her shoulders and they walked together. The boys were in a good mood and playfully kidded with each other. Suddenly, Jepheth stopped and pointed.

"Aba, look. Is that Eldad?"

Noach looked, worry on his face. Eldad was not running as he had the last time. As Eldad got closer, he looked solemn.

He took a seat with the women and waited for the others to reach the group.

As Noach, his wife, and sons sat, Noach gave Eldad a curious look. "What is it, son? Is something else wrong with Saba?"

Eldad slowly shook his head. "It's Savta."

Naamah gasped. Noach looked from Eldad to her and back. He seemed to not understand.

"She . . . she died a few hours ago."

"What?" Noach asked in a state of disbelief. "But Saba is the one who is sick. What happened?"

Eldad shook his head. "I'm not sure. She had me gather firewood this morning, and when I returned, she had collapsed on the floor." His eyes watered, but no tears came. "Saba Methushelach had me place her in bed next to him. He said to come tell you, but not to hurry."

Naamah grabbed Eldad's hand. "Why? Maybe we could have done something."

Eldad shook his head. "No." He looked into her eyes. "She was gone. Nothing to be done."

Noach shook his head, confused. "But why did he tell you to come here slowly?"

Eldad made quick eye contact with Noach, but did not keep it, looking down. "He said . . . " Eldad choked up and then cleared his throat. "He said he knew you would finish the ark today, and I should walk slowly so he could get to the other side before you returned."

"What?" Noach jumped to his feet. "Why would he say that?"

Eldad shook his head. "He just said, 'Today is the day.'"

Noach looked at his wife and then the others. "Pack up everything. We should go."

The women quickly put all the food back in the baskets; the men put everything else away. They hurried back to the village . . .

Once they arrived, Noach rushed into the house and knelt at the bedside. He shook Methushelach's lifeless body. "Saba! Saba!" There was no response.

Noach placed his head on Methushelach's chest and sobbed.

Naamah came over, knelt next to Noach, and placed her head against his arm, rubbing his back. "I'm so sorry, darling. I'm so sorry."

Noach put his arm around her and pulled her close but continued to sob.

The others simply stood watching, tears coming down their cheeks. Each son had an arm around their spouse's shoulders, but they stood motionless, not speaking.

Mikael noticed Eldad stood with them for a while but then turned and walked out the door. Eldad looked back several times, apparently conflicted, not knowing whether to stay or go.

As Eldad walked from the house, Shem turned and followed him out. "Eldad, where are you going?"

Eldad turned, his cheeks wet with tears. He shrugged. "Home, I guess. Or whatever you want to call that place I come from." He shook his head. "I have no reason to stay here any longer."

"What?" Shem went to one knee to be on more of an eye level with Eldad. "You can stay here as long as you want. A flood is coming, you know." He smiled. "You'll be safe with us."

Eldad gave a weak smile. "That's a great offer. But I can't take it."

Shem cocked his head. "Why? You heard what I said, right? A flood is coming. You will be killed if you don't come with us."

"I know." Eldad shook his head. "But my Av won't allow me to come with you. He . . . he doesn't believe in you, your Aba, or his words." He shrugged. "He only allowed me to help your family here at the house, after much begging on my part, and my assuring him I would not help you build the ark."

"But you believe our words, don't you?"

Eldad stood frozen in place for several seconds. "Yes, but that doesn't matter." He shook his head. "My family won't allow it."

Shem gave a sad expression. "Maybe I could talk to him?"

Eldad's eyes went wide. "Oh, no. Doing so will only make him mad."

Shem shook his head, his eyes watering. "After all you have done for my family, why would he not let you?"

Eldad patted Shem's shoulder. "It's okay. I talked to your Saba."

Shem tilted his head. "What do you mean?"

Eldad smiled. "He introduced me to Yahweh. He said I will now always be connected to him. When the flood comes, I will then be with your Saba in Sheol." He shook his head. "So, you see, I'll likely be better off than even you."

"But it just doesn't seem fair."

"Perhaps, but your Saba helped me understand. I'm not a pure-blood. While Yahweh can accept me, my presence would cause a problem for your descendants after the flood. So the blindness of my family is a blessing in the end. The human race will be saved, as will I." He smiled again. "So don't be sad for me. One day, I'll see you again."

Shem stood. "Let me shake your hand, Eldad. Although you are still very young, I have never met a wiser man since my Saba."

Eldad laughed. "Considering those were his words and not mine, that is the only reason."

Shem nodded, then give him a tight hug. "Until we meet again—on the other side."

Eldad turned and walked away. He turned once, waved, and walked on.

Shem went back inside to the others.

Ar'yel looked at him and then the door. "Where's . . . Eldad?"

"Gone."

"Gone? Where?"

"Back to his family, I'm afraid."

Ar'yel shook her head. "I don't know how such a great kid could come from such horrible parents."

Shem nodded. "Yet, let's be grateful they allowed him to help out Saba and Savta."

Ar'yel nodded. "Yes, we were most fortunate."

"As were they."

She nodded.

After Noach grieved the rest of the night and the next day, the family prepared a burial for both his grandfather and grandmother. Various spices were prepared and placed in cloths which the women wrapped around the corpses. Jepheth found a nearby cave he considered appropriate, and their bodies were placed there. They then closed the mouth of the cave with large, heavy rocks . . .

After Noach said a few prayers, they headed back to their once thriving, now empty, village. Noach again prepared a burnt offering and sacrificed a lamb that night.

"Goodbye, Saba," Noach said while standing near the offering. "Goodbye, Savta. I'll see you again one day. Praise Yahweh for such a promise."

Naamah held onto his arm and placed her head against it. "Amen."

CHAPTER 32

Preparing the Ark

Rayneh pulled sweat-soaked strands of hair away from her face. She looked over at Ar'yel. "And I thought we were busy when the guys were building the ark!" Rayneh said.

Ar'yel nodded. "I know. If I have to tie one more jar of olive oil down, I may scream." As she turned, Naamah handed her several more clay jars to fill and tie down. She sighed.

Naamah smiled. "Thanks for not screaming."

Ar'yel stared at her and then burst into a chuckle. "Just tell me this is the last of them."

Naamah nodded as she stood and stretched her back. "All of the oil, at least."

Kezia trudged up lugging a sackful of root vegetables. "Can someone help me with these?"

They all sighed, but Ar'yel came forward with several large clay containers and began filling them; Kezia assisted.

"I feel like we have enough food for an army," Kezia said. "How long are we expected to live in this thing?"

Naamah put another large clay container down for them to fill. "Well, Noach says our stay could be as long as a year, at least."

Kezia's eyes widened. "That long! How will we manage?"

Naamah patted her arm. "With Yahweh's help, my child. With Yahweh's help."

They spent the rest of the day storing other vegetables, grains, spices, herbs, and water—lots of water.

At the end of the day, the women sat with their backs to the wall of the ark.

"We're done?" Kezia asked. "I didn't see anything more outside to bring in."

Naamah, sitting next to her, patted her thigh. "That's all for us to pack and tie down. Now we have to do the same for the animals."

Kezia sighed. "Just when I had my hopes up."

"What have the men been doing all this time?"

Naamah looked over at Rayneh. "Oh, they've been building cages. Lots and lots of cages."

"And that's not all," Ar'yel said. "Shem has asked me to help get the feeding system and watering system together." She laughed. "His ideas are quite ingenious."

"Like what?" Kezia looked over at Ar'yel, who laughed at her.

"What are you laughing at?"

"You," Ar'yel said. "You look completely dead on your feet."

"I am. I really am interested—even though I don't sound like it."

Ar'yel laughed again. "He has developed large vats for grain and another for water that will go to almost all of the cages at the same time. We just have to keep those vats filled and then we won't have to worry about each individual cage."

"Oh," Kezia said, still sounding deadpan. "That's clever. Really clever."

"Kezia, you should—"

She stopped when she heard snoring. Ar'yel giggled. "Is that Kezia?"

Naamah laughed. "Yes, she's now dead to the world."

Shortly, the men arrived. Cham saw Kezia sound asleep and chuckled. He gathered her in his arms. She jerked slightly when he lifted her, but she fell back asleep immediately. He looked at the others. "Aba said we'd all sleep here so we can get an early start tomorrow."

"Oh, joy," Ar'yel said, giving a very tired laugh.

Shem helped her to her feet. "We'll sleep outside where it's cooler," he said.

She leaned into him. "What if it's too cold?"

He kissed her cheek. "That's what *I'm* here for."

She smiled and walked out with him.

Jepheth helped Rayneh and his mother to their feet. "Aba's outside getting everything ready."

Once outside they saw Noach had built a decent-sized fire and had bread for everyone. He opened a bottle of preserved fruit and passed the jar along with the bread.

Naamah gave Noach a kiss. "Thanks, dear. But I'm almost too tired to even eat."

"Well, eat something and then come to bed."

She nodded, took a few bites, and then pulled a blanket over herself and snuggled up to him.

In no time, all eight were sound asleep.

Mikael and Raphael watched them sleep. Such a strange concept. He knew humans needed rest, but Mikael often wondered what that would feel like. Yet he knew this also made them vulnerable. The Watchers did not need sleep, so he alerted his angels to stay ready as he had no idea when they would make a move against Noach and his family.

"Mikael, have you noticed how clever the design of this boat is?" Raphael asked.

Mikael laughed. "Well, the ark was designed by our Creator, so I would expect his design to be nothing but clever."

"I know. I know. But the design is just so ingenious. I mean, who would have thought to have a hole going all the way through the center so wave action can pull in fresh air from the top and then distribute that air throughout the craft?"

Mikael nodded. "And be a way to get rid of all the animal and human waste."

Raphael shook his head. "It seems he has thought of everything."

"Indeed," Mikael said. "Indeed, he has."

The two of them sat and watched the night sky, marveling at its beauty. Mikael still remembered the first night the stars appeared. He had been in awe of them then and still felt the same way. His Creator's unbounded creativity always impressed—always.

When the sun peeked over the horizon, Noach stirred and woke the others. "Up, up," he said. "We have a long day ahead of us."

While the women prepared a quick breakfast, the men finished up all the cages. Then, after breakfast, the women began storing grain and other food items for the animals in clay containers, tying them down so they wouldn't shift and break during their voyage. The men then turned to making the mechanisms that would make the ship run efficiently: water pipes so rainwater could be stored and used to wash out the animal waste, vats feeding grain or water to the various cages, a conveyer system for getting rid of the solid waste, and completion of the middle hole in the ark for waste removal and ventilation of the ship.

After several weeks, Noach announced at one of their evening meals that all was finished.

"Is it really true?" Kezia asked. "I never thought I'd see the day." She glanced at her hands and frowned. "These are all but calloused now."

Cham took her hand and gently kissed it. "I've never seen anything more beautiful."

She gently tapped his cheek with her palm. "Liar." She pulled him in for a kiss. "But I appreciate it."

Cham laughed as he put his arm around her shoulders. He looked at his father. "How much time before the rain comes?"

Noach shrugged. "I'm not sure. I guess not too much longer now that everything is ready."

"Well, we can't start without the animals, right?" Shem asked.

All eyes turned Shem's way. He shrugged. "That's what all of this is about. Saving us. Saving the animals. Us is here—but not the animals."

"Yeah," Jepheth said. "How *do* we get the animals?"

Noach shook his head. "We don't. Yahweh will take care of that."

Naamah, sitting between his feet with her head on his knee, looked up at him. "How will he do that?"

Noach shrugged. "I think . . . they'll just show up."

Naamah's eyes widened. "Well, that will certainly be something."

Noach chuckled. "Indeed, my darling." He bent down and kissed her on top of her head. "Indeed it will."

While they sat around the fire eating bread and dried fruit, they sang . . .

Mikael listened to the words of their songs and smiled. They were praising Yahweh for his faithfulness and loving-kindness. Despite their fate and unknown future, they still praised their Creator.

Mikael sat and basked in their music.

CHAPTER 33

Animals and Prayer Warriors

As dawn broke, they all woke to the sound of a trumpeting roar. All eight of them sat up at nearly the same time.

"What in the world was that?" Naamah asked.

Kezia looked frightened. "Not one of those horrid beasts the Nephilim created, I hope." She glanced at Cham and took his hand. "They are not usually this close."

Noach jumped up and almost did a dance. "They're here! They're here!" He glanced at the others and then stopped upon seeing the blank look on their faces. He gestured to the sound as he heard the trumpeting again. "The animals for the ark. They're here!"

Everyone scrambled to their feet.

"Already!?" Naamah exclaimed with a look of trepidation.

Noach squeezed Naamah in a hug. "Why not? The ark's ready."

"Well," she said, looking at him hesitantly, then adding, "I'm not sure I am."

He laughed. "It's all Yahweh's timing, my dear."

The creatures appeared in the clearing. They had a slow but steady gait. One lifted its long trunk but seemed to almost wave rather than trumpet again.

"Oh, my," Noach said. "Aren't they magnificent?"

"Why so many?" Kezia asked as she continued to hold Cham's hand.

Ar'yel walked toward them.

Kezia's eyes widened. "Ar'yel, where are you *going*?"

She turned and laughed. "To see them, of course."

"Is that wise?" Naamah asked.

Ar'yel continued to advance toward the creatures. Shem and Noach followed closely behind her.

There were six in all. Shem turned to his father. "I thought there were supposed to be only two."

Noach had a twinkle in his eye. "Don't you see, my son? Only the small ones will enter the ark. Their parents are escorting them here. The one from one couple is a male and the young one from the other couple is female." He shook his head. "They both shouldn't be from the same family." He smiled and patted Shem on his shoulder. "This is Yahweh's way of assuring good and healthy breeding stock."

Shem smiled. "Amazing," he quietly said. He turned and waved the others over.

They approached warily.

Ar'yel seemed to have no fear. As she reached the creatures, which stood nearly twice her height, the young one, slightly higher than waist height, rubbed up against her, almost knocking her over. She giggled. "Easy, fella. You're more massive than I am." She rubbed the small creature's forehead and the animal gave a muffled roar, raising its trunk. She giggled again.

Each female parent pushed their offspring toward the ark. The young ones looked back but then followed Ar'yel into the structure.

"Lead them to the far back cages," Noach shouted.

Ar'yel waved her acknowledgement and continued to lead the animals, giggling as she went.

The adult creatures watched their young ones until they disappeared inside the ark. They seemed to give a slight nod to Noach—then walked back into the forest.

Shem looked at his father with eyebrows raised. "Well, that was interesting."

Noach nodded, a big grin on his face. "That was just the first of many."

Next into view was a pride of large cats with two of the females each carrying a cub in their mouths. They deposited the cubs next to Noach. Seeing the cubs seemed to erase the fear both Kezia and Rayneh had exhibited earlier as they both came over, each picking one up to stroke its soft fur.

"Oh," Kezia exclaimed. "They are so cute."

"And soft," Rayneh said as she rubbed her cheek against the furry creature's side. The cub purred loudly. Rayneh giggled and stroked the creature even more.

Kezia held hers up. "You and I are going to have a good time together."

She and Rayneh turned and carried them to the ark. The parents of these cubs watched them carefully until they disappeared inside the vessel. They all turned and left, just as the other creatures had done.

Throughout the day and into the night, the scene repeated itself. Noach realized this was going to be a long process, so he had everyone sleep in shifts. Although a good idea, everyone was too excited to sleep, even though they tried. Yet, over time, exhaustion overcame their excitement, and everyone at least got a little rest.

The next morning, Jepheth got everyone's attention and pointed. They all turned and stood in shock. Towering above the treetops were several approaching behemoths.

Jepheth looked wide-eyed at Noach. "Aba, I think we may have a problem."

Once the animals broke through the forest, Noach laughed. "No, I don't think so." Tagging along with these giants were two miniature duplicates, no taller than Noach himself. Shem put an arm around each of their long necks and led them into the ark. The mature ones again stood and watched until their babies had entered the ark. They also seemed to bow and then head back into the forest.

Naamah approached Noach. "This is all so impressive. I would not believe such an event could occur if someone told me of this—not without experiencing it firsthand."

Noach smiled and nodded. "Yahweh is truly amazing." He looked at her. "We will have some interesting stories to tell our grandchildren."

Naamah laughed. "Absolutely. The story of how Yahweh saved the world."

Shem walked up and put his arm around his mother. "And we were all a part of the miracle."

She put her head against his and then turned and kissed him on his cheek.

The number of animals seemed to have no end. Yet Mikael noticed Noach was extremely meticulous in how he housed them. He had specified places for mammals, birds, and amphibians. He didn't look concerned until the number of cages unoccupied were down to only a few.

After housing two marsupials, Shem stepped out and looked at his dad. "We're almost full. How many more are coming?"

Noach shrugged. "I'm not sure." He turned to Rayneh. "Go count the number of empty cages." She nodded and ran into the ark. After a time she rushed back out, seemingly still counting those the others were leading into the ark. Noach looked expectantly at her. "Well?"

"We have eleven. Only eleven left." Noach then counted the animals still coming. "I see eight."

"So we have extra?" Rayneh asked.

Shem shook his head. "No, I see two more."

Jepheth then pointed. "One more just come out of the forest."

Noach strained to look for others. "That should mean we are full. Does anyone see any more?"

They all waited, barely daring to breathe as they did.

No more animals appeared.

Shem pushed on his father's shoulder. "There. You should have been as confident as I was."

Noach looked at him, a wry smile coming to his face. "You were holding your breath just as I was, so don't get high and mighty with your Aba."

Shem wrapped his arm around Noach's shoulders and laughed. "You did it, Aba. Your ark is full."

Noach shook his head. "No, my son. Yahweh did it. He knew how many cages for us to build." He took a deep breath. "While we feel we have just completed something, we are only at the beginning of it."

Shem nodded.

Noach turned and gestured to the ark. "This is our new home. Likely, a few more days will pass before the rain starts, but we now have animals to take care of, so we will stay here and do that." He paused. "It will allow us to test and make modifications of the equipment before we embark on our journey."

Shem, his arms still around his father's shoulders, looked at him. "Why did you put most as a pair, but some as seven pairs?"

Noach smiled. "Once again, this is all Yahweh's doing. We need clean animals for sacrifice at the same time we need them to procreate. Plus, he knows the reproductive cycle of each and knows how many of each are needed to preserve their kind on our new world."

Shem smiled. "A well-thought-out plan."

Noach laughed. "Indeed, my son. Indeed." He turned to the others. "Let's sleep under the stars again. Once the rain comes, we may not see them again for at least a year. I want to appreciate them as long as I can."

The others nodded.

As Noach and his family prepared for the evening, Mikael knew that if there was going to be an attack, the event would come soon. The rains would come before the week was over. As he looked at the sun nearing the horizon, he had an odd feeling.

Mikael whipped around. "Raphael, prepare the angels. Lucifer's angels are coming."

Raphael's eyes went wide, but he did as Mikael requested. Raphael went to one side and Mikael the other to get everyone in formation.

As Lucifer's angels approached, Mikael saw them begin to blot out the light of the setting sun. He drew his sword and held the hilt tightly. "Prepare yourselves! Do not let anyone through. The fate of the world is in your hands."

Lucifer's angels came fast—and were on them in seconds. The first few Mikael found easy to defeat. His blade made them go catatonic; they fell to the ground. Yet as time went on, his opponents grew stronger and stronger. He had forgotten how many angels Lucifer had taken with him when he was banished . . .

After a time, Mikael could feel himself getting tired. He knew his other angels were reaching this point as well. Although infuriating, he had to be impressed with Lucifer's tactics. Lucifer's angels came in waves, so each wave was fresh while his angels were fighting each wave and tiring. Still, Mikael mustered strength and fought on.

So far, no demon had been able to cross their defenses.

Noach woke everyone. "Shem, Cham, Jepheth, wake up. Wake your wives. It's time to pray."

Jepheth rubbed his eyes. "What? At this hour? We've only slept a few hours."

"I know," Noach said. "But I feel a strong need to pray."

They each woke their wives, who appeared as confused as their husbands.

Naamah took Noach's arm. "What is it? What's wrong?"

Noach stood and turned, looking in all directions. "Don't you feel it, Naamah? Something's wrong."

Naamah looked around. "Feel what, Noach? What's wrong?"

"I don't know. But something is wrong. We should pray."

Naamah gestured for everyone to come near. They sat in a circle, held hands, and prayed.

At first Mikael was unsure why, but he suddenly felt stronger. He attacked his opponent with more force now. The eyes of the demon he fought went wide, as he too looked surprised at Mikael's added strength. His opponent thought he was getting weaker, but Mikael now found himself fighting with renewed strength and energy. The one he was fighting was now the one weakening. Mikael saw his opportunity. The demon went to stab him, but Mikael was able to deflect the blow, using his mighty wing to turn swiftly and deliver a fatal blow. The demon's eyes went wide just before he went catatonic and fell to the ground.

As Mikael turned, he saw Noach and his family praying. He smiled. Now he knew where his strength was coming from. Mikael nodded. Yes, prayer was a powerful defense against Lucifer and his minions. As he looked around, he could see the renewed energy in all his angels.

Mikael prepared himself for the last and largest wave. He knew Lucifer likely had saved his most powerful for last.

Pray, Noach, pray, Mikael thought. Prayer was what would win the battle.

Noach opened his eyes and began to sing. The others joined. Noach had them flow from one praise song into another. As Mikael and his angels heard the singing, he could again feel the power within him growing stronger. He knew Noach likely didn't even know why he felt the need to do this, but Mikael knew Ruach was responsible. And Mikael was grateful for it.

Yes, Lucifer's angels were strong, but the praise to his Creator was even stronger. Lucifer's final angel that Mikael was facing was extraordinarily strong. Even with his renewed energy, Mikael found outmaneuvering him difficult. Yet as he fought Mikael began to see subtle flaws in the angel's strategy.

Mikael began to force him to continue repeating the flaw: the angel lifting his hand just a little too far to increase the force of his swing, leaving his side unprotected. Mikael finally took advantage of it, catching the angel off guard and delivering the fatal blow. The angel's eyes widened, his body went catatonic, and he fell.

As Mikael hovered with his giant wings, he saw the Watchers standing nearby, talking among themselves. Mikael flew to where they stood, landing in front of Samyaza, their leader.

"Your attempt to defeat Yahweh's plan has failed. Now take Lucifer's angels and go."

Samyaza looked at him, hatred in his eyes. "You may have won this battle, but the war is far from over."

He turned his back to Mikael and walked away, the other Watchers in tow.

Mikael turned back and had his angels create a wall between the fallen angels and the ark. As each demon awoke, it immediately teleported away. Soon no one was left but his angels.

"Rest up, my friends. You have fought well. But keep alert. I don't trust the Watchers—or Lucifer."

As Noach finished the song he was singing, this time he went quiet, not starting another.

Naamah looked over at him. "Is your bad feeling gone?"

Noach smiled and nodded. "It is." He looked at each one. "I'm not sure why Yahweh wanted us to pray and sing, but thank you for doing so. I'm not sure what we accomplished, but I know our actions were significant."

Kezia put her head on Cham's shoulder. "Does that mean we can sleep now? Morning will come way too soon."

Noach laughed. "Yes, my daughter. You may."

They went back to their arrangements and were asleep in no time.

Mikael noticed the smile on Noach's face.

Rest well, my friend and fellow soldier, Mikael thought, admiring Noach. *You did well tonight. Very well, indeed.*

CHAPTER 34

The Rain

The next few days were extraordinarily busy for Noach and his family. Even though the rain had not yet come, their home was now the ark; they had many animals to take care of. Noach and his sons were able to test each apparatus they had built to feed the animals and remove their waste.

After two days, Noach had the group gather at midday to discuss how everything was going.

Jepheth seemed excited. "Aba, it all works!" He nodded his head. "Well, at least everything does now."

Cham laughed. "Yeah, unlike the first day when you almost dumped a whole vat of grain into the equine cage."

Jepheth punched Cham's shoulder. "But the equipment works great now. And the grated cage bottoms work great, too."

Cham nodded. "And we can use the equines to power the conveyer to remove the waste." He shrugged. "And the process gives them exercise. A win-win."

Noach patted each of their shoulders. "Great job, boys." He turned to his other son. "Shem, any concerns?"

Shem shook his head. "No, I think the ventilation will work fine."

Ar'yel scrunched her nose. "Yeah, but a bit smelly."

Shem gave her a side hug. "True, but the fresh air will keep the other air in the ark from becoming stale."

She tilted her head back and forth slightly. "I'll take your word for it. I'm just glad we're living on top, closer to the air vents."

Noach laughed. "That's part of the reason we're living there. We definitely need to be above the animals." He turned to each of them. "Any other issues?"

Everyone shook their heads. Noach smiled and stood. Everyone else followed. They held hands and Noach prayed.

"Yahweh, we give you thanks for your protection and for entrusting us with your plan for the world's future. We continue to place our lives in your hands and look forward to what you have for us in our new world."

They sat and completed their meal.

After a short time, Naamah verbalized what they all likely felt. "This is our last meal outside," she said. "After today, we will be inside until the flood is all over."

"I'm excited and apprehensive," Shem said. The others nodded. "I'm excited to have a better world, but apprehensive as I don't know what the next year will bring."

Noach stood and had everyone give a collective group hug. "We are all in Yahweh's hands. He will not let us down."

"Amen," Naamah said.

The group cleaned up and brought everything they had outside back inside the ark. Once they were all indoors, they felt a huge lurching; the door to the large vessel was closing.

Naamah jerked around. "Who did that?"

Noach came over and gave her another hug. "Yahweh has sealed us in. We are all in his hands now."

Noach then motioned to Cham to bring the tar pitch. "Place pitch around the edges to be sure they are waterproof."

Cham laughed. "I thought you said we were now in Yahweh's hands."

Noach swatted Cham's rear end and chuckled. "Now see here, mister! He also gave us common sense. I think he would expect us to use it."

Cham continued to laugh as he carried out his father's request.

After a short time, Ar'yel exclaimed, "Listen! Listen!"

Everyone stopped and stood still. They could all hear a *tap, tap, tap* sound—as if something was hitting the ark.

Ar'yel scrunched her brow. "What is that sound?"

Everyone cocked their head, straining to listen.

The tapping sound became more frequent . . . now harder. Noach's eyes widened. "It's the rain! Water falling from the sky as drops of water."

"Really?" Ar'yel asked. "Falling as drops of water? That will take . . . forever to get this ark to float. Won't it?"

The tapping sound became faster and faster until it was almost deafening.

Ar'yel's eyes grew big as she whispered, "Maybe not."

Shem pulled her close upon seeing her worried expression. They all huddled near the door.

Suddenly they heard a loud banging on the door. The girls shrieked. Their husbands held them, but they looked unnerved as well.

They heard a muffled, "Noach! Noach! Let us in! Let us in! You can't leave us out here!"

Naamah looked at Noach. "Can we? *Should* we?"

Noach gave a shrug. "How can I? Yahweh closed the door." He went close to the door and said, loudly, "I can't open the door. It has been sealed by Yahweh. You had over one hundred years to change your minds. It's too late now. It's too late."

"I'm sorry! I'm sorry! Please! Please, let us in!"

"The ark was open for a week after the animals came. You should have come then. It's . . . it's too late!"

Noach turned, his eyes moist. He put his arm around Naamah's shoulders. "Come, children. Everyone's fate is now out of our hands."

Mikael and Raphael stood at the top of the cliff that overlooked the valley where the ark rested. When the rain started, he and his angels undertook a phasing action so the rain had no effect on them—this was somewhat like being between the physical and spiritual worlds. More and more people now flocked toward the ark, crying out for help. All the angels, now surrounding the ark, looked at the gathering throng and stood ready in case anything went awry.

Hearing noise behind him, Mikael turned and saw Eldad approach. He climbed one of the trees overlooking the valley below. As he sat on one of the higher limbs, Mikael heard him say, "I'll see you soon, Saba Methushelach. I could not be with your grandson, but I can be with you." He looked upward and let the rain fall on his face. Then he laughed.

Mikael was so impressed with this lad. He seemed to hold no bitterness against his family even though they would not let him go with Noach and his family. Yet his security in Yahweh calmed him in the face of the coming storm. He was *embracing* what was coming because he knew his future was secure.

As Mikael looked down, he stiffened. The Watchers had arrived as well. With them were others who had sharp implements in their hands.

They started running toward the ark.

One of them shouted, "If we can't get in, then Noach will die with us!"

The others, already at the ark, gave their approval by joining in their yell.

Raphael looked at Mikael. "What are your orders?"

Mikael saw the other angels waiting for his word. He held up his hand to keep them at bay. He heard . . . no, *felt* . . . something.

Those at the ark began to raise their weapons to start to batter the boat, but they began to feel the vibrations too. They stopped and looked at each other, confusion on their faces. One of them turned, pointed, and shouted, "Run!"

The others looked in the direction the one had pointed and began running. Behind them was a stampede of all sorts of animals. Mikael assumed these to be the parents of those animals now in the ark. The people were no match for the animals. They were unstoppable and ran over anyone in their path. Yet even when the crowd ran in all directions, the animals split into as many groups and either killed them or ran them into the forest and continued chasing them until Mikael could no longer see any of them.

He heard their screams for a long time before they died out.

He then heard Eldad above him. "Yeah! Yahweh wins!" Then, in a sincere tone: "I'm so happy I didn't listen to the Watchers. Thank you, Saba Methushelach. I will see you soon."

Raphael tapped Mikael on his arm and pointed. When Mikael looked in that direction, the Watchers were still there. He couldn't believe they *still* looked so smug. Yet that changed quickly when the rain turned into a deluge as thunder and lightning exploded around them. Concern soon was plastered on their faces, but then the ground near them bulged upward, created a groaning sound, and numerous geysers shot high in the air, even higher than the trees on the cliff where Mikael and Raphael stood.

The Watchers started running, but the bulge in the ground kept growing even as the geysers continued to shoot water into the air. Suddenly the entire ground in the valley gave way, and what looked like a huge wave of water belched out of the ground, sweeping the Watchers away with the swell. The rain came down as sheets of water now, and the valley quickly filled with rushing water. Soon it grew deep enough for the ark to lurch off the ground's surface and begin to float . . .

Before long a large tsunami approached, growing larger and larger as the narrow valley forced the water still higher. The wave grew even higher than the cliff where Eldad sat. The last Mikael saw of Eldad, he raised his hands to welcome the tsunami. "Saba Methushelach, here I come!"

With those words, Eldad was gone.

The wave picked up the ark and flung the structure forward, out of the valley and above the surrounding hills.

Mikael and Raphael teleported into the ark to see what Noach and his family were doing. Inside, chaos seemed to reign—at least initially. When the ark first lurched, the animals grew restless, as did everyone.

Cham ran up to Jepheth. "There is water and grain everywhere."

"What?" Jepheth said. "Where is it all coming from?" He then gasped with realization. "The cages! The water and food vats are still open!"

Jepheth ran frantically to the upper deck. "We've got to shut off the water and food vats! Rayneh, get the ones up front and I'll get the ones in the back!"

Noach then yelled, "Once that is done, come to the middle of the ark. The turbulence should be calmer here. The animals may be nervous, but they should be fine."

Ar'yel went with Rayneh and Shem with Jepheth. They had to stop and hold to a railing or post several times before they had all vats closed.

Rayneh shook her head. "Why didn't I think about this? We should have had them off until the turbulence was over."

"Yes," Ar'yel said as she grabbed a railing again. "But who could have predicted *this* much turbulence?"

"Good point." Rayneh smiled. "Thanks for making me feel not so foolish."

Ar'yel leaned in and whispered in Rayneh's ear, "Besides, we'll say the mishap was all Jepheth's fault."

Rayneh laughed and playfully slapped Ar'yel's arm. They were still giggling when they arrived back with the others. Yet their giggle turned into a shriek when the ark lurched again. Each woman grabbed onto her husband.

Noach asked everyone to take a seat. "I think this may be the norm for a while. The lower we are to the floor, likely the better."

They spent the rest of the day in this position, holding onto each other. The ark would often lurch and tilt, and this caused the women to shriek and even cry. The men put up a brave front, but their expressions gave them away. They were just as concerned as the women.

Noach kept assuring them Yahweh was faithful and all would be fine.

As Mikael and Raphael teleported back outside, Mikael was glad Noach and his family could not see what was occurring with the Earth. The water was continuing to rise, yet now there were numerous dead bodies tossed about on the waves. The world had turned into a massive water graveyard.

It was amazing how fast the water rose. Not only from the water falling from the sky, fast and furious, but from the land itself as the ground split in many places causing water to gush upward in massive swells.

CHAPTER 35

Tartarus

Mikael sat on one of the railings watching Noach and his family sleep where they had all huddled together in the midst of the ship, trying to rest and stay away from the ark's largest movements.

Raphael stood next to him. "Amazing this is all that is left of the population on the Creator's Earth."

Mikael nodded slowly. "Yes, but this was what was required to save the human race from its own destruction."

"Well, that and also from them being used as a giant experiment by the Adversary," Raphael said.

Noach sat up and stretched. The two angels turned their attention to him . . .

Noach reached over and woke the others. They also sat up and stretched.

"What time is it?" Jepheth asked.

"Is it even morning?" Rayneh asked as she looked around. Seeing Noach nod, she scrunched her brow. "But how can you tell?"

Noach cupped his hand behind his ear and gave a smile. "Hear that?"

Rayneh stopped to listen. "The animals are calling."

Noach nodded. "They're hungry."

Jepheth gave a chuckle. "Well, of course they are. We turned off their automatic feeding."

Rayneh cautiously stood. "Well, I'm not sure the ark is any more stable than yesterday. This could be precarious."

Jepheth nodded. "We just have to open the vats for a brief time to feed them and give them water." He shrugged. "I guess we'll have to keep doing that until the waves settle."

Rayneh sighed. "That's going to make a long day."

Jepheth laughed. "And you have somewhere else to be?"

She playfully slapped his arm. "For that remark you owe me a massage tonight."

Ar'yel pulled on Rayneh's arm. "After today, we'll all need one," Ar'yel said. "Come on. I'll help you." She looked at Shem.

He nodded. "Sure. I'll go help Jepheth."

As they went their way, Noach looked at Cham. "Come. Let's go be sure the ventilation shafts are not leaking large amounts of water. With the ship being tossed the way it is, water could be getting in." He turned to Kezia. "While we're gone, see if you can help Naamah prepare a breakfast."

She smiled and nodded, holding Naamah's hand to help steady her as the ark continued to heel every so often. Naamah held an oil lamp in her other hand. "We should probably light some of the sconces along the way. Evidently, darkness will be with us for quite some time."

Kezia nodded. "Sounds like a good idea."

As everyone went about their chores, Mikael smiled. "It seems they are coming to terms with their current responsibilities."

Raphael nodded. "Yes, but it hasn't even been a day. Everything's very new right now. This could get old in a hurry."

"You're probably right." He glanced toward Naamah and Kezia as they walked down the distant ramp. "At least they have each other to rely on."

At that moment, a distortion in what Mikael was seeing stood in front of him, startling him at first. He was unsure why his eyesight was playing tricks on him.

"Ruach?"

"Yes, Mikael. Yahweh desires your presence."

Mikael stood. "Certainly." He glanced at Raphael.

Raphael smiled and gestured. "Go, go. I'll be fine. Besides, I have Noach and his family to keep me company." He chuckled. "At least they don't talk back."

Mikael grinned. "Yeah, because they can't hear you, like I can."

He saw Raphael start to make a comeback, but Ruach whisked Mikael away before he heard it . . .

In only a moment, Mikael found himself standing at the Sacred Altar of Stones. As he turned, he saw Yahweh standing near him. He genuflected instinctively. "My Lord. I am at your service." He then saw others he did not expect to see. His eyes widened. There before Yahweh stood Lucifer, Samyaza, Arakiba, and all the other Watchers.

They were back—in their spirit form. Mikael assumed their bodies had been destroyed in the flood. This time, no one looked happy. Even Lucifer gave no glib comeback the way he typically did.

Mikael simply stood there, unsure of what to say or do. He just waited for Yahweh, who turned to him and said, "Mikael, I want you here as witness to what I am doing this day."

Mikael nodded but had no idea what Yahweh's words meant. "Certainly, my Lord."

Yahweh turned to the Watchers. "Samyaza, you were the instigator of all that occurred on Earth over the last few centuries."

Samyaza looked at Lucifer, but Yahweh continued. "Yes, I know Lucifer is ultimately responsible for inciting these ideas in your mind, but you are the one who implemented your evil desires and made them a reality, taking these others with you." His eyes then panned across theirs. "And they were more than eager to do so."

The other Watchers squirmed knowing these words were truth and they could not deny them.

"And all this to gain favor with Lucifer. Yet what you hoped to achieve will no longer happen and will never happen for any of you."

This seemed to take Lucifer off guard; his eyes and attention shot to Yahweh.

"We are all eternal beings," Lucifer said.

Yahweh looked at Lucifer and nodded. "Eternal, yes. But I control the freedom of your eternality."

Lucifer cocked his head as if not understanding his statement. "And what are you imposing?"

"All the Watchers will be held in prison until the day I reign victorious over my creation."

"But . . . these are *my* subjects."

Yahweh raised his eyebrows. "Yes, they still are. But they are no longer free to impress you any longer."

"Well, that hardly seems fair."

Yahweh shook his head. "Fairness has nothing to do with this. As I have always said: I provide opportunities, you choose your actions, and I the consequences that merit your actions."

Nervous looks could now be seen on the faces of each Watcher. Many looked at Lucifer as if to ask him to find a way out of this.

Lucifer continued. "So, how were we to know you would be so harsh?"

Yahweh calmly said, "You could have asked."

Lucifer then seemed to deflect the point Yahweh was making. "And you just glibly sentenced all of humanity to death and destruction."

Yahweh shook his head. "No, Lucifer. *You* did that a long time ago. You were the one who sacrificed their humanity to turn them into creatures they did not really wish to be, and you cared nothing for their lives as you allowed these Watchers to have them purposefully destroyed in their raids between their children so no pure-bloods would be left."

"So, this is just revenge?"

Yahweh sighed and gave a mournful look to Lucifer. Mikael was unsure if Lucifer really believed this or if he was once again just deflecting.

"Lucifer, you know that is not true. After being so close to me, you of all those here should know my heart."

Lucifer did not crack, however, or show any remorse. "I thought I did, but you were willing to sacrifice almost the entire population on Earth to save your precious Noach."

Yahweh's next words became noticeably more forceful, but not overly so. "And how long did Noach warn every single one of the impending disaster? Plenty of time for everyone to have repented and come to their senses." Yahweh pointed directly at Lucifer. "But *you* incited them to do otherwise. It was you,

Lucifer, who did not care about their lives, or, apparently, about the lives of these who were closer to you than any other. It is you who has brought destruction upon them all." Yahweh shook his head. "Lucifer, your pride will be *your* downfall for certain."

Lucifer stood straighter and held his chest high. "And you are too soft and caring, and that will be your downfall. This was one battle, not the war."

Yahweh shook his head once more. "Oh Lucifer, you have definitely revealed your heart. So be it, then."

Lucifer cocked his head as if trying to decipher the intent of those words.

In the blink of an eye, they all found themselves in an extremely dark and gloomy place. As Mikael turned, he saw a hazy . . . *something*. There seemed to be movement on the other side of a type of barrier that was before them, but the scene was like viewing something through heat waves on a desert floor. He could tell something was there, but the forms were non-distinguishable.

Samyaza was the first to speak, but his voice now lacked confidence. "Where . . . where are we?"

"This, I'm afraid, is your new home," Yahweh said, gesturing to the space around him. "Welcome to Tartarus. You will never be allowed to leave this place because of the actions you and your fellow Watchers have done. You abandoned your station as angels, interfered with the normal living process of mankind, experimented on them, turned them into something against their natural process of living, and even turned them away from each other and from me. If you want to identify with them, you can now identify with them in their death."

All eyes widened. Evidently, the seriousness of their fate was starting to dawn on them.

Samyaza turned to Lucifer. "This is more than you ever said would happen."

Even Lucifer was starting to look nervous. "This seems too cruel a fate for eternal beings."

"Humans are also eternal," Yahweh said. "Their spirits live on after their death. You and those here have destined them to an eternal state of sorrow and regret. I can't think of a more fitting consequence. Beyond this barrier are those whose fate you have sealed. You wanted to be with humans. Here you will get to experience the full effect of being human."

"You made them too weak. Too easily influenced by power."

"Lucifer, your definition of power seems very different from mine."

"Is it not used to influence?"

Yahweh nodded. "Yes, but not in the manner you are thinking. Those in power must first have the heart for others. Their power is used to influence their subjects to be all they can be and then encourage them to influence others in the same way." He shook his head. "Power is not to sway people to do your bidding, but to persuade them to reach beyond themselves. Then you both get what you want rather than getting what you want while they live in fear. True power yields a win-win scenario. Your kind of power yields . . . this."

At Yahweh's statement, bars of plasma—or something that *looked* like plasma—appeared at the barrier. Then this same material, looking something like glowing ropes, latched onto all two hundred of the Watchers' arms and legs. They tried to pull against their restraints, but to no avail.

"Now, Lucifer, go and tell your other angels of their friends' fate. Likely, they will think twice before so willingly being part of your schemes."

"Or," Lucifer said with an acidic tone, "they may be more determined to do so."

"No, no," one of the Watchers said. "No one would want a fate like this."

With that, Lucifer disappeared. Mikael knew his disappearance was Yahweh's doing—he was there when Sheol was first created and had observed how no angel had the power to teleport. As he looked at the Watchers now, he almost felt sorry for them. Yet when he remembered all they had done, he had to agree this was a most fitting consequence.

Yahweh turned to the Watchers. "What you have tried to accomplish has failed. I will be back one day to let you know that Lucifer's ultimate plan has failed. He will not be successful, just as you were not successful." He shook his head. "Yet, I'm afraid, so much destruction will be in his wake." He displayed a determined look. "But his plan will ultimately fail."

Mikael then saw Yahweh turn his attention to him. "Come, Mikael. We will leave this place."

Before teleporting, many of the Watchers pleaded: "No, no, don't leave us here!" Others: "We're sorry. We're sorry! We repent!" Or: "I'll do anything if you just take me out of here. Please!"

That was the last thing Mikael heard from the Watchers. A second later, he was back at the Sacred Altar of Stones.

As Mikael looked into his Master's eyes, he expected to see satisfaction. After all, he had defeated what these Watchers had tried to do against his divine plan. Yet what Mikael saw was something completely unexpected. Yahweh's eyes were moist. While no tears were shed, it was obvious he was sorrowful for what had happened.

"My Lord. Are you all right?"

Yahweh shook his head. "No, Mikael. It is always upsetting when I must punish those I have created and cherished. While I don't regret my actions, I am pained I had to take them."

Mikael nodded. The more he got to know his Master, the more he appreciated and adored him.

Yahweh gave a smile and patted Mikael on his upper arm. "Keep up the fight, my prized soldier. Lucifer has lost this battle, but he is likely already planning the next."

With those words, Yahweh disappeared.

Mikael headed back to check with Raphael.

CHAPTER 36

Afloat at Sea

Over the ensuing weeks, Noach and his family found an efficient routine. There was a feeding schedule for them and the animals. The waste was removed, and the larger animals exercised. They even had time in the evenings for themselves, although a good bit of that time was spent preparing for the next day. Yet there was time for some reading and making crafts or utensils needed to make work even more efficient. Noach also ensured they made time to pray and praise their Creator.

Even though the ark still tossed and tilted, it seemed the motions no longer greatly affected them. Noach had explained how the ark was constructed so the structure always faced into the wind, and this made the ark drive through large waves rather than a large wave hitting them broadside. They now barely had to hold onto a railing while walking—unless a large tilt of the ark was quite significant, and this was now infrequent. The rain also seemed to become a background noise they barely noticed.

One morning as Rayneh and Ar'yel walked and laughed together as they did their chores, Rayneh stopped and grabbed Ar'yel's arm. "Did you see that?"

Ar'yel nodded, eyes wide. "Yes. It was like light passed through the ark."

It happened again. They grew excited and ran back to the others.

"Everyone! Everyone!" Rayneh yelled. "Did you see it? Did you see it?"

They found Noach first, and he looked at them with concern. "What is it, my daughters?"

"We saw light! We saw light!" both women said, almost in unison.

Noach just shook his head; he seemed to not understand what the women were implying.

Ar'yel pointed upward. "We think the sun is peeking through the clouds." She looked at Rayneh, who nodded. "We saw sunlight!"

Rayneh added, "It was only brief, but we definitely saw it."

Kezia ran up to the three of them. "Do you hear it?"

They stopped. Rayneh and Ar'yel paused, trying to contain their excitement.

Rayneh shook her head. "I don't hear anything except for the animals."

Kezia gave a broad smile. "Exactly! You don't hear any rain!"

They looked at each other, eyes wide. They looked at Noach with expectation. He smiled and nodded. As they scurried toward the top of the ark, Noach called out. "Naamah! Shem! Cham! Jepheth! The roof! Meet us at the roof!"

They all arrived at nearly the same time. Shem was the first to speak. "What's going on?"

Ar'yel grabbed his arm and squeezed. "The rain has stopped. Rayneh and I saw sunlight."

Shem stopped and cocked his head, listening. "It has stopped! I've tuned the sound out for so long that I didn't even notice."

Ar'yel nodded. "Kezia was the first to notice."

Shem looked at her. "That is very observant of you, Kezia."

She beamed and Cham gave her a hug. "My sonic woman."

Kezia gave him a scrunched-brow look as the others laughed. She shook her head. "That doesn't sound very flattering."

Cham laughed. "Well, it was meant to be."

She laughed with him but playfully swatted his arm. "You and I need to have a talk about the technique of flattery."

Excitedly, she turned to Noach. "Can we see?"

He nodded and turned to Shem. "Help me open the window to the roof."

They slowly opened the window. Some water poured lightly inside the ark as it opened. At that same moment the sun peeked from behind the clouds and filled the opening with sunlight. They all gasped and then smiled at each other.

The opening was not large but allowed each couple to stand with their torso out of the ark to take in the view. They each took a deep breath as they stood and looked out.

Ar'yel was the first to express her disappointment. "Aw. I can only see the sky and part of the deck of the ark. Can't we go out all the way?"

Shem shook his head. "No, dear. We need to be sure all is safe before we open the ark all the way. It would be almost impossible to close the vents back up quickly if the need arose."

She nodded slowly as her disappointment turned to a smile. "At least seeing the sky is a nice change. Still very cloudy, but they seem to be breaking up."

When the sun broke through again, she lifted her face toward the sky, trying to soak up as much sun as possible while it was peeking through the clouds.

As the two stepped down, Naamah, holding onto Noach's arm, stuck her head through the window as Noach joined her. "Ah, the air is so fresh. Such a welcome change."

Noach rubbed her upper arm and smiled. "Indeed, my darling."

Ar'yel exclaimed, "When the clouds are gone, I'm going to come up here and just bask in the sun for a while. My, how I have missed the sun."

From below, Kezia said, "After so much water, it will take forever for all of it to go away."

Noach shook his head. "No, my dear. It *will* be long, but not forever."

She looked up toward him. "How long?"

He shook his head. "I'm not sure. It's only been a couple of months. It will, though, take much longer for the water to dissipate than it did for the water to come upon the earth."

A loud boom was heard—more like *felt*—as Noach and Naamah descended back into the ark. The large boom was somewhat muffled, as though the sound's origin came from deep under the water.

All turned to Noach. "What was that?" Naamah asked.

Noach shook his head. "Likely, the earth beneath us is still undergoing change."

As Noach reached to close the window, he stuck his head out for a final look. He then slammed the door to the window and held it tight. They all looked at him, not understanding what he was doing.

"What's wrong, Aba?" Shem asked.

"It's a giant wave," Noach said. "Everyone, brace yourselves!"

Just then the wave hit, causing some water to come through the ventilation grids and getting most of them wet. The women screamed as the ark again lurched from the force of the wave and knocked some of them to the floor—including plunging Kezia into the pool of water that had come through.

She stood, water dripping off her. The others suppressed a laugh. She looked at them, dejected. "Well, there goes my enthusiasm for the outdoors."

Cham came over and put his arm around her shoulders while trying to hold back his own chuckle. "Let's go get you into some dry clothes."

She swatted his chest but then leaned into him. Cham looked at the others as they nodded his way. He gave a grimace followed by a smile.

As they left, Naamah said, "Poor Kezia." She looked at herself and then the others. "We're all a little damp, but she got the brunt of it."

As they headed down the ramp, the ark lurched again. Water again came pouring through the ventilation grids.

"I'll come back and get all this water wiped up," Shem said. He shook his head. "I'll be glad when we reach a calm state."

Noach nodded. "As the water recedes, this will occur less, but I'm not sure how long it will take for the earth to get calm and stay calm. Our world still seems in a state of much change."

Shem nodded as he grabbed a railing to steady himself. "It's almost as if the earth itself is fluid, with part of the land crashing into other parts."

Cham looked at him. "What makes you say that?"

Shem shrugged. "What else would be making those muffled booms we keep hearing? Those sounds have to be from something solid hitting something solid."

Cham nodded; he looked deep in thought.

Shem turned to his father. "I don't think the world will look the same. Not as we remember it."

Noach nodded. "I fear you are right, my son. But Yahweh is still Creator and will, I'm sure, give us something wonderful."

Shem nodded and smiled as he went to retrieve some rags to soak up all the water on the top deck.

Raphael looked at Mikael. "What do you think the Creator is doing with the earth?"

Mikael shook his head. "I don't know." A grin shot across his face. "Want to go see?"

Raphael turned up his brow. "What do you mean?"

Mikael shrugged. "Well, think about it: we can't be affected by water. We could go down to the earth's surface and look around, see what's going on."

Raphael's eyes went wide. "I never thought about that." He grinned. "Let's do so."

Both teleported to the Earth's surface, which had certainly changed. While Mikael expected the surface to not look the same, he didn't expect to find what he did. In some places huge trenches had formed. Magma rivers were seen at their bottoms. In other places, magma was flowing up from the interior, cooling when hitting the water and causing mountains of hardening magma to form. Mikael had not realized Earth's crust floated on a sea of internal magma. Some of Earth's plates were crashing into others, one plate going underneath another and raising the upward-forced plate higher and higher.

Mikael instinctively knew large mountains would be part of Earth's new landscape. All these trenches, some very wide now, would likely become seas, lakes, and oceans in the new Earth. Even in the midst of chaos, the creativity of their Creator was quite evident. Mikael shook his head in amazement. Yahweh was truly remarkable.

CHAPTER 37

A Peek into the Future

Mikael sat on a boulder next to a gentle stream admiring the beauty surrounding him. He just had to be here for a while. He had been on Earth for too long and needed some creative peace around him. The Watchers' Earth had been brutal, crass, heartless. Although there had been some beauty still there, most of the world had become marred with all the genetic manipulation and bloody violence the Watchers had brought to the planet upon which Adam was to have reigned.

They and the flood had destroyed it all.

Mikael understood the why, but he needed rejuvenation. Therefore, he left Noach and his family floating on the ocean of water for a respite. He felt a little guilty doing so, but as he looked around, the guilt quickly faded. This beauty was beyond anything even Earth afforded. This was his Creator's creative dimension, and it was beyond compare.

Raphael looked over at him and laughed. Mikael gave a small grin. "What's so funny?"

Raphael shook his head. "You."

Mikael raised his eyebrows but didn't say anything.

"You look content—and guilty. At the same time."

Raphael's words made Mikael laugh. "I can never hide anything from you." He sat up straighter. "I really needed this, though. Earth has become anything but a place of beauty. I needed a taste of creativity to continue on."

"Too bad Noach and his family can't do the same."

Mikael nodded. "Hence, the guilt side." He lay back on the boulder as an extremely colorful butterfly—or some creature like it—landed on his abdomen. Mikael raised his head slightly to see the neon blue and yellow of the creature's wings reflect the sunlight. After a few seconds the creature flitted away, landing on a nearby flower. Mikael looked over at Raphael. "Slight guilt."

Raphael just laughed. His laugh quickly faded as his gaze went behind Mikael. Raphael immediately genuflected.

Mikael quickly turned; his eyes widened. "Yahweh!" Mikael stood and bowed deeply. "My Lord, is anything wrong?"

Yahweh laughed and motioned for both to sit. Yahweh sat next to Mikael.

"Does my presence always indicate a concern that needs addressing?" Yahweh asked.

Mikael chuckled. "No, my Lord." He paused. "But, well . . . often it does."

Yahweh laughed harder. "Perhaps you are right. I should enjoy my own creation even more than I do."

So . . . is there a concern?" Mikael asked.

Yahweh nodded. "You."

Mikael squinted. "My Lord? I am fine."

Yahweh put his hand on Mikael's shoulder. "Are you? Really?"

Mikael gave a slight smile. "Well, I am now. I just needed a little rejuvenation by basking in your creativity."

Yahweh smiled. "It is beautiful here, isn't it?"

Mikael nodded. "Very much so, my Lord."

"Have you ever considered why I made this dimension?"

Mikael gave him a blank stare. Yes, he had wondered that—many times. Yet Yahweh's question seemed to go deeper than just a superficial inquiry.

"I'm sure there is a purpose behind everything you do."

Yahweh chuckled. "I'll consider you in the future when diplomacy is required."

Mikael gave a weak smile in return. He was unsure the direction his Creator was heading.

Yahweh looked around and swept his hand before him. "One day, all of this will be where the righteous dead reside before I reign on Earth."

Mikael's eyes widened. "You mean, all those in Sheol will one day be here?" He sat up straighter. "That's . . . that's great. It's wonderful."

Raphael joined this discussion. "But why not now, my Lord?" He looked around. "Is . . . is it not ready?" His expression indicated he could not see why it wouldn't be.

Yahweh shook his head. "It is not that this place is not ready. The time is not ready. They have died with their sin unpaid."

Mikael squinted. "But the burnt offerings . . . "

Yahweh smiled. "Yes, they definitely show their devotion and commitment to me. Yet there is a price that needs to be paid. Animals are only representations of what has to be done in the future. The sacrifice points to me, Mikael."

Mikael heard a gasp from Raphael. He felt the same. "But how is that even possible, my Lord?"

"When the time is right, I will go to Earth as an infant so I can identify with my human creation and be the human sacrifice needed to save them all—no matter in what time they live."

"But my Lord. That changes everything. You will then always be identified as human. Superhuman, but still human." Mikael shook his head. "I can't even begin to fathom you in such a form."

Yahweh put his hand on Mikael's shoulder. "It will be difficult, granted. Yet the Almighty, I, and Ruach contemplated this even before we created Adam. This was the contingency for which we planned. So, you see, keeping the race pure through Noach was essential to this plan for which I have committed myself. My plan can't fail. We won't let it fail."

"What about Lucifer, my Lord?" Raphael asked. "He wants to thwart such a plan, I'm sure."

Yahweh looked at Raphael and nodded. "Indeed, Raphael, he does." He gave a slight shrug. "Yet his pride has already blinded him to his lack of success. He will try to thwart our plan, and it may even look like his is succeeding. Yet, in the end, we will use his pride against him to accomplish our goal." He produced a very large smile. "Not to worry. Our plan will win in the end."

Raphael nodded. "Yes, my Lord. I know you are all-knowing and can see what we cannot." He smiled. "That is why your side is the only logical one to be on."

Yahweh laughed. "I wish all my angels had your logic, Raphael."

"Then we wouldn't have an Adversary," Mikael said.

Yahweh nodded. "So getting Noach and his family safely through the flood is vital to our mission."

Mikael knew his respite here was over. He stood. "Yes, my Lord. We will see to it."

Yahweh smiled. "I know you will." He stood as well. "Goodbye to you both for now."

With that, Yahweh disappeared.

Both Mikael and Raphael stood in silence for a few moments. Raphael then looked at Mikael. "That was sobering."

Mikael nodded slowly. "Yes, very. It seems our purpose becomes more meaningful every day."

"When do you think our Lord will go to Earth and become human?"

Mikael shrugged. "Well, it can't be the near future. Earth has to be populated again, I would presume. Likely we'll have several more encounters with Lucifer and his angels before that happens."

Raphael put his hand to his chin. "I wonder if Lucifer already knows this."

"I don't know. But he's very smart and will likely figure it out pretty quickly." Mikael sighed. "Then Noach's descendants will definitely be under attack. He certainly doesn't want our Lord to become the answer to mankind's sin problem."

Mikael started walking and motioned to Raphael. "Let's just have one more stroll, and then we'll return to Earth."

Raphael smiled and followed Mikael.

Mikael knew he had to get back to his duty, but he definitely needed to absorb as much of this beauty as possible. He wasn't sure how long it would be before he could return. He looked at Raphael. "So, one day, all the righteous in Sheol will be brought here. Can you imagine the look on their faces?" Mikael laughed. "They will be overcome with joy. I know Paradise is wherever our Master resides, but this will be such a wonderful place for them."

Raphael nodded. "I know it is for us."

Seeing some animals in the distance took Mikael's thoughts back to Serpentess. She had been so content here. "Remember Serpentess, Raphael?"

Raphael nodded. "Yes. The animals seemed to adore her."

"Just think about all the things Lucifer has affected in a negative way. He destroyed the wonderful future Serpentess and Serpent could have had. He persuaded so many fellow angels to be against our Master and meet their fate of doom. He turned a beautiful Earth into a place of wickedness and violence, and then he sealed the fate of most of Earth's population to an eternal future of hopelessness." Mikael shook his head. "And Earth isn't even that old. I can't even imagine what he will do next."

Raphael shook his head and pushed out a deep sigh. "Mikael, we certainly have our work cut out for us."

Mikael nodded. "And I guess we need to get back to it." He looked at Raphael. "Ready?"

Raphael patted Mikael on the back. "Yes, let's do so."

Both teleported back to Earth.

CHAPTER 38

The Olive Branch

Mikael found about five Earth months had passed since he left. When he returned, he found Shem at the window with his wife Ar'yel.

"Shem, will we ever find land?" She leaned against his arm. "I've almost lost count of how long we've been adrift."

"Well, the water must be receding since the sun has been out almost every day of late."

Ar'yel looked out and stared at the sky and then back to him. "I wish we could see more than just the sky."

Shem laughed.

She looked at him in a confused manner.

"First you just wanted to be able to see the sun," Shem said. "Now you want to see more."

She slapped his arm. "And you don't?"

He chuckled as he rubbed her arm. "Just be patient. It will happen. A lot of water still has to recede."

"Maybe it's a lot more water than the sun can handle."

Shem laughed. "Perhaps. But not more than Yahweh can handle, I'm sure. We are in his hands, so one day we will be back on dry land."

"Well, I sure hope it's sooner rather than later."

Shem smiled and patted her hand. At that moment they both looked at each other with eyes growing wider by the second.

Ar'yel's grip tightened on Shem's arm. "What is that sound?"

Shem shook his head. "I . . . I don't know. How . . . eerie."

Mikael heard the noise, which started as a creaking sound but then got louder and higher in pitch. Then . . . the ark came to a sudden halt. This propelled Ar'yel into Shem with tremendous force. He hit his head and Ar'yel nearly fell off the ladder. Shem steadied her back onto the ladder and rubbed his head as he grimaced from the pain. The sound of the ark turned from a high-pitched squeal to a low moan.

Ar'yel gave Shem a concerned looked. "Are you all right? That sounded like you hit your head hard."

Shem nodded as he continued to rub his head. "I'm okay." Yet his expression didn't look convincing.

Ar'yel gave him a kiss on his cheek. "So what happened?" She turned her head. "Listen!" She put her hand to his chest. "Do you hear that? I've never heard that sound before."

Shem nodded. "It sounds like . . . " He stuck his head higher through the window so he could hear better. He looked down at her. "I think the water's waves are lapping against the side of the ark."

Ar'yel's eyes grew larger still. "You mean we're not moving?!"

Shem nodded. "I think we're stuck on something."

"Land?"

"Seems to be. Or something solid at least."

She stuck her head back through the opening. Her hand found Shem's arm and pulled him upward once more. "Come look at this! I can see land sticking up from the side of the ark!"

"Really?" Shem stood next to her. "Must be part of a mountain the ark has landed on."

"That's good, right?" She looked into his eyes as if looking for confirmation.

"As long as we don't have a hole in the hull and are now taking on water."

Ar'yel's eyes shot wide as her hand went to her mouth. "Oh my! Surely not. Yahweh wouldn't let that happen, would he?"

"Let's go see." Shem helped her back down into the ark and they ran to where Noach and the others were.

Shem was panting. "Aba! Is the ark okay?"

Noach cocked his head. "Seems to be. Why?"

Shem shrugged. "Well, we've run aground. I—" He looked at Ar'yel. "We . . . wanted to be sure the ark was undamaged." His gaze panned to Cham and then Jepheth, who was walking to join the group. "No water entering the ark?"

All looked around and shook their heads.

"What's going on?" Jepheth asked, looking like he had little idea of what was happening.

"The ark's run aground," Shem said.

"So that's what that awful noise was all about." Jepheth rubbed his head. "And why my head and the side of the ark greeted each other with such force."

Shem smiled. "Good thing you're very thick-headed."

Jepheth gave him a silly grimace. "Very funny. Anyway, what do we do now?"

All eyes turned to Noach.

"Did you see any land?" Noach asked Shem.

Shem nodded. "Looks like part of a mountain."

"Well, there's only one way to see if any significant land is present."

All eyes turned to Noach.

The patriarch laughed. "We need to release a raven, of course."

"Oh, oh," Ar'yel said, becoming excited. "Let me go get one." She scurried down the corridor and then down the ramp.

"Bring the bird to the upper window," Noach shouted. "We'll meet you there."

They could hear her muffled confirmation.

By the time Noach had everyone at the window, Ar'yel had arrived with a raven wrapped in a cloth to keep the creature calm as she walked quickly with it. She handed the bird up to Noach, who climbed as high as he could, his torso out the window.

"This kind of bird will ensure us if land is out there," he said. Noach threw the raven into the air, and the bird spread its wings and flew away, first making a circle high above the ark and then flying out of sight.

They all stayed in place for quite some time waiting to see if the raven would return.

Naamah suddenly pointed. "I just saw the raven fly by again!"

Noach stuck his torso high through the window, turning from one side to the other. He laughed. "And there it goes again."

After a few minutes, Naamah laughed. "Noach, you better think of another plan."

Noach turned her way. "And why is that?"

Naamah pointed again. "Our raven friend seems happy just to be outside. Their kind are not typically choosy where they rest. The raven could just use twigs or branches that are floating to rest between its flying trips."

Noach laughed as he shook his head. "I should have considered its habits. This raven is just happy to be out there. He's likely not even considering coming back." He looked at the others. "Ar'yel, mind bringing out a dove?"

Ar'yel's eyes went wide. "Oh, great idea, Aba Noach. A dove will be much more persnickety."

Shem laughed. "*Persnickety*? Are you creating new words for our new world?"

She elbowed him in the ribs and he gave an *umph*.

"Mark my words," she said. "People will be using that word one day." She put her face next to his as if in a dare. "Besides, admit it. You knew exactly what I was meaning."

"Yes, dear. But that's because I understand doves."

The others laughed, but she ignored them as she pulled on Shem's arm. "Now come help me fulfill Aba's request."

In a few minutes Ar'yel and Shem were back with a dove wrapped in a cloth, carried just as Ar'yel had done with the raven. Noach carefully took the dove and tossed the bird into the air. The creature also did a quick circle of the ark and then flew out of sight.

They all stayed a little longer, but the sun was starting to set.

"It may be a while before the dove returns, so I think we should go back inside," Noach said.

Everyone heeded Noach's instructions and headed back into the ark except for Jepheth and Rayneh. Noach turned to shut the window. "Jepheth, are you and Rayneh coming? It'll be dark soon."

Jepheth shook his head as he put his arm around Rayneh's shoulders. "We want to stay a little longer and look at the stars." He looked up. "It's been a long time since we've had no cloud cover."

Noach smiled and nodded. "Just don't stay too late. And be sure to close the window when you're done." Noach turned to leave them to themselves but then turned back upon hearing Rayneh.

"It's back! It's back!"

The dove landed on the windowsill. Noach held out his hand and the dove hopped onto it, breathing rapidly. Noach stroked the bird's feathers. "Poor thing. Didn't find a place to land, did you?"

He gestured for Rayneh to hand him the cloth Ar'yel had used to hold the bird.

"We'll try again in a week." He wrapped the bird and took the dove back to its cage.

* * * * * * *

A week later they were all back at the window when Noach released the dove again. The bird did its same circling maneuver and then flew toward the watery horizon.

Ar'yel looked at Noach and said, "You think the dove will find anything this time?"

Noach shrugged. "We've become lodged on something. Likely some kind of mountaintop. There could be other mountains higher still."

Ar'yel grew excited. "Well, if we're stuck on one, then the water can't be that deep."

Noach shook his head. "No, I think this mountain is extremely high. Far higher than any mountain we knew before."

Ar'yel's eyes grew wide. "Mountains that high?" She shook her head. "I never knew mountains that high existed."

Noach gave a light chuckle. "Well, they didn't before. I think our world will be totally different than previously, and we'll find Yahweh has sculpted our Earth anew. All the tsunamis that hit us even after all the water stopped rising has to mean the earth was being reshaped."

Ar'yel looked deep in thought. "Well, I can't wait to see what Yahweh has done."

Noach grinned. "Neither can I, Ar'yel." He turned to everyone else. "I'm going to stay here a while, so everyone else can go about their day. I'll let you know when the dove returns."

"You sound confident it will," Kezia said. "What if it doesn't?"

Noach gave a broad smile. "Then that means the dove found livable land."

"All right then," she said, grinning. "No dove, the faster we get out of here."

Cham pulled on her arm. "Come on, Kezia. Don't get your hopes up too soon."

They went about their daily chores until, some time later, they heard Noach running down the ramp from the upper floor. "Everyone! Everyone!"

As he approached the others, Noach held the dove in one arm draped in the cloth. In his other hand was a small sprig of . . . something.

When Noach saw them, he held up the sprig. "Look! Look! The dove brought a sprig from an olive tree!"

Jepheth reached Noach first and looked at the sprig. "It's green! So we have vegetation already growing somewhere!"

Noach beamed. "Seems to be." He handed the dove to Ar'yel. "Please take our friend back to its cage."

Ar'yel took the dove back to its cage, chuckling as she went. "Come on, friend. Let's get you back so you can rest."

Jepheth looked at his father with eyes wide. "So what happens next?"

"We'll send the dove out again a week from today—and see what happens once more."

Rayneh gave a slight shrug. "Why can't we check now? After all, you just said it proves vegetation is growing."

Noach nodded. "Yes, but the dove apparently didn't feel comfortable staying there." He tilted his head. "Maybe by next week it will."

As before, each went back to their chores. Life once again returned to its normal on the ark.

Mikael looked at Raphael. "They all look a little dejected."

Raphael nodded. "Yes, but who can blame them? They've been cooped up in this ark for almost an Earth-year. Who wouldn't be anxious to get out?" He pointed to Mikael. "Even you had to do that."

Mikael looked at Raphael with the corner of his mouth turned up. "Now don't go and make me feel guilty."

Raphael laughed and patted Mikael on his shoulder. "Just stating what I see."

Mikael shook his head. "You're quite the friend, Raphael. You really are."

Raphael laughed some more.

CHAPTER 39

The Future Promise

When the next week arrived, Ar'yel stood with everyone at the upper window with the dove in her arms, eagerly waiting Noach's arrival. Noach stopped short as he arrived.

"So, everyone seems ready for this," the patriarch said.

Ar'yel nodded. "Absolutely. Here's your friend."

Noach laughed. "Shem, open the window and I'll let my . . . friend . . . fly."

Noach pushed his torso and the bird through the opening. As he prepared to let the dove fly, he said, "Okay, my friend. You gave us hope last time, now give us great news this time."

The dove once again circled and flew out of sight.

Noach lowered himself back into the ark. "Well, there's no use for us to wait this time. The best news is for the bird not to return. I'll leave the window open during the day just in case the dove does."

Over the course of the day, everyone's excitement built; it was palpable by the time of their evening meal. After Noach gave a blessing, and everyone had been served, Ar'yel burst out with the question on everyone's mind. "So, did the dove return?"

Noach shook his head. "No, not yet."

Her eyes widened. "So we can go onto the outer deck tomorrow?"

Noach cocked his head. "Well, maybe not tomorrow."

Ar'yel's shoulders dropped. "But . . . why?" She looked at the others as if for support. "Every other time, the dove returned before sundown. Now that the dove didn't, doesn't it mean it found a place it felt suitable?"

"Well, I suppose."

Ar'yel looked at Shem as if to say: *Talk to your father.*

Shem cleared his throat. "What are you waiting for, Aba?"

Noach stopped eating and looked at everyone. "Just because the dove has found suitable accommodations doesn't mean we can do the same—yet." He shrugged. "I just think we need to wait a little longer. I would say we wait a week and then open the top of the ark."

Everyone looked at each other, disappointment on their faces. Yet no one said anything or went against Noach's argument. However, little conversation took place for the remainder of the meal.

The rest of the evening, and all the next day, everyone seemed depressed, lackadaisical, and worked very slowly. Once back at their evening meal, Noach sighed. "What is wrong with everyone?"

Naamah gave him a blank stare. "You have to ask?"

Noach shook his head. "Okay. Okay. We'll open the top of the ark tomorrow. Satisfied?"

In an instant, everyone's disposition changed. This mealtime became one of the liveliest dinners and most animated discussions the family had experienced in a very long time.

Once the meal was done, Noach calmed everyone once more. "Okay, everyone. Meet me at the upper deck first thing after breakfast tomorrow."

Everyone looked at each other and nodded. Naamah said, "We'll make it a quick breakfast."

Noach shook his head. "I definitely feel outnumbered."

Everyone laughed. Each of the girls kissed his cheek as they left with their husbands.

"That's nice," Noach said, "but I know you're just trying to butter me up."

More laughter could be heard as the family dispersed to get their chores completed before time for bed.

* * * * *

Mikael stood behind everyone who had gathered at the upper deck. He was happy for them to finally get out into fresh air. He knew how pleased he felt with his time out of the ark in the Creator's creative dimension. He knew they felt the same way. A little fresh air would do them worlds of good.

After Noach opened the window he had his sons help him remove the ventilation slats which opened a space leading to the outer deck of the ark. The men climbed up and helped their wives onto the top of the ark. In this area the surface was flat and made a deck for great viewing of their surroundings.

Naamah was the first to exclaim it: "Oh, take in the fresh air! It is divine."

Ar'yel nodded as she took in an exaggerated breath. "I had forgotten how sweet air can be without the odor of all the animals."

Noach laughed.

"Oh, don't get me wrong," Ar'yel said. "I'm glad for the ventilation we had. But this . . . this is absolutely wonderful."

Noach came over and gave her a hug. "I agree with you totally. Completely."

Kezia pointed. "Look! I see land! We had seen part of this mountain, but look, there are many more in the distance."

Cham came over and wrapped her in a hug. "It looks like we're in a mountain range." He glanced around. "There seem to be mountains all around us."

Ar'yel looked at Noach. "You were right, Aba Noach. Yahweh has created tremendous mountains for our new world."

Noach smiled. "And I'm sure this is only the beginning of the special things our Creator has in store for us."

"So when can we actually leave the ark?" Rayneh asked.

Noach turned and held up his hands, chuckling. "Whoa there. We still have a way to go before the world can support us. The exposed ground is still very, very soggy. We can't have the animals get stuck or hurt as they leave the ark for good."

Rayneh cocked her head. "Yes, I know you're right." She sighed. "How much time are we talking about?"

Noach cocked his head. "Oh, I'd say about two more months."

Her eyes widened. "That long?" She looked at her husband, disappointment on her face.

Jepheth came up to her and wrapped his arm around her shoulders. "Well, we can't leave the ark yet, but we can have dinner out here tonight. Right, Ima?"

A huge grin came across Naamah's face. "What a perfect idea. Picnic outside."

Rayneh looked at Jepheth. "And then a time to lie under the stars."

Jepheth raised his eyebrows and nodded. "Sounds like a great plan to me." He looked around at the others. Everyone nodded in agreement.

Noach clapped his hands. "Okay, everyone. We do still have animals to take care of. So let's get our chores done and we can then have an early dinner and sit under the stars." He looked around. "What do you say?"

All nodded. Shem jumped through the opening and helped his wife and the others back into the ark. Each dispersed and went to finish their chores.

Mikael stood with Raphael on the deck of the ark and looked out. "What do you think of the new world, Raphael?"

"Well, it's hard to tell right now. Yet, since Yahweh has created it, I'm certain this new world will be awesome."

Mikael laughed. "Yes, I'm sure it will be. Makes you wonder why he changed all the Earth's topology." He glanced up. "Now, with the vapor canopy gone . . . " He glanced back at where Noach's family had entered the ark and turned back to Raphael. "I guess that will be something else for Noach's family to get prepared for."

Raphael nodded. "I wonder if they realize that. The temperature could get pretty cold in these mountainous areas."

Mikael raised his eyebrows. "Well, their time under the stars tonight may give them a clue. They will likely need blankets. At this high of an altitude, although the days are warm, the nights are likely to be cooler than they're used to."

"This could be good for them, then," Raphael said. "They can experience this now and be planning for what to do when they actually leave the ark."

Inside, everyone worked in a joyous mood. While serious about their chores, they definitely had a more lighthearted approach to their duties.

Rayneh was helping Ar'yel clean up around the animal enclosures where some of the marsupials had pushed food outside their cages. Ar'yel swept up around one of the cages, turned to put the broom away, and then turned back. "Hey, there now." She looked at one of the smaller animals as the creature had pushed food out of its cage again. She bent down, picked up the morsel, and shoved it back in the cage. The animal ate the food as she pushed the morsel back inside. She giggled. "So, you're just wanting attention, is that it?" She reached in and stroked the animal's furry forehead. The creature pushed itself into her finger as if to ask for more. She giggled again. "Now, you're going to go and make all the other animals jealous. They're going to want me to spend just as much time with them." She shook her head, but with a smile on her face. "I don't have that kind of time. I have a date with my family outside tonight." She scratched her furry friend's forehead once more. "Now, you be good, you hear?"

As she stood, the animal started to push another morsel outside the cage. "No you don't," Ar'yel said as she took her broom, laughed, and pushed the bit of food back inside the cage. The little animal then made a grunting noise and scooted farther back in its cage.

"Aw," Rayneh said. "Now you've hurt its feelings."

Ar'yel chuckled. "Well, it has to learn sometime." She turned and put her broom away. "Come on, Rayneh. Let's get washed up for dinner. I can't wait to enjoy our meal outside."

Rayneh nodded. "Oh, and let's take some blankets outside. We'll treat this like a real picnic."

"Great idea. I'll bring some extra ones so we can lie and watch the stars afterward."

Both giggled and ran to get ready.

Mikael watched them run up the ramp to the next tier. He smiled. He was happy they had something to look forward to. This was certainly a change in their routine.

Raphael tapped Mikael's arm, chuckling.

"What is it?"

Raphael pointed.

Mikael laughed hard. The small animal Ar'yel had scolded had taken another food morsel and pushed it back, once more, through the cage's small opening.

The men helped their mother take the meal to the top of the ark and handed the food up to their wives. Once they all had gotten topside, their wives had the food arranged on blankets just as with a regular picnic.

Shem smiled. "This reminds me of the times we would eat as we were preparing the ark." He shook his head. "Seems like so long ago."

Ar'yel patted the seat next to her. The other men sat next to their wives. The sun was low in the sky, peeking through two mountaintops in the distance.

Noach prayed and then everyone ate, talked, laughed, and told stories that made everyone laugh still more. It seemed being out in the open air lifted everyone's mood.

Once the stars started appearing, the women sat between their husbands' feet, leaning their heads again their husbands' chests. Every so often one would point out a star for the others to look at.

Noach sat with his arm around Naamah's shoulders. "With all the other changes, I'm just glad the heavens still look the same. Seeing the same constellations as I remember them helps make the other changes not so bad."

Kezia looked over at him. "Aba Noach, tell us the story in the constellations again. I like the way you always tell it."

Noach laughed. "Oh, all right. But you have to point to the correct constellation as I go through the story." He looked around. "Everyone willing?"

All nodded.

"Okay. Here goes: This is the story of the Mazzaroth. The Promised One to come will be born of a virgin." Noach pointed and looked at the others. "Okay, everyone. Point to the constellation Betulah." Once all did, he continued. "This means he will not be entirely human but will also be deity, coming with a dual purpose of love and justice."

Kezia interrupted. "How is that possible?" She turned and gazed at Noach, looking inquisitive, not confrontational.

Noach shook his head. "I'm not entirely sure, my dear. But with Yahweh, all this can be made possible. It seems his Spirit, Ruach, will be part of the conception."

Kezia's eyes narrowed. "So, like the Watchers, but only in reverse? He will be good and not evil?"

Noach laughed. "Well, that's a unique perspective. Somewhat, I suppose, but he will not be an angel, but be Yahweh. Somehow Yahweh will dwell on Earth as a human yet retain his divinity."

Kezia smiled with her eyes. "Well, I can't wait for that."

Noach smiled and went on. "The reason for his coming will be to pay for the justice Elohim requires."

"Oh," Shem exclaimed. "Just like what our ancestor Chanok taught."

Noach nodded. "Now point to Moznayim." All did so. "He will have to die to pay for the required justice, but this will not deter his other mission of becoming the conquering king. The Adversary will be against him and his efforts."

"Big surprise there," Rayneh said. "I just hope he doesn't make as big a mess of things as he did for us."

"Indeed," Noach said. "Although the Adversary—point to Akrab—is desiring the same crown destined for the coming One, the Promised One will hold him back from obtaining his goal, with the Promised One eventually crushing the head of the Adversary."

"Amen," Naamah said. "Just as Yahweh promised to Chavvah."

Noach patted her hand. "Exactly, my dear. This Promised One will be unique."

Cham laughed and pulled Kezia's pointing finger closer to his. "Kasshat is this way," Cham said.

She looked at him and giggled. "I always forget this one."

Noach smiled. "His uniqueness testifies to Elohim's character, which the Adversary, represented by the supporting constellation Nacash—as that long strand of stars above Kasshat looking like a serpent—is trying to challenge. Praise will go to the Promised One who will overcome the Adversary and cast him into the fire."

"Ah, sweet victory," Jepheth said.

Noach smiled and nodded. "The payment for justice will come in a unique way, for the Promised One will come as a sacrifice, but death will not destroy him but transform him.

"Gedi," Kezia said as she moved her finger toward that constellation. Everyone followed her gesture.

"That's right, Kezia," Noach said, looking happy she was so engaged. "Although the death blow reaches its mark and causes the Promised One from heaven to fall, the Promised One springs back to life."

"I just love that part," Ar'yel said. She shook her head. "Now that's a hope to hold onto."

Shem patted her arm. She looked up at him and smiled.

Noach continued. "What comes next?"

"D'li," Ar'yel said, looking at Noach for confirmation.

He smiled. "Very good, my daughter."

Ar'yel looked back at the sky, happy with herself.

"This act of the Promised One allows the outpouring of Ruach," Noach said, "which is as a sea giving life to those who desire to follow the Promised One. This good news spreads swiftly as those given new life tell others of how the Promised One has changed them into a new creature."

"Do you believe that, Aba?" Cham asked.

Noach nodded. "With all my heart, son."

Cham looked in deep thought. "Seems almost impossible."

Noach laughed. "*Almost* is a great word, is it not?"

Cham chuckled and nodded.

"What's next, Cham?" Noach asked.

"Oh, uh." He glanced back at the sky and pointed. "Dagim."

Noach nodded and smiled. "The Promised One rescues those who have been chained to the Adversary through the rebellion of Adam: those before the Promised One's coming as well as those after his coming. He takes the chains or bands from the Adversary, frees them, and takes them unto himself. They will one day reign with him when he becomes the Exalted One."

"Did Adam regret what he did?" Shem asked.

"Oh, absolutely, my son. He always said if he could go back, he would have done things differently. Yet, as you saw with the Watchers, they played with our pride and many of our friends did things we never thought they would. It was the same with Adam that fateful day."

Shem turned back and looked at the stars. "I'm just glad Yahweh loves us so much he is willing to do all this for us." He glanced back at his father. "When do you think this will happen?"

Noach shook his head. "Not sure. Sometime in our distant future. We first have to repopulate the earth." He continued. "Next comes T'leh." He looked at the others. "Everyone see it?"

All nodded.

"The Promised One who came as a sacrifice becomes the chain-breaker, the conqueror over the Adversary who holds control over all of us, Adam's descendants, due to Adam's rebellion—but we will then be released by this Promised One."

Noach paused as all looked at him. "This was what Adam regretted the most. It wasn't just his rebellion he regretted, but that he plunged all of us into a kingdom ruled by the Adversary."

Noach smiled. "Yet Adam's eyes would almost twinkle when he told this next part."

"Yes," Ar'yel said. "I always love this next part about Shor." She looked at Noach and smiled.

He smiled back and continued. "This Promised One then becomes the judge of fury and the mighty hunter, represented by Kesil—just to the left and down from Shor—who conquers the Adversary by taking from the Adversary his own, who he now protects from the Adversary as he reigns victorious and sends his fury against the Adversary as a river of fire and judgment—this is what consumes the Adversary."

"Job done," Shem said.

Noach nodded. "Now point to Teomim. The Promised One thus fulfills his dual mission by coming as Deliverer and Judge. He crushes the Adversary with his judgment of wrath, comes as the Redeemer, and also as the Prince who rules. The Promised One then provides a place of rest for those restored to him."

"Sarton," Shem interjected.

Noach nodded and continued. "This is also represented by the two supporting star clusters called Mezarim, the protective sheepfolds for his flock. He provides a way for them to travel from their earthly abode to his heavenly abode where they become his and are under his protection forever. The Promised One then reigns victorious forever."

"Ari," Jepheth added with emphasis.

"That's right," Noach said. "Although the Adversary may try to flee, the fury and wrath of the Promised One is released on the Adversary, who is utterly destroyed."

Everyone clapped. "Victory!" several enthusiastically said.

Noach smiled. "Indeed, my children. Indeed."

After a few moments of reflection, Ar'yel shivered and said, "My, it's getting chilly out here." She rubbed her arms, grabbed one of the blankets, and pulled it over her. "Is the temperature supposed to be this cold?" She shook her head, looking at Noach. "I don't recall it getting this cold prior to the flood."

Noach thought for a few minutes. He then spoke, shaking his index finger, as though articulating new thoughts that were just coming to him. "Water came from above and from the earth beneath." He looked up. "Do the stars look brighter than they used to?"

Jepheth nodded. "Yes, I was just thinking that." He turned to his father. "Does that mean something?"

Noach slowly nodded. "Perhaps. Maybe a vapor canopy kept the heat from the sun closer to the earth."

Ar'yel replied. "Oh, like my blanket."

"Exactly. The vapor canopy was like a blanket for the earth."

"And so," Jepheth said, "without the blanket, the earth gets cold."

"Something like that, I think," Noach said. "I think the deluge was the vapor canopy collapsing which produced all the rain."

Shem turned and looked at his father. "You know what that means?"

Noach looked at his son. "What is that?"

Shem gave a look like the answer was obvious. "We have to get down off this mountain after we leave the ark. It won't be as cold near the bottom of the mountains."

Noach nodded, deep in thought. "Yes. Yes, that is definitely a necessity."

Naamah stood. "Well, for now we need to get off the top of this ark and back into its interior. Our blankets, and the animals, will keep us warm for now."

Everyone laughed as they stood and picked up the remains of their meal.

Kezia kissed Naamah's cheek. "You were always the practical one, Ima."

Naamah shook her head and laughed. "Just realistic."

CHAPTER 40

A New World

One day, as Noach was about to pass her during chores, Rayneh got his attention. "Aba Noach, may I talk to you?"

Noach paused and nodded. "Of course, my daughter. What is it?"

"Do you remember what you told us about when we can leave the ark?"

Noach cocked his head. "Not specifically. What did I say?"

"When we had our first dinner on top of the ark and watched the stars that night, you said we could likely leave the ark in about two months from that night."

Noach nodded. "Yes, I guess I did say that." He held up his index finger. "But I did say 'about.'"

Rayneh nodded. "I know, but the two-month period will be in two weeks, so I just want to know if you've considered the exact day."

Noach smiled. "I'll tell you what. Let me look outside again today, and I'll give an announcement at dinnertime. How's that?"

Rayneh smiled and nodded. "That would be wonderful."

Throughout the day, Rayneh told everyone else this news. The excitement grew so strong it could be felt by the time dinner was served. When Noach arrived at dinner, everyone was seated and waiting. Their eager faces looked up at him.

Noach sat slowly as he scanned their faces. "I think I'm in the dark about something."

Naamah set his food in front of him while shaking her head. "No, dear. You're the only one *not* in the dark."

He gave her a quizzical look. She smiled and whispered to him, "When do we leave the ark?"

Noach chuckled as he glanced at Rayneh. "Well, it appears someone has spread some news."

Rayneh laughed. "We're all dying to know your decision."

Noach nodded. "Let's pray, and then we'll talk."

Everyone bowed their heads and Noach prayed: "Yahweh, our Lord, we thank you for the protection you have given us from the hands of the Watchers even before your flood, and we certainly thank you for the protection you have given us during it. Now we ask for your protection, guidance, and continued faithfulness as we leave the ark next week."

Noach opened his eyes and noticed everyone with wide eyes looking back at him. He laughed. "Wasn't that what you wanted to hear?"

Naamah pushed on his arm lightly. "Well, we didn't expect you to deliver the news quite like that."

"What day next week?" Rayneh asked as she passed a basket of bread to Jepheth.

"First day of the week."

Rayneh's eyes grew wide as a huge grin came to her face. "Four days! We leave the ark in four days!"

Everyone else was grinning now as well. The conversation picked up pace and speed, becoming quite animated. There was a great deal of laughter and giddiness throughout the meal.

"Now let's not get ahead of ourselves," Noach said. "We can't let our excitement get the better of us. We need to release the animals in an organized manner."

Jepheth nodded. "Yes, they are as anxious to leave the ark as any of us."

"That's a good point," Cham said as he dipped bread in his soup. He looked at Noach. "I assume we should release the larger animals first so the smaller ones don't get trampled in the process."

Kezia nodded. "Oh, yes. That's a good plan. We should go from the largest to the smallest, just to be sure."

Rayneh nodded. "I'll mark the cages tomorrow so everyone is aware of their order."

"Okay," Jepheth said. "And I'll schedule who leads which animals so we're not wondering who will be doing what."

Noach smiled. "Great plans, my children." Now he too seemed to be getting excited. "In four days, we'll have our Earth back." He scanned each of their faces. "Won't that be glorious?"

They all nodded enthusiastically.

As the day approached, their excitement grew. After breakfast on the fourth day, which everyone ate quite quickly, they congregated at the ark's door.

Noach looked at Cham. "Okay, Cham. Let's open the door."

Cham looked at the door and then back to his father. "And how are we to do that?"

Noach laughed. "Well, how did you close the door?"

Cham shook his head. "I didn't. I only pitched the door's edges with tar after it was closed."

"Yahweh closed the door," Shem said.

Noach nodded. "Then I think we should ask him to open it, don't you?"

Everyone nodded. They held hands and Noach prayed. "Yahweh, our Protector, we thank you for your protection during this time of our journey. It seems our journey has ended, and you have given us a new world to populate. We now ask you to open the ark for us and the animals you have sustained as we all enter your new world."

They opened their eyes and waited. Slowly the ark door swung open and then landed, forming a ramp out from the ark to the ground below. Everyone laughed, cried, and hugged. They all fell to their knees and thanked Yahweh. Each man took his wife's arm and led her down the ramp.

"It's beautiful," Naamah said, her voice a tone of awe. "The mountains look rugged and majestic." Her eyes widened. "And I see some vegetation!" She gasped as she turned. "And flowers." She bent over and delicately touched a brilliant yellow flower in bloom.

They each walked around looking at the scenery that encircled them. When Cham went to the side of the ark, he yelled. "Everyone, come look at this!"

All seven ran his way. "What is it?" Noach asked with concern. He stopped short when he saw what Cham had pointed toward. "Now, that's beautiful." Before them, running down the distant mountain, was a majestic waterfall.

Ar'yel looked up and gasped again. "Look at the sky!"

Everyone looked up and also stood staring, stunned.

"*What* is it?" Rayneh asked.

Ar'yel shook her head. "I have no idea, but it's absolutely beautiful."

Noach chuckled. "Yahweh did it." He shook his head. "I didn't understand how he would, but he has."

Naamah took his arm. "Dear, what do you mean?"

Noach looked at her and smiled. "He said he would put his bow in the sky." He shook his head again. "I just didn't realize it would be something so beautiful."

Rayneh held up her hand and counted under her breath.

Jepheth laughed. "What are you doing, Rayneh?"

She looked at him and smiled. "Counting the colors. There's seven of them. I see seven distinct colors."

Jepheth looked up and squinted. "You can see that many clear lines of color?"

She nodded. "Can't you?"

He shrugged. "I guess. It's hard to tell since they morph into each other."

Rayneh raised her eyebrows. "Well, there's definitely seven."

Noach nodded. "Yes, my dear. The number of perfection and completion. This is Yahweh's promise to us that he will not destroy the world again with water. His judgment is now complete, and he has sealed his promise with his perfection."

Noach turned to the ark. "Well, it will take most of the day to get the animals out, so let's get started."

Slowly, each one turned from the spectacular view and headed back into the ark for what would be some of their final times.

Noach turned to Shem. "Son, we should keep the sheep, cattle, and goats in the ark until we build a small corral for them. I want to offer a burnt offering before the sun goes down today."

Shem put his arm around his father's shoulders. "Certainly, Aba. I think that is a great idea. We certainly want to start in the right way."

Noach patted him on his shoulder. "Yes, my son. Yes we do, indeed."

Mikael stood away from the ark with Raphael. "Well, my friend, it seems Elohim has rescued mankind. Hopefully, they will make wiser decisions this time."

The answer came from a voice Mikael did not expect.

"Oh, but will they? Really?"

Mikael whirled to see Lucifer standing behind them. "And why are *you* here?"

Lucifer smiled. "Well, it may be a resculpted world, but it is still technically mine."

Mikael shrugged. "Maybe, but you lost. Your world kingdom is no more."

Lucifer nodded. "Granted. My efforts did not result in what I wanted." He smiled. "No matter. If Yahweh can start over again, so can I."

Raphael squinted. "And what is that supposed to mean?"

Lucifer looked at him with raised eyebrows. "Come now, Raphael. I'm not talking in riddles."

Mikael wasn't sure what Lucifer was implying, but he knew he was already scheming something. "Well, you certainly can't do what you did before."

Lucifer tilted his head back and forth slightly. "True, but 'can't' isn't a word I normally use."

Mikael gave him a blank stare.

Lucifer laughed. "Oh, no, I can't have angels become humanoid again, but don't think Nephilim is out of their dictionary."

Mikael shook his head. "What? How can you even . . . "

Lucifer held up his hands. "Oh, don't get your wings in a pinch. If I've learned anything, it's that I now know the boundary line." He smiled. "That's important to know."

Mikael cocked his head. He didn't like the way this was sounding.

"Giants are simply a matter of genetics," Lucifer said, giving a slight shrug. "Quite fascinating really, once you get to understand it. Giants really help to persuade others." He smiled. "Simply by their mere size." He raised his eyebrows. "If I control the giants, I control a lot more."

"What are you planning?" Raphael asked.

Lucifer put his hand to his chest. "*Planning*? Me? Oh, I just make suggestions. These humans are really so easily influenced." Lucifer's gaze focused on someone coming out of the ark. "I just have to get the right person interested."

Mikael looked to where Lucifer was staring. Cham had exited with some of the equine animals. Mikael then looked back at Lucifer, who had a small grin on his face.

"You really are evil, you know."

Lucifer's gaze shot to his. "This is *my* kingdom. I do what I see fit. So you can just go back to Papa and do your worshiping."

Mikael shook his head. "What happened to you, Lucifer?"

"Oh, let me see." He paused and then stated his next words with heavy emphasis. "I got kicked out of the club." He shrugged. "So I'm making my own."

"Well, you kicked yourself out of that club."

Lucifer shot him a hot stare. "Whatever. I'm making my own future now." He gave a sly grin. "I have work to do. Give my regards to everyone."

With those words, and a sarcastic chuckle, Lucifer disappeared.

Raphael shook his head. "I guess our work will never be done."

"Evidently," Mikael said. "Not until our Lord takes back ownership of this world and rules from it to show his superiority."

"And when will that be?"

Mikael shook his head. "I don't know, but I think we will have much to do until then."

As they stood and looked down at Noach and his family, Mikael saw the patriarch and his sons gathering stones and building an altar.

Mikael pointed. "But they are starting out in the right way. Giving glory to Yahweh, our Creator, is definitely the right start."

Raphael nodded. "I just hope it continues."

"At least some will." He smiled. "Of that we can be sure. Yahweh has decreed it, and we will help him make that happen."

As they stood and watched, Ruach joined them.

At short time later, toward evening, Noach was burning the sacrifice. The family had gathered around the altar to sing praises to their Creator.

Ruach touched Mikael's arm. "Do you feel their praise? It is wonderful to hear, to see, to *feel*."

Mikael nodded. "Something we should do as well." He turned to Raphael. "Come, my friend. I'll meet you at the Sacred Altar of Stones."

He looked one last time at Noach and his family offering their praise. "We have much to be thankful for as well."

I hope you've enjoyed *Rebellion in the Stones of Fire*. Letting others know of your enjoyment of this book is a way to help them share your experience. Please consider posting an honest review. You can post a review at Amazon, Barnes & Noble, Goodreads, or other places you choose. Reviews can also be posted at more than one site! This author, and other readers, appreciate your engagement. Also, check out my next book, *The Holy Grail of Babylon*, coming soon!

Also, check out my website: www.RandyDockens.com.

—Randy Dockens

COME EXPLORE THE NEXT BOOK OF

THE ADVERSARY CHRONICLES

Discover stories from the Bible in a way not yet told.

Lucifer is preparing for his ultimate reign.

And he has a plan literally out of this world for creating the perfect human who can influence and dominate the earth so he can come to power and rule all. Since the time of the Tower of Babel he has been scheming by creating a planet in a time dilation field where advances in human genetics can be faster than on Earth. A few have arisen to stop his plan at all costs. This involves a couple who unknowingly have almost identical DNA to the ancient rulers of Babylon who created the false religion that is key to Lucifer's plan for ultimate control. Can Lucifer's plan be stopped before this couple must pay the ultimate sacrifice to save their world?

(BEFORE FINAL EDITING)

SAMPLE CHAPTER FROM
THE HOLY GRAIL OF BABYLON
PART OF THE ADVERSARY CHRONICLES SERIES

THE HOLY GRAIL OF BABYLON

CHAPTER ONE

THE TOWER

Raphael's eyes went wide. His gaze went up and up as his head went back. He turned to Mikael.

"Well, it's definitely impressive—by anyone's standards," Raphael told his angel friend.

Mikael nodded. In many ways mankind had made so many advances. The ability to build such a magnificent structure like this massive, towering ziggurat was one such example.

"Well, I see Yahweh's spies are here."

Mikael turned when he heard the words spoken behind him. There was Lucifer with a smug smile on his face. Mikael found Lucifer could be irritating just by being in his presence.

And to think this was the one who every angel looked up to in the early days prior to his Creator making this world.

Mikael gave a forced grin. "Just checking up on *you*." He glanced back at the tower. "What are you up to this time?"

"Me?" Lucifer placed his hand on his chest with a look of shock. "I'm simply giving everyone what they want." He looked from one angel to the other. "And what's wrong with that?"

"Nothing is ever that simple with you, Lucifer," Raphael said. "You don't do anything for others without it benefiting you."

Lucifer's eyes widened. "And what's wrong with that? A win-win scenario is always a good thing, isn't it?"

"It always comes down to motives. You know that, Lucifer," Mikael added. "Your track record for motives is not at all good. You have to admit that."

"Oh, I don't have to admit anything." Lucifer suddenly pursed his lips and gave a slight squint. "And I certainly don't have to justify myself to the likes of you." Lucifer produced a smile and held his arms out wide. "But I'll share my creation with both of you." His tone turned condescending. "After all, you have to go back and report *something*, right?" He shook his head ever so subtly. "I can't let you go back with nothing to report. What kind of a host would I be then?" He gave a chuckle, leaning in slightly, but still had a tinge of sarcasm in his voice. "Don't want the Ancient of Days to think I was inhospitable to his two . . . *reporters*." He produced a broad smile. "So come. Come see my creation."

Lucifer placed one hand on Mikael's shoulder and his other on Raphael's. The next thing Mikael knew, they were in a room with several other humans. Being next to a window, Mikael could see they were high in the tower itself. Other than the people, the only thing in the room with them was what looked like some type of sculpture on a high pedestal. The piece was beautiful, composed almost entirely of various colored and varied-sized crystals arranged roughly in the shape of a large square, forming a three-dimensional cube structure with two sides open so one could see through it.

"Well, your artwork is beautiful," Mikael said, looking at Lucifer. "But what is its purpose?"

Lucifer smiled. "All in good time. All in good time."

Mikael noticed the people in the room were guards of some kind. Two men stood on either side of the structure, spear in one hand, with one end pointed at the ceiling and the other end on the floor. Their torsos were bare except for a wide necklace-type decoration around their necks that seemed to be composed of beaded material which contrasted with their dark bronze complexion. Two other similar guards stood at the door of the room just inside the hallway. Each wore a loin-cloth, which were ornate in design. These men were evidently not ordinary guards.

"You must think highly of your sculpture to have so many guards protecting it," Raphael said, looking from the guards to Lucifer.

Lucifer gave a forced smile. "Well, once you understand its importance, you will understand why."

"Importance?" Mikael asked. "What do you mean?"

"Today," Lucifer said, "we are embarking on a journey that will be heralded by all in the days to come as the triumphant pinnacle of humankind. And since you are here, you will be able to witness it."

Mikael glanced at Raphael, who shook his head lightly. Evidently, he didn't understand Lucifer's cryptic message any more than he did.

Mikael looked back at Lucifer. "What are you talking about?"

Before Lucifer had time to answer, the sculpture began to glow. The crystals refracted the light being produced and formed a kaleidoscope of color on the walls of the room.

The guards in the hallway looked in, their eyes widening.

One of the guards next to the structure pointed at one of the guards near the doorway. "Go tell the queen he has returned," the first guard said.

The man nodded and quickly trotted down the hallway. Mikael could hear the *pat-pat* of his bare feet growing fainter the farther away the man ran. The other three guards genuflected, facing the structure. Evidently, they expected someone to appear.

Lucifer turned to Mikael and smiled. "This is the beginning of a journey to bring me and my chosen greatness beyond greatness. My chosen will go beyond the heavens and bring Heaven to earth."

Mikael sucked in a breath. "You can't be serious! What are you saying?" He didn't know what Lucifer had done, or was doing, but this did not sound like a good thing—at all. The fallen angel was talking almost as if he was God the Creator himself.

"And what do you think you are achieving?" Raphael asked.

A smile slowly came across Lucifer's face. "Something wonderful," he proclaimed.

ERABON PROPHECY TRILOGY

Come read this exciting trilogy where an astronaut, working on an interstellar gate, is accidently thrown so deep into the universe that there is no way for him to get home.

He does, however, find life on a nearby planet, one in which the citizens look very different from him. Although tense at first, he finds these aliens think he is the forerunner to the return of their deity and charge him with reuniting the clans living on six different planets.

What is stranger to him still is that while everything seems so foreign from anything he has ever experienced . . . there is an element that also feels so familiar.

Available now!

THE STELE PENTALOGY

Do you know *your future*?

Come see the possibilities in a world God creates and how an apocalypse leads to promised wonders beyond imagination.

Read how some experience mercy, some hope, and some embrace their destiny—while others try to reshape theirs. And how some, unfortunately, see perfection and the divine as only ordinary and expected.

Available now!

THE CODED MESSAGE TRILOGY

Come read this fast-paced trilogy, where an astrophysicist accidently stumbles upon a world secret that plunges him and his friends into an adventure of discovery and intrigue . . .

What Luke Loughton and his friends discover could possibly be the answer to a question you've been wondering all along.

Available now!

Why Is a Gentile World Tied to a Jewish Timeline?

The Question Everyone Should Ask

Yes, the Bible is a unique book.

Looking for a book with mystery, intrigue, and subterfuge? Maybe one with action, adventure, and peril suits you more. Perhaps science fiction is more your fancy. The Bible gives you all that and more! Come read of a hero who is humble yet exudes strength, power, and confidence—one who is intriguing yet always there for the underdog.

Read how the Bible puts all of this together in a unique, cohesive plan that intertwines throughout history—a plan for a Gentile world that is somehow tied to a Jewish timeline.

Travel a road of discovery you never knew existed. Do you like adventures? Want to join one? Then come along. Discover the answer to the question everyone should ask.

Available now!